This fifth Glas collection of Russian women's writing, this time by women in their 20s and early 30s, reveals its evolution through two decades of upheaval, from lack of awareness of their dependent and downtrodden position in society through a realization of the need to fight for their rights, to complete confidence in their equality. So much so that women today often write in men's voices. When they impersonate men it is obvious that they don't think much of their role today. Contrary to the belief that male and female texts tend to become undistinguishable, the typical features of both still stand out while the thematic range and settings change.

Russian women, who increasingly occupy leading roles in society, take a sober view of the present-day world. With typical female emotionality and attention to detail, women today speak openly on formerly forbidden subjects, including specifically women's issues, and leave no taboos unturned.

Whatever talented women write about is already interesting by definition because female vision is always sharp, unexpected and paradoxical. Particularly fascinating are these women's frank self portraits and merciless portraits of the opposite sex.

Interestingly, half of the authors in Russia are women and, according to publishers, their books are invariably in greater demand.

Contributors to this collection are all winners of the Debut Prize for young writers.

GW00722704

GLAS NEW RUSSIAN WRITING

contemporary Russian literature

in English translation

Volume 55

This is the fifth volume in the Glas sub-series presenting young Russian authors, winners and finalists of the Debut Prize founded by the Pokolenie Foundation for humanitarian projects in 2000. Glas acknowledges its generous support in publishing this book.

Still Waters
Run Deep

*Young Women's Writing
from Russia*

glas
MOSCOW

GLAS PUBLISHERS
tel./fax: +7(495)441-9157
perova@glas.msk.su
www.glas.msk.su

DISTRIBUTION

In North America
Consortium Book Sales and Distribution
tel: 800-283-3572; fax: 800-351-5073
orderentry@perseusbooks.com
www.cbsd.com

In the UK
CENTRAL BOOKS
orders@centralbooks.com
www.centralbooks.com
Direct orders: INPRESS
Tel: 0191 229 9555
customerservices@inpressbooks.co.uk
www.inpressbooks.co.uk

Within Russia
Jupiter-Impex
www.jupiterbooks.ru

Editors: Natasha Perova and Joanne Turnbull
Cover design by Igor Satanovsky
The cover includes details from photographs by Anastasia Perova and by Jan Yugai
Camera-ready copy: Tatiana Shaposhnikova

ISBN 978-5-7172-0095-0

Отпечатано типографии ФГУП Изд-во «Известия»
127994, ГСП-4, г. Москва, К-6, Пушкинская пл., д.5.
тел.: 694-36-36, 694-30-20; e-mail: izd.izv@ru.net
Зак. №2150

CONTENTS

Irina Bogatyreva

UNIVERSUM

Translated by Arch Tait

1

Perhaps it was because she was the only person who never tried to pry into his life; or perhaps it was because they didn't see each other too often, so that he hadn't tired of her. Whatever, it was Makha that Max called and asked to come and do the job.

"You'll find it straightforward," he said. "I've tied up the loose ends so you won't need to meet customers, just answer their emails. But get it right. I don't want them put off. Your replies have to keep them happy."

Makha was worried, but didn't let it show. "Why not set your mailbox to auto-reply?"

"I've just told you why."

"No problem," Makha said, trying not to sound excited. "My neighbour has the Internet. I can easily check your emails for you now and again."

"No, you're not listening. I want you to stay at my place while you're doing it."

She could only stop talking and agree.

"Maybe everybody he knows is busy and I'm the only one at a loose end. Otherwise, I can't imagine why he would choose me."

Makha had always presumed Max had lots of friends, any one of whom would be happy to do him a favour almost before he asked for it. That was why she had never tried to push herself forward. They would have an agreeable, if brief, conversation when they met, and then quite likely not see each other again for a month. They would phone only if there was some urgent need. Like now.

For the week before Max's departure, she was walking around as proud, mysterious, and pleased as could be. She and Max had friends in common, but none who knew anything about his private life, and certainly none who had ever visited him at home. The prospect of living in his apartment put Makha in a different category. It was her secret and she was happy.

Without a word to her roommates or anyone else, one day Makha packed her belongings and left the college hostel.

The district Max lived in was equidistant from every halfways interesting part of Moscow. It was the kind of area you don't get out of if you are unlucky enough ever to move there. He had a single-room apartment on the ground floor of a thin-walled, prefabricated residential block. The cellar below was occupied by stray neighbourhood cats, and the apartment above by a large Azerbaijani family. Max was sandwiched between them in his kitchen, which boasted a stove, a sink, a wall cupboard, and a couch under the window on which he slept and which had a table and computer in front of it. The computer was old, with a small rounded monitor. The serious technology was in his room.

The room was Max's workshop and den and the windows had long been tightly curtained. The computer which lived in there could recreate accurate images of our transitory world which were no less, and perhaps rather more, convincing than reality. A huge printer drank white tubes of coloured ink and reproduced in any format the masterpieces Max took with his Canon.

"I would appreciate your not going in there," Max said as he was about to leave Makha in charge.

"Bluebeard locked and barred his secret room."

"Why would I do that? I know you won't go in unless you need to."

Before departing, he pointed out to her all the food shops on the way to the metro, each with its own pack of dogs keeping a watchful eye on things.

"It won't be long before I can recognize all of you," Makha thought as she passed the dogs on her way back to Max's hideaway. The wet asphalt was mottled with rag-like leaves, and Makha pictured dull days ahead of her, standing in for Max in this grey district of high-rise apartment blocks.

She surveyed once more, but now more intently, the accommodation entrusted to her. The furniture included, besides the table and couch, a wardrobe which stood in the hallway and had a solitary winter jacket languishing in it. Makha found some old jeans, a sweater and shirt neatly folded next to the couch in the corner of the kitchen. Max was not untidy: this was just where those items stayed. In the bathroom, in a basin under the sink, a pile of dirty laundry was biding its time. The plumbing was uniformly the mournful colour of fallen leaves. As she was washing her hands, Makha automatically looked above the sink to see herself in the mirror, but saw instead a wall with old tiling.

Max was not untidy, just thoroughly accustomed to living alone. "A single person needs very little," Makha thought, "especially if they're a man." It occurred to her she should have done some shopping on the way back. In the crockery cupboard she found eggs, crackers, and a jar of coffee. Under the sink was a bag of potatoes and a bottle of cooking oil. She could see why Max was so thin.

"My parents won't phone the hostel, and nobody there will miss me," she thought contentedly. She felt as if she had won a sea cruise. It wasn't that the apartment was like being on holiday after the grimness of the hostel. She had stayed over with friends before, and looked after pets while their owners were away. Those people, however, had all been provincials like herself, often even from her region, people who had somehow managed to rent a place in the capital. Max was something else.

She and Max belonged to different worlds. He was a real Muscovite. Not first generation, but someone whose long-forgotten (if still living) ancestors were cozily ensconced in pre-revolutionary rooms on Pokrovka and Malaya Bronnaya Streets. After generations of living in this stony urban habitat, they had become remote and introspective, as if no longer rooted in the soil but floating in the sky on balloons. Next to him, Makha felt like a rosy-cheeked peasant girl, strong boned and tireless as a horse.

It sometimes seemed to her that Max did not really know life, particularly when she observed him interacting with ordinary people: manual workers, drivers, porters or market traders. At such times, he struck her as comical. After a while, however, she came to believe that he had some greater, deeper understanding of life, because these ordinary people would suddenly soften and be happy to do whatever Max asked of them.

Absolutely everybody liked him. Nobody knew why, or what magic Max possessed to make everyone, even the most stuck-up or morose, turn to him with a smile. It happened spontaneously. He knew a great many people, but didn't allow anyone too close. Anybody was welcome to discuss the meaning of life with him, but nobody was quite sure where he lived. Everybody knew he was a photographer, because he carried his bug-eyed, round-shouldered Canon with him everywhere, but nobody had ever seen his work.

That was why Makha felt she had won the lottery. Now she would know things other people didn't know. Now she was seeing things other people never saw. Yet she knew with a happy certainty that she would say nothing to anyone. Even though she was overwhelmed with pride and joy, she would never tell anyone that she knew more about Max than they did. He hadn't asked her not to, but whoever knows a secret is its guardian. Makha purred with pleasure at the thought.

"My parents won't phone the hostel, and nobody there will miss me."

As she was finishing washing the kitchen floor, she suddenly realized that the insistent beeping was coming not from the alarm of some imported car parked outside the window, but from the computer. She moved the mouse to wake up the screen and saw an exclamation mark which warned her that the mailbox was full. Max had mentioned she would have to download his emails from the server to his computer. When she had finished, Makha settled down to answer them.

He had told her to make the answers concise and not too specific. She should ask for clarification of every question. (The file with prices and comments was open.) If there was anything she did not understand, she should be evasive, but take care that no one should guess that it was not Max himself who was replying. She should cheerfully accept new commissions, but without discussing deadlines or other details. "In short, you need to be fluid and flexible, but as you're a woman, you will adapt easily. That's nature's gift to you."

From the first of the emails, she realized Max was not just a photographer. He was also a computer graphics artist and a website designer, and he conducted online seminars. He created layouts for billboard advertisements, he could create virtual worlds, and, in short, his work was in an area of which Makha knew nothing.

"But he told me it wasn't that difficult, so it doesn't matter if I don't understand what it's all about. Of course it doesn't. No problem!" Makha positioned her fingers on the keyboard, feeling like a pianist about to perform in front of a large audience. In the concert hall, nobody moved, nobody breathed, everybody waiting for those first chords. Makha found she had completely forgotten the music.

"Dear Mr T.," she forced out of herself. "Regarding your enquiry in respect of the cost of designing a webpage for the Cynology Association, I have pleasure in informing you..." Her fingers ran over the keys and then stopped. Makha listened. There was a strained silence in the hall. Her audience did not recognize the tune. She was playing all the wrong notes. She decided to take a look at how Max replied, and opened his sent emails folder.

Her immediate impression was that she would never dare to write the way he did in case she scared all the customers away. Here, for instance, was someone wanting a site about Asian dancing. He wanted the home page to reflect the texture of a drumhead made from the leather of the wild Arkhar mountain sheep, with red pompoms hanging down the sides. "It would certainly be possible," Max wrote in reply, "at your expense, to skin an Arkhar mountain sheep, but within your budget the best we can manage is a goat. And you will need to forget about the red pompoms."

The terse sentences and sharply focused descriptions had an uncompromising clarity and directness of vision. Where she would have written five words and agonized over whether to include a sixth, Max used two and moved on. If she tried to imitate his style it would result in mere rudeness, but all those polite, business-letter cliches she had at her fingertips were no good either. They would give the impression that Max was a soft touch.

Makha decided to try lifting phrases wholesale from Max's old emails but, after firing off several such collages, sensed she was only alienating people. The end result was a faceless golem, rather than an email which would make people glad to wait for Max for as long as might be necessary, and delight them when he finally did anything for them.

To reply appropriately, she needed to match his confidence. It was essential to believe firmly that you were capable of anything and that people would be delighted with your work. You needed to be a professional down to your last pixel. You needed to be Max.

After setting up the auto-reply, Makha decided she had no time to re-invent the wheel and should get into her new role without further delay. She had to be reincarnated in order to do the task set, and to do it well.

The only trouble was that she and Max were complete opposites. He was a man: she wasn't. He had a good head for mathematics, which she had always found hard going. He a Muscovite born and bred, which was far from being her situation. Moreover, Max was older than she was, and had long been living his own, independent life. Makha, on the other hand, was still only learning not to worry about what her mother might think of everything she did.

She sat down and mulled over how to get into the role. She tried to imagine where, in her place, Max would have started. This got her nowhere, so she put on his clothes.

She had always supposed she was shorter and plumper than Max, but his jeans fitted her round the waist, and she rolled up the legs. She loved the way the sweater hung on her like a sack. It was old and soft, and the jeans worn and faded. She poured boiling water over the coffee grounds, took out the crackers, and settled herself in front of the monitor. Perfection! She really had everything she needed.

The emails came flooding in, but she took her time. She needed to get the tone right, and the rhythm. Right, here was a customer wanting to know whether Max could do this and that. How soon? How much would it cost? How was she to respond? Being obliging and courteous is what women do, so she would cut out "of course" and "naturally". No reckless inflating of the price, though. No use of "easily" or "in next to no time". As for such diffidence as, "do my best", and "see how it goes", that would betray her youthfulness. Max had his feet more firmly on the ground. So what was she going to say?

She gave the customer's email another careful reading. He was obviously completely at sea, and afraid he would end up paying over the odds. As a woman, she wanted to set his mind at rest, to spell out all the stages of the job, give him a price, and reassure him he was getting good value for money. She immediately realized, however, that, if she did try to set his mind at rest, he would turn into a complete pain in the neck and demand reports at each stage. He needed to be compelled to do something for himself.

"Do you actually know what it is you want?" No, that was too abrupt and carried a suggestion of spurious superiority, the kind of thing a man would write in order to show he was the top dog.

"By and large, that kind of job does fall within the category of work I undertake, however ..." Makha could stop there. She drank some coffee and glanced out the window to see that, in the sodden November twilight, the streetlights were coming on. Their light shining down from above Max's window tinted the drizzle yellow. Her reply now came easily and naturally, like inspiration: "Tell me in detail what you want."

Her fingers ran confidently over the keys, the music as pure as fresh air. The audience heaved a sigh of relief.

2

The Azerbaijanis upstairs woke early. The head of the family drove for a transport company and left while it was still dark. Makha heard a choral polyphony of voices coming from the family's single room on the first floor, when she finally curled up on the couch after her all-night vigil before the computer screen. She woke to the beeping of the full mailbox signal at around two in the afternoon.

Striking the right note, she felt the work was going well and was pleased. At first, she needed to make a special effort before beginning each email, but then got into her stride and the only problem was keeping up with the sheer volume of enquiries.

She soon saw how convenient it was to have a bag of potatoes and a bottle of cooking oil in the house. Not long afterwards she understood why the plumbing was the colour of autumn leaves. Later she accepted that the dirty laundry in the basin would have a long wait before its time came. If at first she had viewed all these things as a woman and wanted to put them all to rights, now she stopped noticing them. She became Max, and Max was content with what he had, and just like Max she had no time for anything but work.

"I am getting to know him better than I thought," Makha reflected, "even without entering the forbidden room."

"Hiya. Haven't heard from you for an age. I've posted some pix on this page. Take a look?" Followed by a link. "Spam," Makha decided and deleted it, shuddering to think what kind of pix these might be.

The next day, however, another email arrived from the same address, even more perfunctory. "Did you look? And?" This time there was no link. "Not usual spam," Makha decided, but still did not reply, focused as she was on customers, and now acting her part so well she even allowed herself to improvize.

The Azerbaijani children went to school and came back. They were all ages and had different shifts. In the morning, the older ones listened to black rappers. In the afternoon, the younger ones watched cross-dressing Ukrainian comedian Verka Serduchka. Their father parked his truck directly in front of Max's window, and after that the music upstairs was of a different order: an opera of family quarrelling, with arias from wailing children. Makha had the full benefit of it through the kitchen ceiling.

"Why no reply? Nadya here. Sorry for using this mailbox. My computer's gone down and taken your email address with it. I got this one from the Net. How do you like the pix? I'd really like to know." The email was from the same address. Makha gave a low whistle. "Looks like I'm going to find out more about Max than I expected. More than he expected."

With the indicator light of her feminine curiosity glowing brightly, she set aside the rest of the emails, ransacked the computer, but failed to find any trace of other mailboxes. There was nothing besides business correspondence. If Max had anything else, it must be on the computer in his room. Makha paced to and fro in front of the closed door, like a cat patrolling a refrigerator. No, this was insufficient justification for breaking a promise. She returned to the couch. Max always had lots of women around him, effortlessly attracting them like bees to honey. He was not irresistibly handsome, never promised them anything, indeed never did anything for them, yet still they were attracted, without knowing why or what it was they wanted from him. At least, it was a mystery to Makha. She didn't doubt that, since this happened within the modest circle in which she knew Max, it must be the same in other circles where she couldn't see him.

Even so, his personal life was shrouded in mystery, and there had never been rumours of romance. Max would talk to anyone who wanted to talk to him, would chat on the phone, even go out with them. Usually the girls came back from these assignations fresh and radiant, as if they had discovered something important about life. In the hostel it was easy to read other people's moods.

All the women Makha saw with Max struck her as exceptional. Other girls, her fellow students in the hostel, who chatted with Max for an hour in the smoking room, acquired a mysterious aura. The other women she didn't know, but whom Max sometimes mentioned, she pictured as being as wise and beautiful as Greek goddesses. She was enviously attracted to them by a feeling akin to celebrity worship. They were beyond her reach, but each of them had something that distinguished them from the rest, and had marked them out from the rest for Max.

This Nadya was now one of their number. Makha could, of course, ignore the email and any others which might come, but the light of feminine curiosity was flashing as obtrusively as the visual alarm on a deaf old lady's telephone. Behind this email lay the life Max never let anyone into, his private life. She would lift up a corner, peep in quickly, and retreat.

That wasn't cheating or breaking her promise. He had asked Makha not to go into his room and she wouldn't, but he had also asked her to answer his emails, and she would.

She wanted to send an email that would make the girl spill the beans about herself, to let Makha get to the bottom of the mystery, but knew that would only frighten her off. She needed to be patient, to take a deep breath, to lie motionless on the ocean bed. She needed to pretend to be Max.

"Hi. Snowed under right now. I'll look asap. Haven't heard from you for ages either. How's it going?" Of course, if they were really close, she would be surprised by the coolness and that would be immediately evident from her reply. Actually, so would everything else. This was bait.

Nadya swallowed the hook, line, and sinker, replying just fifteen minutes later. "Everything's fine here. The computer packed in, but now I've got a job with Internet access, so I can email you any time. Cool? Don't worry, I won't pester. If I do, just tell me, okay?

"Nikita was sick last week. Mother and I took it in turns to sit with him. He's better now. I'm learning to view them the way you told me. It seems to work some of the time and then I feel light and free, but later hemmed in again.

"I feel strange looking at this city now, seeing both what I remember and what you taught me to see. There's a kind of transition, where you don't know which of the frames is more real.

"We've had snow on the ground for a month now. Don't expect you have any yet. How are you anyway? Just let me know how you're doing. We haven't been in touch for ages."

It was an email freighted with overtones of separation, failed marriage, dissatisfaction with life, and babies' diapers. Makha's face was ashen. "What a drag to get stuck in someone else's soap opera. Only, what if it's my – that is to say, Max's –

child?" she thought with a start. She shuddered. Even if it was, Max was not there now, and there must be a reason for that, which Makha had no wish to know. In fact, she had no wish to know any more about this relationship. She felt a mannish distaste for a woman's misery and left the email unanswered.

The following day, Nadya again emailed, evidently guessing Max's reaction to her whining. She wrote in a quite different vein. "Hi. I was on my way to work just now and managed to snap some robins. I take a camera with me everywhere now, just like you." (Smiley face.) "Five bright red robins at once on an ice-covered branch. It should come out really well if I've done everything the way you said to. When it's ready, I'll upload it to the same page."

Makha smiled. "Good girl," she thought for some reason and wanted to reply. She wrote about the rain outside the window, the jobs piling up and threatening to swamp Max. She hesitated, then took the bull by the horns and casually asked how Nikita was. If he was their child, the reply would make that clear. In fact, the reply would make everything clear. "Not that I care whose child it is."

Nadya's smile could be sensed in every line of her reply. "Yesterday a girl came to see Nikita. Mother kept tiptoeing past the door, shushing me and saying Nikita had a girl visiting him, top of his class, helping him keep up with his lessons. Mother kept knocking on the door to ask whether they wanted a cup of tea. She didn't leave them alone for more than ten minutes. I asked her, 'Are you afraid they'll start kissing?' She was indignant. 'Whatever will you think of next? Children in sixth grade kissing!' She still went in again to ask if they wanted some tea. By the way, you never told me if you've got someone there. Like brothers and sisters?"

Makha had no idea whether Max had brothers and sisters, or anyone at all, but she felt she now knew all about

Nadya and, to her surprise, was greatly relieved. What a lot of nonsense, she muttered. She cut Max's advice to a novice photographer on how to edit colours in Photoshop out of one of his old emails, pasted it in, and sent it off to Nadya. "That's to help with your robins," she added herself.

In the morning one of the upstairs children had a birthday. Makha heard them all shrieking and clapping, and then saw a herd of well-fed, smiling faces with black hair and eyes, all festooned with balloons, come scampering round the corner and pile into their father's truck. The head of the household started up, and off they all went.

She carried on replying to emails, but without much enthusiasm. She was almost rude to one enquirer. She visited several forums which Max frequented, read the professionals' postings on various threads and no threads, and left. She fried some potatoes and ate them straight out of the frying pan, holding the handle with a greasy black towel and gazing out the window.

Outside, the wind was stripping the last traces of gold from the trees in the yard. A black plastic bag snagged on the streetlight outside the window, rustling forlornly. "Why doesn't he at least get himself a cat?" Makha wondered. Finally admitting to herself that she had absolutely no desire to deal with any more emails, she went and put the laundry to soak.

Something wasn't right today, but she couldn't put her finger on what exactly. Time seemed to be standing still, as if until very recently everybody had been looking over in the direction of this apartment, bombarding it with emails and orders, avidly seeking advice, but had suddenly stopped. Nearly everybody. Time was standing still, as sticky as fingers that have squeezed an orange, and something was missing. Makha went to do the laundry and remembered it was Saturday.

"That's why she hasn't written," it dawned on her. "It's the weekend and she only has Internet access at work. Of course. How obvious."

With lightsome heart she finished washing and rinsing the laundry, went back to the computer, and replied to a couple of emails which had come in. Through the window she saw the truck disgorging dark-haired children, now clutching McDonald's bags and decked with paper hats and other tat, with toy mutants which were even rounder and smilier than the children were themselves. Music and yelling soon had the ceiling reverberating.

"I'll write to her myself," Makha decided. "She may have been offended by getting such a short reply." She would have liked to write about the autumnal scene outside the window, and the woebegone flapping of the plastic bag on the streetlight. She would have liked to write about how the tap dripping in the kitchen during the night seemed to be drumming out the rhythm of some antediluvian jazz hit, about how quickly the world had forgotten she ever existed and allowed her to just disappear. What was required, however, was to write about Max, and how was she supposed to do that? She didn't even know him properly. Would he have noticed the black and golden hues of autumn, heard jazz coming from the sink, and be hoping friends would call? If, indeed, he had any.

For heaven's sake, the man's in love with himself! He hasn't got anyone and he doesn't want anyone! He's an arrogant, blue-blooded, Mr High-and-mighty Intellectual! Afraid to live in the real world, that's why he only talks to people over the Internet. What does he have to say to this poor girl? What does he have to give her, other than hackneyed advice about how to live her life? She is so obviously in love with him and the sad goat can't see it!

She paused, and then started pounding the keyboard.

She wanted to reply in a way that would please a girl from the provinces. She wrote to the effect that Max had never forgotten the time they spent together; that, who knows, they might even meet up again some day; that nothing in this world happens without leaving a legacy; and that if even the slightest trace of warmth was left in this dank autumn, etc., etc.

When she had finished, she re-read it, hated it, and deleted it. She had no intention of representing Max as a slobbering moron, and besides, she didn't know whether the two of them had even met. Writing that kind of stuff, she might just saddle Max with real problems. Overcome with emotion, this Nadya might take it into her head to turn up here with all her worldly goods. The thought made Makha laugh. If she ever really wanted to wind Max up, this would be just the way to do it.

She pondered some more and suddenly wrote, "If someone had told me that today I would be where I am, doing what I'm doing, knowing what I know, I would have thought it hilarious. Now, though, I know it is wiser to laugh after the event, to learn to see ordinary things in new ways, to learn to keep people you have known for a long time at a distance, to see them for themselves and not just to react to the attitude you have developed towards them over the years. This is only the first step on the road towards changing yourself. Sooner or later, fate will place you in a situation where you seem to see the world through someone else's eyes. At that time, like it or not, you will begin to see everything in a different light. What will you see? Who knows? You may even see yourself as you really are, separate from this person whose eyes are looking at you. God grant that what you see does not drive you mad."

Makha re-read the email, unable to make head or tail of it. She was not even sure whether she or Max had written it. It sounded the way he spoke, but what he was getting at she had little idea. After reading and re-reading it, she decided there was nothing to add or take away, and sent it to Nadya.

3

She first met Max in an autumn like this. She and her fellow second-year students had been abruptly taken away from their classes for a week and sent off to do their "summer" fieldwork prematurely. They stayed at their institute's new holiday centre near Moscow, where they were to paint murals on the newly plastered walls. As future architects, they were even entrusted with designing the interiors for the buildings. They discovered later that the centre was owned by a relative of the dean, who was exploiting them as free labour, but at the time they didn't care and pitched in enthusiastically. There were no visitors because the guest rooms were being refurbished and they lived in the staff accommodation, tight little double rooms with white-painted walls.

Max was staying there too. The owners had invited him to take photographs, and he always carried two cameras, one digital and one which took film. With the digital he took interior pictures, including some of the girl students standing on stepladders and covered in paint. He explained that these were for the Internet. His traditional camera was for views of the surrounding woods and the sad muddy little river. For the frame, he said.

Max was not stand-offish, but neither did he try to be chummy with the students. He treated them as colleagues and enjoyed discussing colour schemes and decoration with them, but didn't turn up to their guitar-playing parties. The girls came to see him as a kind of summer camp counselor. He was the recipient of anonymous poems, and bouquets of maple leaves and melancholy michaelmas daisies were left at his door. He was invited to join them after dinner, and asked to tell them "something interesting" before they went to bed. He was whispered and gossiped about.

Makha and a fellow student spent a long time painting white classical columns on an azure background in the gym. It was one of the more remote buildings, so she barely encountered Max. She saw him at meal times, but he never made it as far as their building with his digital box of tricks, and she never happened to talk to him when the day's work was done. Not that she particularly wanted to. She tried to spend all her spare time as far away as possible from walls which reeked of paint thinner. She would go for walks around the holiday centre and in the woods.

That was how she got lost. The woods were quite sparse and she thought you would need to be blind to get lost in them. They were crossed by two dirt roads with weathered ruts, and numerous smaller and larger tracks which all led to a crossroads. One of the dirt roads emerged on to a tarmac which led to the nearest village, while the other led off to the fields. It didn't seem like a forest you could hide in, let alone get lost in. Within a couple of days, Makha had crisscrossed it completely, keeping to the roads and tracks and always managing to come home before dark.

The firm, springy moss between the trees proved her undoing, and made her stray from the track. With every step, her foot sank into something damp and dark, which disappeared as soon as you took your foot away. This was so delightful and primal that Makha was seduced and walked, or rather floated, over the moss, mindful only of the dark footprints which appeared and then were swallowed up by the moss.

As dusk fell, Makha became aware that she had no idea where she was going. She pressed on for a little, thinking that a light patch between the trees was a track or one of the roads, but it was only more moss. She tried retreating, but that didn't help. The moss was the same, as alluring as it had been millions of years ago.

Makha felt so much at home among trees that she had never believed you could lose yourself in a wood. She was sure she had a special awareness of every one of them. Each was different. How could she get lost among them? But now, here she was – lost. She looked around but saw no trail to lead her out. She scrutinized the ground and saw no trace of any footprints, which the age-old moss had long ago devoured. The trees became an undifferentiated grey background. Darkness fell quickly, although that is too anodyne an expression for the unsettling reality.

She didn't feel she could scream, so hushed was the stillness all around. She wasn't frightened enough to seek desperately to save herself. Everything seemed just too magical: the woods and the moss, her being there alone, even the fact that nobody would come looking for her. She knew that, because she had been lucky enough to have a room to herself. She had no close friends in the group and, being a loner, had never talked to anyone about her walks in the woods. "That's what I chose for myself," Makha thought, conscious of the darkness making her strangely blind. "It is what I always do choose for myself."

She groped her way forward, her eyes growing accustomed to the night, and tried to remember the trees. At one point she thought she did recognize something and supposed this might be where she had turned off the track, only there was no track. She wondered optimistically whether moss was warm to sleep on, but could feel how disagreeably damp it was. Makha began to fear she was walking into a swamp, and was about to turn back when she heard the sound of water and came upon a stream.

In the darkness, the stream looked like molten tin. It had a very deep, comfortable channel and flowed almost without a murmur, gleaming and white. She squatted down and drank, scooping up the delicious water. When she looked up for a moment she seemed to be looking into a mirror. There was somebody across from her, or perhaps not a person but the night which had condensed into the form of a person. She was scared to death, her body felt as cold and heavy as cast iron. She was incapable of saying or doing anything, until the next moment there was no need: a face materialized in the night and she recognized Max.

Makha had not seen what it was he was photographing there in the darkness. When they emerged together from the woods, she was even a little regretful that her adventure had ended so soon and so undramatically. Next morning she found a broken mirror on her locker, a dozen safety pins in her bowl of porridge, and the top rung of the stepladder she shared with her co-worker had been broken. She threw the mirror in the bin, took the porridge back to the kitchen and dolloped out a new helping for herself. The girls spotted the damaged rung straight away and just avoided painting too high. She had no more encounters with Max in the woods, and the terror tactics stopped.

He became a friend, a companion, just someone their whole group liked. Makha didn't notice it happening. Max was invited to all their get-togethers, and started showing up at the institute. He had business and shared interests with some of them, and began to be invited when they were defending their degrees. Makha talked to him no more and no less than everybody else, but she always remembered his still eyes dwelling on her that night from the other side of the stream. She remembered, and was always trying to catch that look again in his warm, lively glance when he was there with all of them, talking and laughing. She watched him in silence, gazing at him, not letting him out of her sight. Max was aware of it, got used to it, and barely reacted to the fact of her following his every move.

When she got a cell phone, she gave him her number. He thanked her, wrote it down, and a week later called and said, "When you see something you can't understand, the bravest thing to do is allow it to remain just as it is – uncategorized."

Makha did not recognize the voice. She felt chilled and for a long time stayed silent. Then it connected in her mind with her image of Max and, just like that time at the stream, her fear was instantly dispelled. "Oh, hi!" she said. "I'm glad you called."

"There, – you see?" he said. "You have turned me back into something you can recognize." He laughed.

At the weekends, she cleaned all the territory to which she had been granted access, and spent a lot of time in the forums. There were few emails, and she replied to them immediately. Nadya was not emailing and the forums were her only entertainment. She did not post messages herself, but the forums' regulars soon detected Max's presence and she began to receive personal messages along the lines of "Hi!" "How's tricks?" "Why aren't you posting?", and the like. Makha ignored them with an easy conscience, reflecting that Max too was disinclined to chat, but also taking a certain pride in the fact that people were pleased he was there. She checked out the links, instructional and professional, and began to feel she was accumulating expertise. "Soon I'll be able to reply to the emails no worse, no less knowledgeably, than Max," she thought.

The weekend over, the mailbox was again full to bursting. New customers arrived, old ones returned. Now Makha not only quoted prices, but allowed herself to discuss details. If things turned up that she didn't know about, she got on the Internet and gained the best understanding of them she could. This information did not stack neatly in her brain. It tried to escape, became muddled and squashed. Makha felt her head swelling, like a big bubble with eyes in it. "It is just impossible to master all this," she thought in horror. Then she thought about Max and wondered how he could know so much. She meekly continued replying to the emails. Time condensed again, and speeded up. She hardly left the computer.

When an email arrived from Nadya, Makha did not immediately realize it was not an enquiry. "If I always understood you," Nadya wrote, "I would have attained Enlightenment long ago." (Smiley face). "But with you everything is always so simple. I imagine it's because you are older, have experienced all these things, and now don't even remember what they are like." She went on to tell him how much she hated living in her gloomy little town where nobody had any time for anybody else, how fed up she was with her mother, who was completely preoccupied with trivia and did not understand her, and how she missed having a close friend she could talk to in her backwoods. Well, perhaps Nadya didn't actually write all that, but Makha couldn't be bothered to read the email more carefully. It bored and irritated her.

"She hasn't understood what I wrote," Makha thought indignantly. "She has completely missed the point of what I was trying to say, what Max wants to tell her. She is still hoping someone will come to her rescue. Oh, sure! Any minute now I'm going to turn up, marry you, and take you away from your hell-hole! Why do women have to be so stupid?"

Makha got up and started pacing up and down in front of the window. It occurred to her that, if she was a smoker, she would assuredly have lit a cigarette. Or if Max was. Though what was the difference? Neither she nor Max did smoke, and it was pointless to be thinking like this. But how stupid women are. Fools, the lot of them. Stop!

No. That was not how Max would think. That was the way she thought. Max would quite certainly know how to reply. He would write something detached and full of wisdom. That was precisely what attracted them all to him, that was why these girls were emailing him. First, they were attracted to him, and then they quietly fell in love with him, and it was because he didn't get angry, didn't want anything for himself, and could understand them. Or if he didn't, at least he could see more in them than just a woman with problems. He could point that out to them: "Look, there is more to you than that, you can do more. Why do you want to cry and cling to someone else?" He could write like that, Max could. How come?

She had asked him once. Yes, Makha remembered, she had asked him about it and he had immediately replied, as he did to all her questions, explaining what it was about him that attracted everyone. Makha had not understood then. Her mind had been on other things.

"You treat everyone in exactly the same way," she had said. "It seems to make no difference who you are talking to: a man or a woman, what age they are, what they want out of life, or from you. That's so strange. Why are you like that?"

"What difference is there?" Max asked in surprise. "A man, a woman ... There is only you and the sky above. Did you not sense that when you were lost in the swamp?"

They had had that conversation in May, standing on a balcony at the hostel, and looking at the red fringed horizon. The swamp had been far from Makha's thoughts, but right now it seemed close. Very close. She looked down at her feet, half expecting to see the linoleum in Max's kitchen covered in moss. Her feet might sink into it up to her ankles, but she had only to take a step and the footprint would be gone. You would pass by and no trace would remain. The moss would close over your tracks, your thoughts, your hopes, leaving nothing. What difference did it make who you were, what you were thinking about, what you wanted, whether you were a man or a woman? There was really only you and the moss, which saw no difference.

"Learn to see yourself and the sky above. Learn to see that everyone is equal. Rise, become wiser than yourself. Become Max. But then, what will remain of me?"

Max seemed to have moved beyond certain boundaries, within which a person is still a person with weaknesses, problems, personal opinions, and a private life. It was as if he were not above all that, but removed from it – and Makha could not understand, frantically at a loss how that was possible.

"If for you everybody is equal, you don't love anybody," she had wanted to say there on the balcony, but hadn't, and never did. She just let him go, incomprehensible, enigmatic, and a month later went back to her parents for the vacation, keeping Max in her heart as her warm, agreeable Muscovite mystery.

She was calm now, as if she had taken a breath of fresh air. She sat down at the computer and carefully re-read the email. See the person behind the problems, not yourself and your own problems, but prodigal Man. See him and lead him out of the woods, just as Max had led her out of the swamp.

Makha clicked "Reply", closed her eyes, collected her thoughts, and her fingers sped over the keyboard. The email was concise, clear and simple, the way she would have liked Max to write to herself from that other place, that realm of non-being into which he had vanished.

"The more we know about a person, the more estranged

from them we become. They turn into their biography, a data set, a telephone number, habits, a memory. Their essence escapes. The same is true of ourselves. The more complete our knowledge of ourselves becomes, the less we know who we really are. A baby, who has no conception of itself or of the world, is closer to true understanding than someone who believes everything has long been perfectly clear.

"Allow yourself to change in the way that water flows. Allow yourself the luxury of knowing nothing about yourself. You will see how the world around becomes equally uncategorized, – and wonderful."

4

Time, like a metronome, passed at its deliberate, pre-determined speed, only now it was outside a window which Makha looked out of less and less.

Nadya never emailed again. Makha was not surprised, and soon forgot all about her. By now she was no longer just replying to the emails: she had learned how to do Max's job. Some things she found easy, particularly designing posters, calendars, and billboard advertisements. Makha could do that herself, and soon proudly received her first fee. Payment was made electronically, however, and the supply of potatoes in the cupboard was running low. She might soon be obliged to meet customers in order to be paid in real money. She giggled, imagining how astounded they would be when, instead of Max, they were confronted with her. There was no certainty, of course, that any of them had actually known Max in the real world.

She was resigned to the fact that she would never work Max out. Something told her, beyond all gainsaying, that that was impossible. He had taken everything personal with him, if there had been anything personal, and there remained no trace of him in the apartment. She did not even notice that it no longer troubled her.

Makha stopped looking over her shoulder to him, relaxed, and began appearing on message boards under his name. No one noticed any difference. She took part in discussions, gave advice, and people listened and appreciated her. The moderator of one discussion proposed a date for an online seminar. ("Somehow we've neglected this topic and should put that right.") Makha thought about it and agreed.

She performed with unexpected ease, if not without a little anxiety, but that only added spice. She replied to questions like a laid-back professional. When one neophyte began going on about how all work has to be informed by creativity and inspiration, especially work like theirs, and that everything depends on talent, Makha laughingly replied, "You are wrong. No one is irreplaceable. All that matters is experience and expertise. It's been a long time since anyone cared about your personal attributes. That's not what people pay for." Max was listened to as a new guru.

When, towards midnight, the seminar was over, Makha felt a different person. She didn't turn on the light. The monitor's milky screen was bright enough to illuminate the kitchen, for her to sit cross-legged on the couch, to look into the void, listen to herself, and try to understand what had happened. Suddenly, with a terrible certainty, she knew that Max never would come back. He had disappeared. If, indeed, enigmatic Max had ever been there at all.

Makha sat stock-still. She felt she had taken his place, occupied his niche, and nobody but she herself had even noticed. In this world, who you are is of no importance, what kind of heart you have, whether you can hear jazz rhythms in a dripping tap or see the cosmos in a puddle of rainwater. In the world which Max inhabited, and in which she now lived, it did not matter to anyone what kind of person you were. Unless to someone who loved you. Max hadn't seen that. He had just dissolved. Much simpler.

Makha resolutely got up from the couch and went into his living room. That was all right now. She opened the door and turned on the light, not knowing what she was going to do. Would she switch on his computer and search through his private emails? Would she look in the cupboard and find photos of his family, notebooks, personal belongings, dried flowers pressed between the pages of yellowed pads of writing paper? Something, anything that would prove Max had existed?

She did open the cupboard and a sheaf of photos fell out. They were large format, on high-quality paper, landscapes and unexpected sketches, portraits of ordinary people, a texture of wet stone, simple, wistful flowers, puddles and lights reflected in them, all the photographs taken on film and intended, as Max had said, "for the frame". They fell out at her feet and Makha looked down at them, as shocked as if they had been dead birds.

None of these real things were any longer needed. They were things in which there was more of Max than in any of his other work; things he did not want to use as wallpaper for his site, or turn into a poster, an advertisement, or a wall calendar. None of them were needed any more, and they lay in a heap on the floor. If, until that moment, she had retained some hope at least that Max might be in Turkey or Egypt, lazing on a beach, sipping a cocktail through a straw and joshing girls in bikinis, gazing at a warm, delightful sea and trying to forget about Moscow and work, now Makha could delude herself no longer, and everything crumbled. She would never work him out, never get to know him better, and he would not come back. His place had been taken by her. The world did not care who performed a particular job, a man or a woman, old or young. It made no difference.

Closing the door of Max's living room, she returned to the kitchen and for several minutes stared dully at the blackness outside. Then something stirred in her, perhaps in its death throes. "No, I'll leave this place. Tomorrow! For Christ's sake, I am not you, I don't want to be you, and I am not going to be you! It's impossible – and wrong!"

She yanked the computer plug out of the wall. Its background hum, never absent from the kitchen, deflated like a balloon. The silence was so unfamiliar that Makha, in despair, started listening to the night. Somewhere far away, on the verge of inaudibility, a car alarm was wailing.

Makha went to bed and looked at the white ceiling with its bright spot of reflected streetlight. She almost hated this apartment, although she was virtually a part of it. She almost hated that car and its alarm, although she was also comforted by it as the only sign of life in an empty world.

"Perhaps he never existed. Perhaps I've always lived here and been him. Perhaps nothing was ever different." Eyeless, sorrowful solitude encircled her, and insomnia. It no longer mattered how Max had lived in this place.

"Perhaps because I loved you too much. So much that I wanted to be your shadow, to fuse with you, to do everything for you. So that problems and sadness should never trouble you. So that life should be easy for you and you should never again have that terrifying look in your eyes that I saw in the swamp. Otherwise, I cannot understand how all this has come about."

Her parents would not telephone the hostel, and nobody there would miss her. Makha prised open her cell phone, which had been silent all these days, and flushed the sim card down the toilet. She went out to the mailbox at the entrance, scooped up all the paper spam, found the slips to pay for the apartment and the Internet, and was unsurprised to find them in her name. Going back inside, she went to Max's room and took particular pleasure in working out how to operate his wonderful, expensive Canon.

In the morning, when the older children upstairs who had not yet gone to school turned on their rap, Makha called the customer whose job she had completed during the night. She would not have been surprised if the silence at the other end of the line had resolved itself into the dial tone as the customer declined to speak to her. It was so long since she had been outside the apartment block that she no longer quite believed in the existence of the rest of the world, but answer he did. He was not puzzled to hear a woman's voice, but pleased, and promptly made an appointment, agreeing to everything and prepared to pay immediately.

When she was describing herself to enable him to recognize her, she was tempted to say, "I am small and tired with eyes sunken from lack of sleep. HTML and computer graphics are driving me crazy," but she did not. Max would never have spoken like that. She arranged the meeting and replaced the receiver.

Seizure

Translated by Arch Tait

I was hitchhiking from point A to point B through the indeterminate vastness of our boundless land, not alone but with a lean, contemplative lad whom the well-meaning owners of my most recent place of rest had suggested as a companion. Our travel plans coincided but we were making slow progress.

It was a hot summer, the asphalt melting and yielding beneath heavily laden trucks, radiators overheating. In a single day we abandoned two vehicles with boiling radiators, leaving them, like horses ridden into the ground, to their fate on the road. We were crossing the steppe in the Volga region but there was no water anywhere near the highway. The drivers had no choice but to wait for their engines to cool and we were in a great hurry. What could we do but abandon them and hitch on? The road, however, is unforgiving towards the egotistical and in the end nobody was stopping for us.

We split up to make ourselves more mobile, standing well apart and thumbing on our own account. Almost immediately, I was picked up by a truck headed for a suburb of Point B and thought we had been well advised to separate. No truck would pick up two hitchhikers. Only a couple of days later did I learn that my mate had got himself a lift in an air-conditioned jeep. We would both have fitted in nicely, backpacks and all. He travelled the rest of the way with the wind in his sails, arrived by nightfall, and then had to wait twenty-four hours for me at our pre-arranged crash pad. I proceeded at a more leisurely pace with a talkative trucker.

His name was Vlad and he was not only talkative but exceedingly amorous. After driving for an hour he announced he fancied a session in the sack with me. This came as a considerable surprise and I was fairly sure he must be joking, because by this time I was a month into travelling freely round the country and had presently been five days on the road. If I wasn't exactly stinking, I had been well kippered by campfires. When hitching I always dressed so as to make it hard to tell whether it was a boy or a girl standing at the roadside. More to the point, in my tribulations I invariably forgot what sex I was and all matters relating to feminine allure. Summer was the road, tramping, mountains, sun, barbarity, solitude, and hitchhiking. I was an unkempt, asexual freak bearing a backpack as big as myself. My trucker's proposition had me laughing hysterically for a full five minutes.

Except he was serious, and I had to employ all my rhetorical skills to persuade him he was deluded in seeing me as an appropriate object for his lust. Not for an instant did I consider getting out of the truck: everybody knows you shouldn't change horses in midstream. But my driver proved an obstinate nag and tried tenaciously to persuade me I would not be disappointed.

"I've got a boyfriend," I said, searching for a straight-forward human excuse. "What, that drip? The one standing ahead of you? Call that a boyfriend? He's never going to show you a good time. You don't know what love is, kiddo. What you need is a real man."

"I make it a principle not to do it on the road."

"Quite right too! We won't do it on the road, we'll find a turning this evening and have it off there."

He had a huge belly, although he wasn't old. I looked at him, increasingly surprised at his persistence. "Good roadside tarts have died out," he lamented. "The whole way from Nizhny Novgorod I didn't see one you could fancy. If it isn't little schoolgirls it's old woman pushing fifty. What's happened to the fanciable ones? Gone off and got married, have they? What sort of perve would I be to go after skirt like that?"

I sneaked a glance at myself in the side mirror. A freckled, snub-nosed, almost animé face looked back at me, wild-eyed, with dirty, matted hair. I looked barely twenty, although I was older than that. What could he be seeing in me? I looked away from the mirror with a sigh.

"What is it? Don't you like me?" Vlad asked, without turning to me. "I do like you, as a person." "Well, great! Let's do it!" "No. It's precisely because I like you that we're not going to do it." "I don't get it." "I don't want to ruin your life." "What do you mean?"

"I mean literally. I'm a witch. Sleeping with me is dangerous," I blurted out. Now it was his turn to laugh, as if demons were tickling his armpits. He let go of the steering wheel and practically swerved into the oncoming lane. I sat beside him, unsmiling and dismayed.

"Come on, kiddo, don't lay it on too thick! This isn't my first day behind the wheel." "It's not my first time hitching either, gramps." "Well, go on, prove it!" "How?" "Well, what can you do, witch?" "Oh, just little things. I can treat a few ailments, colds, patch up family quarrels, bits and pieces. Nothing too difficult." I faltered, hoping he would let it drop, and not, of course, saying a word about the odd, cruel gift which has burdened me all my life, giving me nightmares and headaches and my sick, unsociable personality.

"Can you put the evil eye on someone?" he asked. "I won't if you don't keep pestering me." "No, I don't believe it. It's a load of garbage. You need to show me something." "Show you what?" "Okay, not a striptease! Just show me something you can do."

I scrutinised him for a moment, and then I lost it. I started telling him about his life: that he had a jealous wife, that he didn't love her, and that she was always going on at him about not earning enough. I told him he had piles and gastritis and catarrh. I told him he loved his five-year-old son and sometimes took him with him on shorter trips. I told him his elder brother had been killed in a headlong collision two years before while drink driving, and that his boss at the transport firm where he worked wanted to fire him but he shouldn't worry about it. If he did get fired, he would find a better job with better pay within a couple of weeks and things would work out for the best. Unless, of course, he harmed me now.

I don't know what had startled him most, but half an hour later he was still sitting there as white as a sheet and it wasn't just the heat making him sweat. He kept intoning, meditatively, the same obscene word. I could see the state he was in. It scared me and I kept very quiet. After all, he was the driver and, as they say, the Devil is always at your elbow.

But what had I told him anyway? All those ailments just go with the territory of being a long-distance trucker. The only one I had left out was rheumatoid arthritis, because for the moment I couldn't remember all the varieties. He had told me about his wife himself, and the fact that he was obsessed with anything in a skirt made it clear there were problems at home. His son's toy Kamaz truck was in the cab with us, and his little baseball cap was tucked in behind the sun visor. I guessed the kid's age from its size. He had been grumbling about difficulties with his boss, and I just made up the bit about his future prospects to lighten the rest of it and encourage him to think positively, as a psychic on television when I was a child was always urging. I had dropped a brick, of course, with the bit about his brother, which came from my hellish innate gift.

"Well, Christ, I mean... Shitty death! You should be advertising in the newspapers! I could bring my friends to see you." "Oh, come on. It's just peanuts." I was pleased. It looked like I could relax, imagining there would be no more talk of sessions in the sack. Alas, his sexual fantasies now burst forth in a new direction. "Hey, I heard that if you sleep with a witch you won't have any more problems in your life. Is that right?" "Vlad! Who's been putting that kind of nonsense in your head? Everything has to be by consent, otherwise..." "Yes, I understand that. I won't say another word. Hey, I've never been with a witch. How do you do it with a witch?"

Oh, spirits of light! I was facing a whole day and half a night of this, trying to rein in my benefactor's rampaging libido.

The road had become a morass and time was now the wilting pocket watches painted by that psycho, Dali. My thoughts turned wistfully to my travelling companion and I longed for our squat, a shower, and my own dear, warm sleeping bag.

In the end I started feeling sorry for poor Vlad. By now he was fantasising about carrying me off to his parents' village and installing me in a new house smelling of wood shavings. We would go every Saturday to the bathhouse, and then leap naked into a stream and jump through fire all summer long. I would shield him from disease and nothing bad would ever happen to him again. He would be top dog in the village and all the chicks would jump out of their skirts and straight into bed with him. In his pagan erotic fantasies I figured as a cross between a water-sprite, his personal magic goldfish, a leprechaun leading him to the crock of gold, and a magical huntress bestowing adamantine potency on all who shared her fragrant, coniferous couch in the depths of the taiga and showing them the way to the treasure. From these sudden outpourings of his subconscious you could have researched the folklore of the planet. Who would have thought it, looking at that beer belly?

In reality he was just a fat, sweaty, kind man hungry for love. His wife despised him. He lacked the education or upbringing to rise above his life, to gain insight into it from some break in the pattern of his existence. All the force of the love within him was focused on his son, whom his wife was always telling that daddy was bad. He hated her and was scared. He was longing for love and inside him there lived a hurt little boy. There was nothing I could do to help, if only because, whatever else he saw in me, he could not see me as a person. I sensed the indistinct shade of his dead brother hovering by my side window. He whispered his life story to me, eager to escape the captivity of death, a life just as unfocused and senseless. Their two incessant, piteous voices made my head ache and spin. I looked through the glass into the eyes of the spectre and listlessly gave the command, "I release you. You are free." That was all he needed. It is the only reason they come to trouble me, and I am used now to doing it without worrying about the details.

The spectre vanished like a swarm of gnats dispersed by the wind, and at that Vlad took a turn. It occurred very suddenly, before I had time to figure out what was happening. His face went red and he grimaced, his eyes bulging. He started rocking forward towards the steering column. The truck veered to the left, I grabbed the stiff steering wheel and heaved it round towards myself. The truck swerved. Vlad instinctively jammed his foot down on the brake, and we came to a halt on the verge, facing a ditch. Just as well the road was deserted.

"Where do you keep your water?" I asked, clambering back. Long-distance drivers generally keep everything on their bunks. He gestured backwards, wide-eyed and afraid. His nose was bleeding, either because he had hit it on the steering wheel or from high blood pressure.

I found everything we needed, water, his first aid kit, dampened a bandage and put a cold compress over his nose and forehead. I opened the doors and a slight breeze, cool now as night was falling and, more importantly, fresh, entered the car. When Vlad recovered a bit, I got him out and we sat on the verge.

"My brother used to have that," Vlad said, already getting over it. He was docile now, small and pathetic. "Fits. He wasn't allowed to drink, or to drive either, but he did drive, very carefully, and only his Lada Samara. He didn't drink though, not a drop, only that one time. His wife had left him, so he did drink. You couldn't even call it drinking, just a beer. The guys in the workshop poured him one, a Friday it was. They were a bit surprised but he didn't explain and just drove off. He was coming to see me. I think he had the same as happened to me just now."

I said nothing. His brother had just whispered all that to me, apologetically, saying goodbye, only I hadn't been listening. I was feeling ill. Perhaps it was hearing it all repeated now, or the sad voice of one of the living, that made me feel suddenly cold and wretched. We sat side by side, our backs to the road, not many cars passing. The terrain was hilly and there was an abandoned field downhill from where we were. Further along, the slanting rays of the evening sun lit up some woodland which cast a long, dark shadow over the road.

"Do you get that often?" "What? Oh, that. No. I didn't get it at all before my brother died. He was older than me. Genes, they say, but anyway, not often, not often at all. I don't know why it happened just now. Just bad luck, I suppose. I haven't been drinking. Perhaps it was you got to me. You're hot!" He smiled archly.

"Is anything hurting now?" "No. Actually, yes. My head. Here." I got up, stood behind him, and began healing him with my hands the way I knew, a light massage. He relaxed, loving it, leaned back and rested his head in my lap. Ten minutes later I asked, "All right?" "Not bad," he murmured, opening his eyes and looking up slyly. "I feel great. As if we'd just slept together."

I smacked his forehead and went to the truck. I was minded just to take my pack and say goodbye, but it was getting dark, there were no cars on the road, and I didn't have a tent. Hitching on your own at night would be worse than travelling with a preoccupied driver. The road is a gamble: you never know what hand it will deal you next. At least with Vlad I was more or less in control.

He crossed the road to the bushes and came back looking

pale, with a tight grin on his face, as if he had found a corpse. I asked what was there but he didn't reply, just started the truck and we drove off. It was only after we had driven a few kilometres, he said, "Did you know you saved my life?" "How come?" "Back there on the left was a quarry. They've dug the sand out twenty metres down, right by the roadside. Moonlighters, damn them, digging away, no warning signs. They didn't bother to make good afterwards, the shits."

We drove half the night and stopped at 3.00 in the morning at a café with good night-time parking for trucks. I felt out of place in the empty, echoing cafeteria. The woman serving behind the counter eyed me up impudently, like a competitor. I cringed inwardly. Vlad bought me a meal and we went to sleep in the truck.

"Come up here. Don't worry, I won't touch you," he said, and we lay together on his bunk shelf, leaving my pack on the seat. We shared a single scratchy blanket.

He was soon asleep, wheezing, hugging me, patting my back, mumbling to himself as he did so. It was cramped and stuffy and the windows soon steamed up. There was fog outside. Dawn began to break and I imagined the face of Vlad's brother through the glass, although I knew he was no longer there.

Vlad woke up after three hours, as promised, and was surprised I wasn't sleeping. "What's wrong?" "It's too warm in here." "I bet you've been casting spells," he said with a grin, and added wryly, "witch."

I could tell that everything that happened to him the previous day had been water off a duck's back. His robust, workman-like personality was resistant to change. I let go of the reins I had seized yesterday, relieved we had almost reached our destination.

Vlad gave me ten roubles and told me to buy myself a coffee. "Do you want anything?" "You," he answered shortly. I said no more, not feeling like coffee, and even less like meeting up again with the woman in the squalid café. I shoved the tenner in my pocket, ran to an evil-smelling toilet, walked around in the dewy grass behind the café for a while and came back. Vlad had already started the engine and was smoking out the window. "What took you so long? Did you get a drink? Right, let's go."

We drove almost the whole way in silence. Vlad seemed almost embarrassed by my presence, either that or by his weakness yesterday. He was ill-mannered and spoke only to swear, calling his wife to say he was on his way and she should have a meal ready for him. The boss phoned, bawled him out for being behind schedule, complained he should have been back long ago. Vlad threw the receiver at the dashboard, was silent for a time and then muttered, "What was that you said yesterday? If he fires me I'll find a better job? Perhaps I should just leave now, eh? Why wait?"

I said nothing. He was immersing himself once more in his life and I was again just a girl he had picked up on the road and who, when he dropped me off, he would drive away from and forget. I had no wish to be involved in his life.

He let me out at his turning. He passed me my pack and, while I was sorting it, lit up a cigarette, not driving off but looking at me appraisingly. I didn't care for that. It was time to say goodbye and I was already thinking ahead, looking for a good position for hitching my next lift.

"Well, goodbye then, witch," he said, just a little too casually. "Too bad we didn't make it in the sack. Nothing doing, when you could have sorted my life for me."

He grunted loudly, slammed the door and drove away.

Yaroslava Pulinovich

NATASHA'S DREAM

Translated by Noah Birksted-Breen

NATASHA is 16 years old. She's in a courtroom, dressed in a tracksuit. Her fists are clenched and she keeps looking around. She's missing a front tooth.

NATASHA. Well, to cut a long story short, that's bullshit, what you just said … That didn't fucking happen… What? Tell you what happened? And what else? You'll want to do it to me, yeah? Who's swearing? Not me… (*She's silent, looks straight ahead, then begins quietly*). Alright. It happened… Eh? I'm not mumbling, I'm telling you normal like… (*Speaks a bit louder*). It happened last year, September. We'd just got back from summer camp. I was like happy that we was back. 'Cos there was nothing at that camp, 'cept mosquitoes and they put Tanya SquintyEyes in my tent, so at night I was looking at mosquitoes and her arse, and I wanted more than that. The only sick thing was that Vitya pulled Lyosha's pants down, we pissed ourselves laughing, but I felt like a bit sorry for Lyosha – I mean, was it fun for him? So yeah. They told us – pack your things, we're going home, and when we was packing, I took Tanya's hairclip, the one with beads, why does that fat cow need a hairclip? Then we got in the bus and I like got upset because I realized that I couldn't even put the hairclip on – then Tanya would know it was me. I decided that if I get a bloke, I'll put on the hairclip to go and meet him. But until my bloke shows up – it'll stay where it is. I mean, seriously, I must have seen it in the tea leaves! 'Course, I had a bloke – look, I'm not a div, but me and him were just, we just got together at all the piss-ups, we even kissed a couple of times. His breath smelled of potatoes but I didn't think it was rank. Then I kissed him at a club once, I kissed him and thought – what if I suddenly start smelling of potatoes but I just don't notice it myself? And even if I didn't smell of it before, I'll stink of it now. Then I ran into the ladies' and washed my mouth with soap for ages. And then my lot, the girls, dragged me into one of the cubicles – to smoke, so I went with them. Sveta was knocking it back, and she opened the window and says: "Too scared to jump?" I say to her: "You thick shit, have your brains rotted? Jump where? It's the second floor!" Sveta stares me out and goes: "I know you won't jump." I go, "What d'you mean I won't jump?" She's like, "You won't jump!" I'm like, "Yeah, why wouldn't I jump?" She's like, "Well, jump, jump!" I reply, "You stupid pair of tits, have you lost it?" And at the same time, I threw the window open. No, of course, I did become a little bit scared at that point but there was nowhere to walk away – and I won't look like a div in front of Sveta! I look at her, something like, "You're a cow" – and I jump… I don't remember what happened next. But as I was falling, I was afraid it was the end, game over. And I made this wish – I want love. With a wedding veil and chocolate sweets. And with all the girls walking behind us and envying us. Only that's not the main thing. The main thing is he loves me, he comes up to me and says: "Natasha, you're the coolest girl on earth, marry me." Then I'll marry him on the spot.

I never thought that jumping from the second floor makes a wish come true. Really, it does, anyone who doesn't believe me should try it. Only you have to say it quickly 'cos you're falling for almost no time. I came to in hospital. They told me that some clever looking guy had come to see me, and I'm thinking – Sanek, is it? 'Course, Sanek's a nerd, but that don't mean he's clever. And I don't have any other intel- ... intellectual friends.

And then he came in – I knew immediately it was 'im because who else'd come and visit me in hospital? True, he didn't talk about getting married. He said he was a journalist from *The Country Spark*, that it's one of the oldest papers in the town, and that he really wants to write about me. I just needed to tell him about my life, nothing special – just any old crap. Are they cruel to us, do they feed us well, how much money do they give us an' that sort of thing. And why I jumped out the window, just 'cos or did they drive me to it? Last year I got a bit rattled 'cos Irina was interviewed – she won the wood-carving competition. But they didn't ask her about growing up, they asked about her artistic plans, that's what was in the paper:

"Irina, tell us about your artistic plans?"

"I am planning an artistic project to carve some wooden planes for Victory Day and give them to all the teachers."

And also a large photo – stunning. All the girls were jealous. I was also a bit jealous but then I thought, anyway I'm a natural blond and Irina dyed hers and that calmed me right down. But Sveta was fuming about it and when no-one was looking, she put that newspaper into the cubicles instead of toilet paper, so everyone would piss themselves laughing, but nobody did – I even felt a bit sorry for Irina.

The journalist – Valery – came to see me the next day with this thing called a dictaphone, you can say all these words to it, and then it repeats them all back. Valery asked me: do the kids at school pick on me? Yeah, right! I can kick the lock off the cubicle door, so what do you think, I'm a div who lets other kids pick on me? And he also asked about my parents – do I remember them or not, and what happened there? I give him a look and say: "Valery, my mum wanted to abort me but I went and survived anyway." Well, I wanted to make out like I'd seen life, so he'd know who he was talking to. What, I'm gonna tell him about Vlad the pimp, should I? How he bumped off my mum? And then Valery asked me: "Natasha, what's your dream?" That's when I understood it was him. Because nobody else had ever asked me what I dream about. And there it is, he just went and asked. I said to him: "Valery, you and I are adults, what's my dream? I have to work." But to myself I was thinking – now ask me again. I was stupid to answer like that, I should have told him straight away about my dream so he'd understand and say: "Natasha, you're the coolest girl on earth, please marry me." But I was afraid of that thing of his... Which was recording... Because, sure, I can tell him about my dream but what if someone else hears it? They'll piss themselves laughing! So that's why I answered him like that and he didn't say anything much, just said he hoped I'd get better soon and said I should come to the office for a paper when they discharge me. They discharged me a week later and told me to take it easy and not carry heavy loads. But the bruise was still sitting pretty on my arm, it looked a bit like a cat. I wore short sleeves specially so everyone would see it. I came back and right away I take Sveta by the arm, "Come on," I say, "let's have a smoke." We went into the toilets and I grabbed her hard by the hair, "You half-baked bitch, I say, what's the idea? You lost the plot?

D'ya at least understand who you're against, yeah?" Sveta squeals and I drag her across the floor by the hair. Then I got bored and went to the bedroom, slipped under the blanket, pretending to sleep. But I keep saying to myself: "Natasha, what's your dream?" "Natasha, what's your dream?" I kept saying it, again and again, and then I actually fell asleep. I didn't have to go to school... I woke up and it was already the afternoon. The girls have come back from school and they're getting changed. And the carer comes in, to check our school marks or something. And she stares at me. "Are you not well, Natasha?" she asks. "I'm not, Raisa Stepanovna, look at this bruise." So she's like, "Then how come Tanya saw you dragging Sveta around by the hair?" What a rat, I think, that fat stinking cow, did she work out what happened to her hairclip or something? "Nah," I say, "there was nothing like that." Then Sveta raises her eyes, she was standing lookin' through her bag, and she says, "Yes, Raisa Stepanovna, there was nothing like that, we just... we were mucking around." And she lowers her cute little blue eyes to the floor. That's when I understood that even if Sveta's a spotty div, she's also my best friend. I call her over in the canteen at lunch, "Sveta, I say, something's up." And I told her all about the way it was, with Valery. She understood that I gotta talk to him, get myself ready and march down to the office. And she's like – you shouldn't be alone, let me come with you, I'll take a look at him, too, and I'll tell you as a friend if it's him or not. Fine, to hell with you, little red riding hood, let's go, I think to myself. I say, just don't put too much makeup on, we're not going to a club, we've got to make him understand from the start that we're not tarts, and we may be from an orphanage but we know our own value. Well, we got ready, I put on SquintyEyes' hairclip, and we slipped out. We arrive, all business-like, we ask some old guy something like, where would one find Valery? He says, over there. In that office. There was a really cool sign: *The Country Spark* Newsroom. Well, we went in, and there was a crowd of seven or eight people sitting there, buried in their computers, smoking, all of them. 'Cos of the smoke I didn't even know where to go, at first, and then I look and there he is, my love, sitting in the corner by the window. I go over to him, "Hi Valery," I say, "how's things." And he says, hi, Natasha, all good. You've come for a paper, yes? And I'm like, well, yes, and generally to find out how you are? He goes, yes, fine, and he hands me a newspaper. So I understand that if I don't tell him now, we'll part ways like ships in the night. Valery, I tell him, I didn't tell you everything, we should talk. He goes, yeah? Well, let's talk. I go, well, not here, can we go for a walk? And then he says, come tomorrow at six to the park, the one near the newsroom, I'll be waiting for you there. Even my armpits started sweating from joy, see you there, I say. And he goes, well fine, okay, bye then. And I left. I'm walking and I can't see a thing. I even bumped into Sveta, who's standing by the door lighting up the office with her crimson spots. She and me are walking along the street and she's like, what, well what, tell me, what happened? But I can't say anything. I'm walking and my head's spinning: "Natasha, what is your dream?" "Natasha, what is your dream?" Like a broken record... I don't even know how that day passed. Every five minutes I ran to look at the clock in the hall, come on, when will it be tomorrow, I'm thinking, when will it be tomorrow? And when we arrived, Tanya SquintyEyes saw her hairclip and she went nuts. Shut it, you fat stinking cow, I say, but I don't feel like swearing. I've become so nice I can't even believe it myself. Any other time I'd knock her over but now I don't even feel like swearing. I waved her away and went into my room. It's good she's not in the same room as me or I'd have strangled her a long time ago. I got into bed, but after the bell rang, I went to the toilets and took out the paper Valery had given me from my pyjamas. I'd decided to read the paper myself first and then I'd give it to the girls to read. 'Cos it's written about me there – so I should read it first. Sveta bugged me the whole way back – come on, show me, show me, I'm telling her, Sveta, forget it, learn to read first! I got the paper out, and I'm reading, I'm reading – there's nothing about me! There should be but there isn't. I read everything, I even checked the crosswords – it's nowhere! And then on the last page, right on the fold, in print that's so small it's hard to read, there's something about some cop's murder, about two cars crashing and about me. Yeah, about me. (*Frowns, remembers*) "A girl from an orphanage, Natasha Banina, jumped out of a second floor window. To a journalist's questions, the girl answered that it was an accident, and she did not intend to kill herself. At present, Natasha's health gives no reason for concern." But no photo. I wasn't happy about that – first name, surname, but no photo. I remembered Irina. I thought, Sveta was right to put that paper in the toilet... But on the other hand, I'm friends with a journalist now, you think he won't print my photo?

The next day, I literally count the minutes – is it now, is it now? And I think, you know, I need to be late, totally normal like. And then I think, oh yeah? And what if I'm late and he doesn't wait, he thinks that I haven't come, so I changed me mind. So in the end I turn up in that park at half five, I sit on the bench, I don't even smoke, I chew some mint gum. I don't know how long I sat there, I even started worrying that he wouldn't turn up. I sit and I sit and suddenly there's a voice behind me – hello, Natasha. I was terrified, but I didn't show it, I turned around ever so slowly, hi Valery, I say. But everything inside me's turning upside down. I've even forgotten how to breathe, something's going boom-boom in my chest, and I'm gulping for air with my mouth. Well, tell me, he says, what's going on? I sit like that, shaking my head like a horse. Sure, I say, let me just gather my strength. Are they cruel to you in the children's home, he asks. I'm like – well, yes, it happens. And why did you jump out of the window, did you want to kill yourself? Obviously, I didn't want anything like that, it was all 'cos of Sveta, that idiot, but anyway I say – yes, I did. Then he says – Natasha, maybe you want some juice or fizzy water? I say – yes, and cigarettes too, if that's okay. He goes off and brings back juice, got himself a beer and hands me a pack of cigarettes – Parliament. We sit, me and him, we smoke, and I pour out my life to him. I don't even know what comes over me, normally only divs pity themselves but am I a div? In primary school, we used to catch kids like that and trip them up, what's the matter, little shit, life's hard, is it? But as soon as I start talking, there's just no shutting me up. I'm talking to him and I'm thinking he'll tell me to get lost any minute now and then it's all over. You flee-bitten orphan, he'll say, and walk away. But he's sitting there, listening, and then he even takes my hand, so gently, as if I'm a little girl. Even in kindergarten nobody held my hand that way, well, only if they were taking you to see the head teacher. But I'm not a little girl anymore and inside my heart is – boom-boom. What an idiot, I think, I should have got some cream from Sveta to moisturize my hands, what if I've got rough hands? And me and him sat like that for a long time, I told him so much other stuff. I told him about us girls, about Irina, about my best friend Sveta. About our club nights. Then he says, come on, let's go, Natasha, I'll walk you back. And we set off. We're walking and I think our bastard-of-a-town, why is it so small? We won't even get a normal walk. If we were in Moscow, we'd walk all night, I'd tell him everything – everything, and then, when it was morning, he'd say to me: "Natasha, you're the coolest girl on earth, please marry me." If we were in Moscow, he'd have definitely said that, but not here, because for that you need to gather your strength, and for that you need time. And what time is there if you can walk around the whole town in an hour? And then when we said goodbye near the orphanage, he hugged me and he says: "Natasha, take care." Can you imagine? Natasha, take care... Natasha, take care... I don't remember how I came in, how I fell asleep, what I said to the carer. It was the first time that's happened to me that I can't remember anything. Even at the piss-ups, I always remember everything, and now, it's as if I'm ill. I'm lying in my room, the bell's already gone, but I can't sleep. The shadows are creeping over the walls and I look at them, and in my head it's "Natasha, take care, Natasha, take care, Natasha, take care..." And then it began, I've never had this before. Yeah, me and Rusya kissed, yeah, but I never thought about him, and now I just can't get him out of my head. I sit in the classrooms but I'm thinking about him. I smoke with the girls in the toilet, but I'm still thinking about him. I even got a good mark for my essay, about this Tatiana, from that book, what's it called... anyway, I can't remember. Sveta even said "Natasha, you've turned into an airhead, what's going on? We talk to you and you're nodding your head like a horse..." Should've got her by the hair but I don't say anything. Yeah, I'm an airhead... And all the time I'm looking out the window, what if he suddenly shows up? Well, I'm an idiot obviously, I know he won't come, I mean, does he know what room I live in? But I keep looking anyway. My eyes start aching from the staring. The girls are like – what's up wiv' you? But I'm like – nothing, and carry on staring...

And then one day I come back from school and Mrs. S is like, "Natasha, come in." I knew right away: this isn't good,

I've screwed up somehow. I go into the office but Mrs. S is holding a newspaper in her hand, well, Banina, she says, you want to go to Orphanage 9, yes? That's how she always scares the shit out of us but now her face told me that she might do it, without thinking twice about it. She'll scribble down a couple of chits and that's it, goodbye girls. But what's happened, I ask. She's like, "I see your life here is so hard that maybe you'd be better in Orphanage 9?" "And that bitch grabs my arm, hissing like a snake, and says, have you gone fucking mad, when were you beaten, who's ever laid a finger on you?" I'm thinking – ha, just try it, if you hit me, next thing you know you'll be counting the stars. I remember when I was ten, how the same Raisa Stepanovna once hit me on the head so hard it hurt for a week. Well, does that bitch think I've forgotten? I don't forget anything, and I don't plan to forget, just try me... And then I think, what's she on about, what's she actually talking about? "What are you on about," I ask? She holds out the newspaper to me, says, "there, read it, my little princess. Journalists are interviewing her, you see..." And she stares at me: "you know, people want the best for you, Natasha, who has it in for you, mm?" I just hate when she talks like that, it makes me want to spit in her face. I take the newspaper, I go off to the toilets, I sit down and read it. And there's everything almost word-for-word that I told Valery. What the hell, I think, why the fuck did he write that? I told you, I told only you, don't you get it? I was so upset... I sit there, staring at one spot. Bastard, I think! And then I think why's he a bastard? He didn't know that he shouldn't write about that because they'll kill me afterwards. Maybe he wanted to protect me, he wanted someone to come and take me away? I mean, he doesn't know what it's like here... But there was this one phrase: "This girl has lived through so very much in her short life. It is terrifying to think what else lies ahead. Will she even survive?" And I started feeling so good that he was afraid for me. It's the first time someone's felt afraid for me. Then I felt stupid 'cos I'd thought he was a bastard. I even kissed his name, on the newspaper... Fuck the carer, I think. Now a real power has appeared behind me, what's she gonna do, go head on against this paper, is she? She hasn't got the balls! And she doesn't care about me but Valery does. Maybe he'll even take me to live with him, why do I need that disgusting hag now? And then it hits me like an electric shock to the head – but what if she chucks me into No. 9? She already swore she'd do it three times. What if she decides to do it this time? I look for Sveta, I say, they're sending me to No. 9. Sveta's like – so what, they took Max there, and he wrote to Gulya that he became a real bloke there, that he doesn't mind at all. Don't worry, he says, it's so sick there, even better, the people are cool, if you're a div here, you'll be a div there, if you're cool here, you'll be cool there. You see what I'm saying? I guess so, I reply. That's something I'd kinda thought of before – so yeah, let them send me away to No. 9, even No. 10, for all I care. Do I need to hang on the streets, do I? Peeps reckon the school's cooler, and even if you don't show up to classes, you still get good marks at the end of term, and you can still do whatever, you just can't leave the grounds. And that's when I think – then how will Valery and me see each other? And tears fill my eyes. I run to the toilets, sit on the bog and cry like an idiot. Sveta knocks – open up, she says, what's going on? And I'm like – fuck off, you cow. And I sit there and cry. I think, I'll fucking kill the carer if she does that to me. And then I remembered mum. She wrote me a letter once. I was four, and they'd taken mum off to jail for six months. I lived with her friend, Anya. Auntie Anya never beat me like mum but she always screamed at me and stopped me from touching things, even though I was never touching her stuff anyway. She had a video player and she was afraid I'd break it. And once she came and brought me a letter – dance, she said, there's a letter from your mum. I'm like – dance? She's like – go on, dance! Well, I danced a bit. But she's like – you dance and take off your dress. And she's laughing so hard it sounds like a horse neighing, she was very drunk. I said – I won't. She's like – well then you won't get your letter. And she went into her room. I waited and waited, then I went into her room – give me the letter, I say. But she's already snoring… I took the letter from her pocket, unsealed it and looked at it. And I understood what she'd written: Natasha, I love you and miss you. Yeah, that's what she'd written, even though I couldn't yet read. I'd take that letter out a lot to look at it. And when mum came back, I showed her that letter. And she took it from me. She probably thought, why do I need the letter now she's back. And I remembered that I have two photos of mum but they're in the carer's office. Once we had a piss-up, and the carers did a search in the morning looking for drink in the bedside tables, stupid tit-heads. Well so, Mrs. N found a bottle of beer, goes on looking and finds the photos. Well, she decided to punish me by taking away the photos. It's just that it wasn't Mrs. N on duty now, it was Raisa Stepanovna Well, you fucking give them to me, you cow, I think, or I'll fucking teach you, right now. I went to the office, and I said to her, give me back my mum's photos. I'm thinking, you can put me in solitary confinement for all I care but I'm still going to punch your ugly mug, I was so angry. But Raisa Stepanovna looks at me hard. Where are they, she said? I say, look in Mrs N's desk. Well, she looked, and rooted around, and found them. She gave me back the photos but she had a look on her face… Not the usual one. Well that's it, I'm thinking, I'll be sent to No. 9. I went to the toilets and I looked at the photos. My heart started pounding. There's one photo which is so, you know... mum's sitting there, all made up, so beautiful, next to some bloke. Mum's sitting at a table, the table has been laid for a big meal. My mum knew how to live, no doubt about that. And the second photo – she's fourteen years old. And, well, I don't really look at that photo where mum's with a bloke. I look at the fourteen-year-old one. The photo's black-and-white and mum's so little in it, and sort of frightened. Well, she's more beautiful in this one, with the bloke, but I look at the black-and-white one, at my little mum, with her frightened eyes, standing there, all tensed up, completely like one of the divs here, 'cept I don't think that about her because she's my mum. And because she's tensed up differently. I want to pity her 'cos of that, pull her to me and say – mum, mum... Do you remember when you wrote me that letter? Did you really write what I thought you did? And then I look at the photo and I think – my mum just wasn't lucky, basically, nobody, except me, really needed her. And now Valery needs me. He's afraid for me.... And there's nothing I can do, my tears drip, drip onto the patterned tiles... I was thinking about that, over and over, and dammit I even forgot about the club that evening!

Something like two weeks passed. Seems the carer forgot about No. 9. And I'm walking around, still thinking only about Valery – how's he doing? Where is he? I want to see him. I don't have the strength. But I don't know what to do so I call over to Sveta and I say, Sveta, I think I'm, um, you know... There's some unhealthy shit happening to me. And Sveta's like – what are you doing, Nat, don't you understand that you need to take action? Go to him, tell him, hello my little hare, I'm your little rabbit, that sort of thing. Put your makeup on, make yourself beautiful, why waste your chance, you've only got one life. Basically, Sveta's some sort of idiot, but sometimes she says things like that, I mean, you gotta wonder where they fucking come from. So I'm thinking – yeah, I gotta take action. I put on makeup, clipped on SquintyEyes' hairclip and I'm off to the newsroom. I arrive like some Madonna, go into the newsroom, and I look – there he is. He's at his desk. Writing something. I'm all – hi, Valery. He's all – hello, Natasha, want some tea? I'm all – I do. He says – sit at this desk, next to mine, I'll put the kettle on. I sat down, and I'm sitting there but I dunno what to say. No, I get it all, I get that 'e's a man who's, what's it, highly fucking cultured so it needs to be about music or films. But what films do we get at the orphanage? I want to try music but in my head I'm stuck on: "Take me away now, take me over a hundred seas..." It's that song, maybe you know it, we're jumping around to it at the clubs all the time. But he gets out sweets and says – help yourself, Natasha, don't hold back. Just I have a lot of work to do, I need to write, and he buried himself in his computer again. So I'm sitting, gobbling up the sweets, and I'm staring at him the whole time. He's handsome. Long eyelashes like a girl's. Well, I never thought I'd notice shit like that, and here I am thinking – eyelashes like a girl's... And he keeps writing and writing.. And I'm staring, I've already finished my tea, it's sort of already time to go, but I keep staring. And, the main thing is I dunno what to say! First time that's happened to me... Then he says – Natasha, your carers are probably missing you. I say – nah, nah that's okay, and again I'm staring, at his eyelashes…. Come again if anything happens, he says, if you have any problems. I'm like – fine, don't worry, I'll be back… Well, I think, the man's really frightened for me, "come by again if you have any problems". And I realize that I have to leave, or he'll start thinking I'm… Well, that was that, I left. I'm walking and working it all out, what problems do I have? They have to be big, to be very serious, so I go again… I get back, I say to

Sveta, Sveta, I need to think of a problem, otherwise how can I go back to him? Sveta's like – well, I don't know, maybe you've got AIDS? Are you a fucking idiot, I say?! And she's like – why not? Everyone feels sorry for ill people, I, when I had to go to hospital, even the carer felt sorry for me, and the science teacher gave me a passing mark instead of failing me. What, don't you think it's a problem or something? I say – no, find another. Sveta thought and thought, went to the toilet, comes back and says – I know, maybe someone wants to adopt you? Some Spanish guy! And you don't want to. Maybe your future daddy, he's, what's it called? A pedophile? And you know that but, can you imagine, nobody believes you? And they're sending you to Spain! I'm saying – Sveta, have you been smoking? What Spanish guy, what are you on about, girl? You been listening to too much death metal? No way. Sveta and me thought and thought about my problem, but 'cos we couldn't think of anything, we went to bed. But anyway I couldn't stand it and the next day I went to see him again... Like the wife of some writer. Writers always had wives, didn't they? And that's when I understood he's mine... That I won't give him to anyone now because I had never had anything of my own, and now I do. And why the fuck should I give something that's mine to anyone? Only it's not mine like SquintyEyes hairclip or you know like jeans, or like an exercise book... It's mine like something you can't just stick in your pocket, and you can't throw it away, and you'll never get bored of it. It's something that's just mine-mine-mine, and that's that. And I can't even explain how much it's mine. It's just mine and that's it. And it was such a good feeling, and right here, in my chest it was so, just so warm...

And then... And then I don't know... There's nothing to say. I don't even know wha' to tell you. I started going to my Valery every day. We drank tea. And he also gave me a little book. By Kuprin. Called "Olesya". It's about one beautiful witch and about how the bastard Kuprin dumped her and it's about how he wrote about that as well. I don't like reading, I prefer to listen to music. But I read that one. And I even wanted to be a witch, too, like Olesya. Really cool, no need to fight, you don't need anything, just wave your hands and that's it – don't fucking move, you bastards! Everyone's terrified of you. And also Valery walked me back twice. Even though his mum's really ill. He walked me back anyway! Basically he was at college in another town, he hadn't been living here for a long time. But his mum's ill. So he lives here now. If Vlad-the-pimp hadn't beaten my mum to death, I wouldn't leave her side either. I had a beautiful mum. She put on bright lipstick, bright enough to make your eyes water. I got up onto her knees as a child, she's like – go away, I've got my lipstick on, you'll smear it. And I'd say to her – will you give me your lipstick when I grow up? And she'd say – Sure… She promised to give me everything – the lipstick, her dresses. It's just after mum died, Vlad took away all 'er things He came in a car and took 'em. So nothing was left for me. I should've killed that bastard Vlad! But someone got there first and killed him, three years ago… I told Valery all that and I wasn't ashamed to tell him. And you know… I actually wanted to tell him, I think… I don't know… And he said to me: "Natasha, you've got beautiful eyes." Rusya said my arse wasn't bad but that's the first time someone said anything about my eyes… I kept waiting for Valery to kiss me. But he only looked, didn't kiss. He was probably afraid 'cos I wasn't eighteen. I kept going to see him like that for three months. Every day… I even skipped sewing classes and I like sewing. I couldn't look at the other girls, let alone tell them…. And I was really rude to Rusya, told him to fuck off... Everyone in Valery's office started calling me by name, greeted me, they say: "Hi, Natasha". And Valery bought more sweets for me, I arrive and he pours the tea, then he pushes over a paper bag with sweets – help yourself, Natasha, he says, I bought them specially for you. Nah, if a person doesn't care, will he really start buying sweets? And he even taught me to play Patience on the computer!

And then... and then... No, I don't want to... No, 's no need, 's no need, I won't... What are you looking at? What are you all looking at? Am I guilty of something? I didn't want it to happen! I went there and I was told that Valery wasn't there. A guy came to the front door and told me. And he wouldn't even let me go into the newsroom. Well, I was like, fine, and I left. The next day I came back, and that guy says it again – Valery's not here. And next day same thing again. And the main thing is he won't let me in! Takes me by the arm and leads me out the street, nah, not nasty, none of that, all polite... But he won't let me in! And I kept coming back, I just kept coming... I was told that he didn't work there any more, that I didn't need to come back, but I didn't give a damn, I could feel he was there!!! I felt it here, in my heart, in my lungs, in everything! And I started walking around town alone, I don't mind if someone kills me now, if some maniac sneaks up on me and suffocates me, or a car runs me over! One time I even didn't go back for the night, I huddled up on a bench and sat there half the night. And then I saw him... With her. With that bitch... They were walking along, holding hands. And then, when they'd gone up to the doorway, he hugged her... and kissed her... And I suddenly wanted to die, to become tiny-tiny, I suddenly wanted to become a dot, just the dot like they draw on the board in maths, I wanted to be dead, to forget everything... For there to be nothing, nothing, nothing... I didn't even cry. Just stood and looked. And thought: "Mum, mum, mum, take me away from here, take me away..." And then, when I was walking back in the morning, I was filled with rage for that bitch. What right does she have to kiss him? What right to take him away? Who does she think she is? Mine, he was mine, I didn't want to let anyone have him, and here she came along and that's it! Bitch! Cow! Cunt! Cunt! Cunt! Little cunt! I mean, doesn't she have anyone else? She's got everything, everything, she's got parents, she has a home, she's got earrings, makeup, lipstick, all sorts of clothes, she probably eats biscuits by the pound... What right did she have to take him from me? Didn't she have enough of her own stuff? I found him first, I fell in love with him first!

And then... No, I don't want to tell you... Can I have some water? (*Drinks water*). Basically, I got back, gathered some girls, I say, time to teach that bitch a lesson... Well, we waited two days for her by that doorway. I remembered her, that cunt, even though it was dark. And then... Well... Let's go and talk, we said... And then when we were behind the garages... We didn't want it to turn out like that!!! It wasn't on purpose. I just dragged her by the hair and Sveta hit her ugly mug... It was Gulka started beating her heels down on her head... I didn't know it would be like that. I didn't think she'd turn out to be so weak... And there wasn't any prel.... Preliminary agreement as they're saying here! There wasn't! None of it is true! We didn't want her to fall into a coma, we didn't want this... to cause this "especially grievous damage", as they're... It's the investigator Prokopenko who wrote that. "They wanted to..." So, I ask you, the court, to examine my case again. (*Pause*). You know she didn't actually die in the end. She'll survive, the bitch, yeah? Don't people come out of comas or something? Her parents have loads of money. I'm told she'll get better. And I've got to do time because of that slut, yeah? And what am I guilty of? I just loved Valery, I just wanted him to be mine so we could walk together, drink tea, and then he'd come and say: "Natasha, you're the coolest girl on earth, please marry me!" Natasha, you're the coolest girl on earth, please marry me. Natasha, you're the coolest girl... Because she'll be told that ten times, that cow, she's got those clothes, and me? Who'll say that to me? Rusya? Not Rusya, he doesn't have enough brains to say that, yeah and I don't want Rusya to... I didn't want her to go into a coma, I didn't want that to happen to anyone, I just wanted – the wedding and the sweets... And all the girls to walk behind and be jealous... I just had that dream. Don't you have dreams? Is it really fair to destroy a person's dreams? If he actually loves me, is it really right? Is it really fair? And SquintyEyes' hairclip broke in my cell... Only the beads are left. See...

Natasha unclenches her fist – several shining beads lie in her palm. She looks at them. She smiles.
Darkness.

The End.

Victoria Chikarneeva

I Only Wanted to Live

Translated by Anne Marie Jackson

And so my story begins. I'm seventeen and in hospital.
Not for an ulcer or laryngitis, or even anorexia. It's far
more serious. The doctors suspect acute leukaemia – cancer
of the blood. I've heard the word "cancer" plenty of times
before, known it was a dreadful disease, painful and difficult
to cure, and that on the whole leukaemia is fatal. But I never
imagined that I, someone innocent, charming, and young,
might have it myself one day. It never even crossed my mind.

I often ask myself – why me? What offence before God
have I committed in my seventeen years to deserve this? I
haven't killed or stolen – I haven't broken any law. I'm just an
ordinary girl who wants to live and love, who wants to have
fun and do what she likes. I keep asking, but I can't find an
answer.

Why? Why am I and thousands like me suffering? My
veins, my fingers, my body have been pricked all over –
pricked by a multitude of needles, five times a day. I take
pills and other rubbish by the handful. I hate pills. I know
at firsthand about catheters, chemotherapy and biopsies.

Every day is a struggle. I want to live. Every day I pray to the heavens above for salvation.

For me each day is a miracle – a miracle through pain and tears.

I'm in the haematology unit of the children's wing. You don't live all that long with a disease like mine, although it's possible to recover if you can get a cell transplant. But it's hard to find donors and very, very expensive. Siblings often provide cells for transplants, but I don't have siblings. My only family are my father and grandmother – my mother died five years ago in a car accident. Sometimes parents will have a baby who can be a donor, but this is no help to me because the baby has to be a full-blooded sibling, and my mother is gone. It's that kind of a story, a real tearjerker. Although my life got off to a happy start. I thought it would always be that way.

Spring. The Beginning

It all started in April when my temperature got up to 39.7 a few times. I took paracetamol but it didn't help, so I took something stronger and made some vinegar wraps. My temperature came down for a few days, but then it went up and stayed up. I didn't have a cough or a cold and I wasn't nauseous; I just felt weak and my bones ached. I didn't want to go to hospital because final exams were just around the corner, followed by college entrance exams, and after that I was off to the seaside! I was ready for my exams – I'd studied with a private tutor. I wanted to study economics and become a real professional. Get an honours degree, find a prestigious job that paid well, buy an apartment, a car, get married, have three children, and live a long and happy life. Long and happy. In short, they were the uncomplicated dreams of a seventeen-year-old.

Finally I ended up going to the hospital for blood tests and was admitted as an outpatient. But on the May Day holiday, my fever went back up to 39.7. I sank into bed, holding compresses to my head and neck. I'd had plans to go with friends for a barbecue at a dacha, but I didn't make it.

After the holiday I had more blood work done and was diagnosed with viral hepatitis. I was admitted to hospital – my bilirubin level was high and my liver was enlarged. I was feverish and spent all my time in bed. I felt awful. My head was splitting, like someone was hitting it with a sledgehammer. I had no appetite and the pain in my joints and bones was so bad I couldn't move. This went on for several days.

In the middle of May I began to receive injections. My temperature was continuously high. If I took something for it, it would go down, but by evening it went back up again. It was unlikely that I had hepatitis and I was starting to get other symptoms. The doctors at the hospital were bewildered. They talked to my father a couple of times but didn't tell me anything.

I was burning up. I'd close my eyes and the heat would spread all over my body, from the top of my head to the tips of my toes. I was absolutely roasting. My head was aching and I couldn't make head or tail of anything, yet I had exams coming up! I had no idea how I was going to take them. I had stopped seeing my tutor because of the hepatitis. My father and grandmother had come to see me a few times. A friend from class visited once, but we had to talk through a window. She told me about the preparations for the graduation party. Naturally there wasn't any role for me. I sat on the window ledge long after she'd gone, crying and gazing up at the May sun, high in the sky. Why did I have to get sick now of all times? Olga Erokhina, not surprisingly, had taken the best role for herself, and Dimka would waltz with Zhenya Ilyina instead of me.

Oh well, I thought, just wait until I get out of hospital and I'll show them. But getting out of hospital wasn't in the cards.

Spring. May

At the end of May I was transferred to the diagnostic treatment ward. Here I would get a diagnosis and be referred for treatment. They drew lots of blood – from a finger and a vein, took some tissue for analysis, and I had an X-ray and a cardiogram. The results were okay, but my haemoglobin level was low and I was deficient in white blood cells and red corpuscles. The doctors said it was probably anaemia.

On the 25th of May, I persuaded them to let me go to school for "the last bell" celebration – it was only for three hours. There was a nice concert and congratulatory speeches, and we, the graduates were solemn in our uniforms, as is the custom in our school. I had a word with our group advisor and she gave me permission to sit only two exams, Russian and mathematics; I was exempted from the others. After assembly, the entire class went to the park to mark the end of the school year, but I headed straight back to the hospital and my drip feed. It had been a rite of passage of sorts for me, too. My spirits improved somewhat. After all, I'd seen my classmates, friends and teachers. And I only had to take two exams! Although I'd rather take all six than be stuck in hospital.

Summer. June

After endless rounds of tests, taken in the most unnatural fashion, I received a provisional diagnosis: leucopaenia – a blood disease that was treatable, although the treatment took several years. I was moved to the fifth-floor haematology unit – a long corridor with cold walls and a great many wards

3*

where children were walking with their parents. There were many young children wearing caps because their hair had fallen out after chemotherapy. The unit had a play room that was open three or four hours a day, a TV, and a cafeteria. The food was okay, but it was hospital food – steamed, without any fat or salt. Over time you can actually get used to it. If it was going to take a long time to get better, then I'd put up with it and fight for my life. My father came to see me – we decided to take our time over college enrolment. An awful lot of money was going to pay for medical bills at the moment, and even though my father was foreman on a construction site, he wasn't a millionaire. I'd wait a year and then study part-time – that was better anyway – and I would get better.

In June I took my exams and got Bs on both of them. As for the other subjects they gave me As. I had a hard time getting leave from the doctors, but exams are really important, so they let me go. Everything at the school seemed big and unfamiliar, like something half-forgotten. I seemed to stand apart from it all – from my friends, the classrooms, the lessons. How ironic! But everyone had changed. Their problems, their plans, their goals and affairs were completely different from mine. They had their lives, and I had mine: the hospital, the drip feed, the tests, and a diagnosis we couldn't be quite sure of. All they talked about was going to college – who was going where. Some were going to become lawyers, some doctors, others economists. But there was nothing for me to say. Just: "I'm stuck in a hospital. We don't quite know what's wrong with me. I'll go to college the year after next." That was all.

After the last exam I returned to the ward and cried for hours, until I began to choke. I was full of shame, hurt, and bitterness. These feelings overwhelmed me, demeaned me, made me kneel down before circumstance. I realized it was beyond my power to change anything. But why? Why me? Why did I have to get sick with who knows what? Why did people have to get sick anyway? Wouldn't it be better if we just died from old age, because we'd worn out our bodies? But no! For some reason we must die before our time and from any old illness. Why did it have to be me who got sick?

I grew hysterical, roaming the ward, wailing and wringing my hands. Natasha, who had the bed next to mine, tried to calm me down as best she could, but it didn't help. I went on ranting despite her five-year-old son Alyosha who was frightened by my fit.

I'm such a lame duck! Ever since I was a child! I don't have a mother! Only a father! And on top of that I'm sick with something stupid that no one even understands! How can it be? Wouldn't it be easier if I just jumped out a window? All my problems would be solved just like that! A few anxious moments, a flash of pain, and that's it. No more suffering! Quick, easy, and effective. But what about your love of life, I asked myself. What about it? What does anyone need with my life?

I cried and I wailed. Natasha had to take Alyosha out of the ward. I began to settle down around five in the evening, when I started to feel very poorly. I slept fifully, talking and raving. I had reached rock bottom.

In the middle of June they decided to perform a biopsy in order to make a final diagnosis. I emerged from general anaesthesia with difficulty and in real discomfort. And a couple of days later I found out the results. I had a disease with an incredibly difficult name that might turn into either anaemia or leukaemia. It couldn't be treated straight away – we had to see how my body would react in the longer term, and so in the meantime I was being discharged and sent home. But every two weeks I would have to come in for a check-up and blood tests. I had to wait to find out just what I had. Can you imagine? It was anaemia or leukaemia! Life or death!

Hurrah! They sent me home! I've got out of hospital and my two-month incarceration. My joy is boundless. I don't want to go back into hospital. I DO NOT WANT TO GO BACK! Now I'm at home. Home sweet home. Lying on my beloved little sofa, watching films on the computer and doing nothing at all. That's it, I decided. I'm not going back into hospital no matter what; otherwise they'll get me again.

When I was discharged, my grandmother decided to take my treatment in hand herself. So began endless rounds of visits to diviners, shamans, psychics, and soothsayers. Did I believe in them? I don't know. Maybe I believed what I wanted to believe. All I wanted was to survive and I was ready to believe anyone who could make that happen. I didn't care what they looked like, whether they were a doctor or a soothsayer – I just wanted someone to help me! I was waiting for help, begging for help. Grandmother and I waited in long queues for hours on end. I drank holy water by the litre and participated in rituals of all sorts. But there was no improvement. I blamed myself for doing something wrong – not drinking the right amount of water, not crossing myself correctly. Each time I went to see some new miracle man, I believed blindly that he would help me. I'd be let down and I'd believe again. I believed over and over, right to the end, to the very last, when I could no longer walk on my own two legs. I lunged at life, reached out for it with both hands, trying to keep hold of it. But life was trickling away. It was abandoning me irretrievably.

I particularly remember visiting a healer who lived on

the outskirts of a small town. We took the back streets. It was dusty, stifling. Not surprisingly, the roads were unpaved. When it rained this place was just a sea of mud. And it was so hot not even the insects would fly. Passing cars trailed columns of dust, tickling my throat and making me cough. At last we reached an ungainly mud brick house with long windows and shutters. The fence and gate were wooden, flaking with green paint – they obviously hadn't been painted in years. There were a few cars parked by the gate and a number of people sitting in front of the house. We took our place in the queue. The garden was dirty and unkempt – it was revolting. Here and there tomato plants, eggplants and peppers had been planted which were already beginning to wither. Dogs, cats and chickens were running around a yard that was littered with cigarette butts. The smell was putrid and it made me nauseous, but still I believed.

Finally we made our way into the shed where the woman healer was receiving. She was forty, perhaps; big, stout, and slovenly. A gypsy, maybe, or a Moldovan, or who knows what. Her name ... well, really that's beside the point. She asked a great deal about my illness and said the doctors were all idiots and didn't know what they were treating. In actuality I'd been cursed and it was my pancreas that was hurting. She claimed that she could see this and that she could heal me. She also read coffee grounds for us. Everything she said, almost down to the last word, was a lie.

"Your mother is very ill, my child."

"I don't have a mother," I said, flinching.

"Yes, she died recently from a serious illness," said the seer, as if in confirmation.

"She died five years ago in a car accident. And she never had anything more serious than the flu."

"Yes, yes, that's what I meant to say. And soon your

father will get a promotion at work. But you do not have leukaemia, my child. You may come see me starting on Tuesday, and I'll exorcise the curse. Bring candles – wax only, water and wine."

We left.

"We'll do it," said my grandmother on the way back home. "Who knows, it might help."

Yes, I know, visiting a quack is foolish, but we started seeing her – and we paid her and we were grateful. How I wanted to believe I was getting better and the hospital had been treating me for the wrong thing. It was ignorant, foolish, childish. Naturally I didn't get better. The visits only wore me out.

Graduation day: the 25th of June. I spent the morning with my grandmother and the seer from the countryside, and in the evening I went to our graduation ball. I didn't have a graduation dress. My father had offered to get me one, but I didn't want it. I'd grown so alienated from my school that I'd quit thinking of myself as a graduate. Besides, I would have been ashamed standing next to my classmates with these dark circles under my eyes, and as emaciated as I'd become. I was going only to get my diploma. I arrived a bit early and went to the head teacher to request that my name not be called out. This surprised her, but she agreed. She handed me my diploma and asked how I'd been doing. After that I withdrew completely from the affairs of the school, from the past. Hardly anyone took notice of me, and if they did, they pretended they didn't recognize me. Thank God for that! After all, people only want to talk to you if you've got something in common, and we no longer had anything in common. Whatever there once had been was now gone and forgotten.

I liked the graduation ceremony. It was beautifully put

together, and the presentation was interesting. Everyone looked so beautiful and grand in their graduation dresses. I sat in the back row wearing jeans and a cap, the diploma in my back pocket. Face pale, cheeks sunken, but eyes bright. I'd grown very thin during my illness – I'd lost eight kilos, and my bones stuck out everywhere – but my eyes I was proud of, my deep, shining, beautiful eyes.

Strangely enough I didn't feel the slightest twinge of envy during the ceremony. There I was, sitting in the auditorium, sick and terribly thin, while my former classmates, beautiful and full of life, the future stretched out ahead of them, were performing on stage, thanking the teachers, giving them flowers, and waltzing. They themselves were building their lives. And they were responsible for their own lives. As for me, I had to undergo my cure.

After the ceremonial part of the evening, I went home. My father and grandmother were worried about my emotional state, but I just had some dinner and went to watch TV. By the next day, I'd already forgotten about the ceremony. We went to see yet another omniscient old woman who also claimed the doctors were all stupid and who said I had a diseased liver and kidneys. And once again I believed. She also promised me life.

This all went on for several weeks. Naturally I hadn't been going to the hospital – I was afraid to. But around the middle of June I began feeling very poorly, even though I'd already been feeling poorly. I had just grinned and put up with it – I'd even cleaned up my room. I kept telling Dad that everything was wonderful and I was doing fine. But when I could no longer get out of bed, I became terrified. Dad literally had to carry me into the hospital in his arms. Once again I was admitted as a gravely ill patient.

Summer. July

It's July now. The heat is stifling, scorching. I'm back in hospital. I've recently had a blood transfusion. My joy at being back home didn't last long – just over three weeks. I saw my father talking to the doctor recently. His hands were trembling. I could tell it was the beginning of the end. I'm frightened.

My condition has deteriorated sharply. I can barely walk – it's too difficult. I'm doing incredibly poorly. Grandmother comes to see me every day. She is helping me as a carer. All I feel is weakness and helplessness.

They recently took a specimen for analysis from one of my lungs because they'd found fluid in it. They used an enormous needle to withdraw the fluid and inject medicine. I was in a state of constant flux: poorly one moment, then okay, then poorly, poorly, poorly. My temperature was always high. It was hard to bring it down and it always went back up again. We tried to reduce it several times a day. I'd grown accustomed to my insides always feeling hot. Like my organs were being fried up in a saucepan. I could sense my kidneys, liver, stomach, lungs. When you've had an operation like that, it's impossible not to sense your lungs. I'd always been afraid of being injured, getting injections, being cut open, getting stitches. When I found out I was going to have this operation, I just went into a trance. At the very thought of the needle going into my breast, of that metal thing going into my body! It repelled me. I have a sensitive, squeamish nature, so I couldn't help but imagine the needle in my breast. But it had to be done, so I had to reconcile myself.

After the operation I spent a couple of days in intensive care. Now I was back on the ward and Grandmother stayed with me during the day. She never went anywhere and would never leave me by myself – it actually made me sick. But at night she went home. A few days ago I was taken for a CT scan. I managed to secretly copy the record:

Liver and spleen – enlarged, density increased

Pancreas – not enlarged, composition homogeneous

Kidneys – size and position normal, areas of pathological density – none

Abdominal lymph nodes – not enlarged

At long last I got a diagnosis – aplastic anaemia. But, as ever, the diagnosis was provisional. Confirmation was needed from Moscow. Which is why my father had taken my tests and specimens and gone to Moscow. We received a response a couple of days later – the diagnosis hadn't been confirmed so I'd be sent to the hospital in Moscow for a full examination, but only when a place became available. Grandmother would go with me, because someone had to look after me. Oh, joy. There was nothing more to say.

The day was too hot, the blue sky too high, the walls of the ward too close. Everything was just too much! Everything was excessive! I should have been taking my first entrance exam today, but Dad and I had agreed to postpone college for a year. In my present state I couldn't even study part-time. I felt like I'd already spent an eternity in hospital. I hadn't the faintest glimmer of hope of getting out of here. My diagnosis was still uncertain. It was a sheer enigma of nature! They suspected leukaemia or anaemia, but these were only suspicions. Good grief! My chances of survival were slim. Too slim. Although it's better to know what's making you sick, what to treat, and to have some small, utterly small, hope of getting out of hospital and recovering, rather than living in this state of suspense! Between heaven and the hospital!

By now I'd stopped complaining about the endless rounds of injections, capsules, pills, and so on. Somehow I was losing the ability to complain, whine and cry. I desperately wanted to live, to gaze at the sun and the heavens, to feel the wind and the heat. I began to understand that life was a miracle, and how painful it would be to part with this miracle; I began to sense that something was slowly and irretrievably abandoning me, and that you could never get that something back again. You couldn't get it back! I began to dread going to sleep – I was afraid I might not wake up again. I was afraid of not having enough time, of not knowing. It's so frightening to realize you're running out of time... out of life.

Summer. Beginning of August

We're getting ready to go to the hospital in Moscow. We're literally sitting on our suitcases. As ever, my blood is drawn every day. I get a transfusion; and my temperature, which is always going up, is brought back down again. I take my tablets. It's business as usual, moving along under its own steam.

Summer. Middle of August

On Wednesday, my doctor, Lidia Filipovna, said they were expecting me in Moscow on Monday. The same day I was discharged from the local hospital and I spent Thursday, Friday and Saturday at home, collapsed on the divan. Now I would be given a final diagnosis. On Sunday, my father and a friend of his drove Grandmother and me to Moscow. And so began my life in the Moscow State Hospital.

I should mention that in our local hospital, I was always being moved from ward to ward, or someone else was being moved into my ward. I met lots of people and made friends. As you'd expect, there were lots of young children. They all had their mothers or grandmothers with them. I remember Vadik. He was five. Half Dagestani, half Russian. We often went to the playroom together. We built buildings from blocks and painted pictures, and I would read stories to him. Vadik had acute leukaemia. At the end of July he was sent to Moscow. I wondered how he was doing, how they were treating him. I hadn't heard anything. But I'd grown very attached to him.

I remember Zhenya, too. He was a tall fifteen-year-old. He died just before the First Feast of the Transfiguration. He'd been very ill, and he suffered. He used to watch television all the time; he said he needed some kind of background noise so that he could distract himself and not pay attention to the pain. I visited him frequently and we watched films together. He died in intensive care one night. I spent all the next day in shock. How could it be? How could he have died? We'd just spent the evening watching some ridiculous comedy and we'd argued about it. I couldn't take it in.

Summer. End of August.

I'm in Moscow. At Moscow State Hospital, Department of General Haematology, 6th floor, Ward 2-1. The wards are individual, two beds to a room – one for me, one for grandmother. And two bedside tables, a table, a chair, a basin and a table to eat at. Some doctors came to see me almost immediately – one of them was even a professor. Straight away they drew some blood. My spirits rose a little – surely they could cure me at the country's leading hospital! Dad went home the same day. He left me some money – all he had. There were lots of tests to pay for, and they weren't cheap – the doctors had warned us.

I was under the spell of the city. I'd never been to Moscow before, although I'd always wanted to visit. There was a view of the avenue from my window, and there was even a comfortable windowsill. I loved sitting there looking out at the sky. I wanted to stroll around the city and hoped

I'd at least get the chance to see Red Square, the Cathedral of Christ the Saviour, and the Tretyakov Art Gallery. I wanted to see more, of course, but I'd just see how it went. The hospital food wasn't bad either; better than at the local hospital – it was actually edible. I was giving a lot of blood for tests, and Grandmother was going all over Moscow delivering specimens to various medical institutes. I believed, I really believed, I wanted to believe that I was going to live. I was going to get better!

I liked my new doctor. She was a woman of some forty years of age, and completely unlike the others, although you couldn't tell straight away. But first impressions are almost always misleading. Irina Anatolievna spent a long time asking me about my illness and studying my case history. She said she'd do all she could to help me get better. I trusted her immediately. She filled me with hope, peace, and confidence that I hadn't felt for a long time. Irina Anatolievna was like a cliff – underneath it was always calm and you could always find shelter there. The truth is, I missed my dad so much ... and my mom, that I grew attached to her with all my being. As a rule, I try not to get stuck on people. It's a form of self defence, because it's hard for me to let go later. It's easier that way: if you don't get attached, it's easy to forget. Perhaps I'm strange, but I've never felt close to my relatives. Other than my mom and dad, I didn't consider anyone to be one of my own. Not even my own grandmother. I'd only started calling her "grandmother" recently – it had just got awkward around her. I hadn't felt close to my aunts or uncles or cousins. Not anyone. Ever. Only my parents and friends. I hadn't seen my aunt for more than a year and a half, even though we lived in the same town. There were no feelings between us. No remorse. We just didn't have feelings for each other. It couldn't be helped.

But I immediately grew attached to Irina Anatolievna. Even inordinately. Frightfully. I soon saw that she was different. My instincts about people never let me down. She was an incredibly interesting woman. Unpredictable. And she was my attending physician.

I too had always been different, but I was only now beginning to see this. Before I had always wanted to be like everyone else. Just as chatty and silly and cheeky. It was ridiculous, but I desperately wanted to not understand the poems of Tsvetaeva and Akhmatova. I wanted to make fun of Sholokhov, and really not believe that he wrote *Quiet Flows the Don* at the age of 23. I wanted to skip classes, laugh behind the backs of those weaker than me, invent farfetched explanations for being late to class. I wanted all this, but from the very start I was different. Unlike the others. It used to bother me, but, as of late, I'd somehow changed. I'd begun to get a sense of my individuality, my otherness ... and I'd begun to take pride in it. Understanding what poems and stories are about is fantastic! And it's fantastic having a mind of your own that's independent of anyone or anything else. It's fantastic just to be yourself! The way you are, without pretending or hiding. Not trying to come across like a superhero or a supermodel. It's fantastic admitting to your mistakes, your vulnerabilities, your fears, without burying them deep inside, afraid they'll suddenly show and people will find out about them. It's absolutely brilliant to love life and revel in it.

Being different had been really hard. I was embarrassed by my own individuality. It became a complex, even a form of self-torture, if you will. Mostly I was afraid of criticism. For some reason, I don't know why, criticism just flattened me. And so, afraid of being ridiculed, I wore a mask. I became either too talkative or too reserved. Always "too". I was always different. Even when I was talking to my cousins, their dull practicality annoyed me. I was genuinely amazed – how could they fail to understand something so basic! But worst of all was that somewhere deep inside I wanted to be like them. It had always seemed to me that down-to-earth people had easier, simpler lives. I failed to see the most important thing – you have to appreciate, tend, and cherish your otherness. Be grateful to the heavens above. Only then will you reap your reward. I only became aware of these ideas here, in hospital. Better late than never. It's dreadful to imagine that if I hadn't ended up in hospital I would have stayed that way. Ruining my uniqueness. An ordinary person.

Summer. 29 August

What an extraordinary day! How happy and cheerful! My grandmother bought me soap bubbles. I know they're for children, but I really wanted to have a festive day with soap bubbles! I filled the ward with them. It was a sunny day, so the bubbles were brimming with colours. Lots of bubbles! Lots of hues! Lots of spots of light on the walls. It all reminded me of a holiday. Of my childhood. I was eight. It was Victory Day, and I was out walking with my parents in the park, wearing a huge bow in my hair and snow-white knee socks. I had an ice cream cone in my hands. Music was playing and there were lots of people and lots of colourful balloons, which invariably drifted up into the sky. The bubbles reminded me of those balloons, my childhood, and my mother. I'd always loved her. Her death was a terrible blow for me. As it was for my father. I'd been sitting in my room sorting things in my desk when Dad came in. He looked terribly pale and scared, like a harassed child.

"Mom is dead," he said.

"What?" I whispered.

My textbooks remained in disarray. I can hardly

remember anything else, and what I do remember is only fragmentary. I remember my grandmother's tearstained face. She was trying to calm me down, but she only made things worse. I remember the neighbours whispering furtively behind my back. I remember my aunt sitting in the corner in an old armchair. But I can't remember my mother in her coffin. Thank God for that! I was only twelve at the time and, although I didn't understand much, I already knew this was a serious wound I'd carry around for the rest of my life. I often recall that first night without my mother. I raved in my sleep. I sensed her there next to me, but she wasn't – she was lying dead in the sitting room. I'd tried to scrub all those horrible events from my memory; but to this day the room where her coffin stood frightens me, and in the darkness I hold out my arms so I won't bump into the red box that held my mother's body.

Somehow my thoughts have strayed – I shouldn't let myself think those sad thoughts. And at a time when the whole ward is glistening with soap bubbles! They're everywhere, spinning and bursting. Like life itself.

Autumn. 1 September

I was wandering round the hospital. Here I was in Moscow but I felt no joy at the fact. How I'd yearned to visit this city – I'd seen Moscow as a place out of the ordinary, magical, magnificent. But now that I'd been here a month, I didn't feel anything at all, because I was in hospital. We didn't go out into the city. Here in the hospital you had to wear a mask just to walk down the corridor – there could be no question of going for a walk outside. And even if it had been possible, there's no way my grandmother would have allowed it. So I merely gazed at Moscow from the hospital window. The image of Moscow was more attractive and more interesting anyway because it was out of reach. As soon as you get hold of something forbidden, as soon as you savour its taste, it loses its appeal. And so it happened that sitting on the windowsill everyday looking out upon the city's avenues, I lost interest in the city as such. I couldn't feel its soul. Every place has a soul – something not defined by its beauty or attractions, or by its number of monuments or the prosperity of its inhabitants. Soul is something else, something that can be felt but not seen. And I couldn't feel the soul of Moscow.

On the whole, I had begun to spend a lot of time thinking. I'd thought a lot before my illness, but those were different thoughts. I thought about school and my friends, how unfair life was to me. If I'd known what was on its way, I'd never have thought that way. I'd resented my friends' jokes and wondered why they acted the way they did. I'd wondered how I could be the same as everyone else, yet still stick out from the crowd. It's bizarre, I know, but I wanted to be the same and different at the same time. Different in that I'd be brighter, cheekier, and stronger than everyone else. I had thought about my future life, about what I wanted from it. I aspired to become the managing director of a huge company. I pictured having lots of money, a posh villa, enormous apartments, flashy cars that I drove on alternate days. A husband and children who put me on a pedestal, but resented me behind my back because I didn't pay them enough attention. A string of young lovers. The dread and deference of my colleagues, and the opportunity to run other people's lives. What an idiot I was! I'd been yanked out of those fantasies into the real world with all its shortcomings.

All this was now dawning on me. I despised myself. Not for my dreams, but because I'd dreamed against myself, against my own nature. I'd only wanted these things because that's what everyone wanted. I had been a rather weak person.

I still couldn't say I was strong, but I'd become much more genuine. And I could recognize as much.

Autumn. 3 September

Today my sense of loneliness has overwhelmed me with despair. It washes over me in waves. One wave, a second, a third... the ninth was the most powerful, like Aivazovsky's famous painting *The Ninth Wave*. Wave after wave. Strangely enough, I didn't want to be rid of the feeling. I sat on my bed, feeling the presence of loneliness. I felt like I could actually touch it.

"Hello, Loneliness," I said, trying to start a conversation. Maybe I was just hallucinating, but I pulled it off.

"Hello," Loneliness replied.

"Why are you ripping my soul apart? Are you enjoying yourself?"

"Let me ask you the same question. Maybe it's you who enjoys it."

"Me?"

"Yes, you."

"Is that a joke? Who could possibly enjoy loneliness?"

"Think about it. You're educated. You've been to school."

"How strange. Maybe it's true, and somewhere deep inside I like feeling helpless and sorry for myself."

"You're on the right track."

"It's possible. You know, hiding in your shell, shutting yourself away from others, you create a world inside yourself. Whatever kind of world you want! You're the boss there. In that world you can do whatever you want. No one can criticize you or make fun of you. No one! But you call this loneliness. You like it, and you're afraid to admit as much even to yourself. Because it's scary feeling sorry for yourself and enjoying it. There's always another way out. Or practically always." I berated myself, "What nonsense I'm spouting! What rubbish!"

"It's not rubbish," said Loneliness, "it's the truth. Well, I'll see you round."

"Good bye," I mumbled, thinking, "I'm obviously going mad, having a conversation with Loneliness. If anyone gets wind of this I'll end up in the psychiatric unit. Although it's better there than here – they have fewer fatalities. And maybe the things that Loneliness and I had to say were true?"

Rather than get further bogged down in these thoughts, I went and watched TV.

Autumn. 5 September

This morning Irina Anatolievna, came and examined me. I was the last patient on her rounds, and grandmother had just gone to find me some tablets. Irina Anatolievna and I sat and talked. As I've said, I'd taken a real liking to her. I cried on her shoulder. For some reason I was feeling bad, wronged, and hurt.

"I don't want to die, Irina Anatolievna. Please help me! I'm only seventeen. I want to live."

"Don't cry, kitten. You're going to live. I'll do everything I can to make that happen."

"Do you really believe that?" I asked through my tears.

"We've cured all kinds of sick children. Of course I believe it."

"I haven't even been diagnosed! My disease is a mystery!"

"We'll soon find out what it is, kitten, I promise." Irina Anatolievna soothed me as best she could. "Only don't cry, it will make your temperature go up."

"But it goes up anyway, whether I'm crying or not. What does it matter?"

"In principle, what you're saying is true, but all the same, please don't cry. You know, kitten, life is relative... You can't measure everything and everyone by the same yardstick. That's contrary to the laws of nature. You may not believe it, but the universe has laws of its own and they're very powerful – the most powerful. Do you understand? We must give in order to receive. Right now you're giving your health, your strength, your youth, and you don't realize that you're going to get something in return."

"What if I receive death in return!" I cried.

"How do you know there's nothing after death? You can't know that. After all, you're not God."

"No, but..."

Irina Anatolievna interrupted me...

"Every person bears only as much suffering as he can withstand. And you've already borne so much! You're very strong, kitten. And... very out of the ordinary. Believe me, everything will be okay in the end. I'm sure of it. If you don't believe yourself, then believe me. I must go now, but please, please, please – believe."

Irina Anatolievna left. Wow, I thought. She's really extraordinary. It would be so interesting to find out a little more about her.

All day I sat and thought. All day I watched the sky.

I love gazing at the sky. It's a shame that most of the time I had to do so from the hospital window. How I love the sky! Unlimited and unearthly! Today there were lots of clouds, but I could see the azure through their ragged edges. I raised my left arm to the sky – there was a catheter in my right – pressed my palm to the window and whispered:

"Heaven above! Please forgive me for everything. For everything I've done and will do. For wishing ill upon others, when I've had no reason to feel mistreated; for crying when I should have been content. I've only demanded; I haven't given anything in return. I've only cared about myself. Please, please forgive me. Even if I don't get better, if I die, I won't feel wronged by you, I'll understand. May your will be done."

My palm had grown sweaty and cold, and, feeling serene and somehow at peace, something that happened quite rarely of late, I left the window and went to bed. I had sweet dreams.

Autumn. September

There's a boy named Kostya in Ward 3-1. He's fourteen. I've only ever seen him through the doorway. His condition is very serious. He had secretly stopped taking his tablets, and his condition deteriorated sharply. There are doctors with him all the time. Kostya can't get up – frequently he yells and cries, but recently I've stopped hearing his cries – he can no longer speak. I saw today that he was being discharged. They were wheeling him down the corridor on a trolley. He was being sent home. To die. The doctors said there was nothing more they could do for him.

For a long time I stared after the trolley, at Kostya's head. My God, how dreadful it was! How frightening! Suddenly I imagined that it was me they were wheeling away, my father and grandmother weeping beside me. I could picture their tears, and I understood everything, but I couldn't say a word! My legs gave away. How terrible it was to die, just like that, unable to say anything, unable to burst into tears, to get up and walk around the room. Poor boy, I thought, beginning to feel the injustice. Whatever had he done to deserve such a punishment? What? I didn't know. But it was terrible.

Autumn. 12 September

Alla, in the ward next to mine, had a visit from her cousin Ksiusha. I went to see Alla and met Ksiusha. She was nineteen, studying at a prestigious university to become a lawyer. Ksiusha was a rather depressing type who didn't see any meaning in life. We quarrelled. She said it was better to spend half your life in hospital than to live the way she did, pointlessly. Living each day thoughtlessly, hoping the next day would be different, but, as soon as there was a ray of hope, running away from it in fear of failure and disappointment. In other words, Ksiusha thought we were lucky because we'd already spent half a year in hospital and we no longer had any reason to worry about tomorrow. I flared up.

"Just what do you think you understand about my life? Who wants to die at seventeen? Only someone without an incurable disease. You can get up and go where you want. You can go to the cinema, or a club, or just walk down the street. But I can't! I'm sick. I'm weak. I can only look at the sun and sky from the hospital courtyard, that's the only place where I can pick dandelions, but at your feet lie all the glades of the world. You have a future – that's wonderful. You can do whatever you want – you're free to make mistakes and try again. But I'm not! You know, sometimes I think I'll go out, I'll run away from this courtyard and pick dandelions wherever I like, I'll look at the sun from a great big field of wheat. I dream about a home, a family, a job that I love. But I have practically no future. Do you know what's really awful? I might die a month from now, or a year from now. I want to know why the heavens bestowed life on me if I have to die so young. I've only had a breath of life, a fleeting experience of flight, and now my wings have been clipped. And you say that you don't see any point in it all, that you don't know what you're living for, that you're capable of suicide! Do you know what it's like for me to listen to this? You keep saying you don't want to live. As for me, I've sunk my teeth into this bloody life. I've sunk my teeth in."

That was the gist of my harangue. I ran out of Alla's

room, fell into bed and began to weep. "How can you not love life?" I cried. I puzzled over the question for a long time but couldn't find any answer.

Autumn. October

I want to describe something that happened to me here in the hospital. I can't get it out of my head. It was in the beginning of September.

Katya was sitting on a couch, ever so pale. Her mother, Yulia, had asked me to keep an eye on her. Katya hardly spoke. She kept her silence, merely nodding at my questions or shaking her head. She'd already spent a year in hospital. Katya had acute leukaemia. I'd seen her childhood photographs – she looked like an angel. Gently curling blond hair, bright blue eyes and a broad smile. As a little girl Katya had been plump and healthy. But now she was as emaciated as me.

"Katya!" I said, trying to give her a hug, but she just sat there, as motionless as if she was dead.

"Come on, Katya, give us a smile!"

Katya pushed my arms away and began to cry.

"I want my mama. Please find her."

"Your mama will be back soon, Katya. What if I read you some fairytales?"

I took a picture book and began reading, but Katya wasn't listening. She had withdrawn. I tried to get her attention, but to no avail. I sat with her for several hours until her mother returned. Katya was a difficult child. She had been through chemotherapy and in hospital she had grown very quiet and withdrawn. It wasn't hard to see why.

Afterwards I began visiting their ward. One time I ran in at the sound of screams. There were a lot of people in the ward, and Yulia was cradling her daughter. Katya had died.

Slowly but surely the world was slipping away from

me. I stood there looking at Katya's motionless body. Horror coursed through me, down my spine. Yulia was pressing Katya to herself, unable to let her go. She was choking on her tears and begging for Katya's body not to be sent for an autopsy. How long we were standing there in the ward, I don't remember. All the following week I was in a state of shock. It was horrible to remember Yulia's face, distorted by torment. When they had taken the body away, she began pacing the ward with Katya's beloved teddy bear in her arms. Then she began packing. She packed with care, silently and steadily: t-shirts, handkerchiefs, shorts, her own things, Katya's toys. And from time to time she would take the bear and hug it and walk with it around the ward.

I stood in the doorway for a long time. I couldn't believe it. It had all happened before my eyes, as if in slow motion. How could it be? How could Katya die? How? How could a child die?

Autumn. October

The days pass, one is like the next. Slowly, slowly, moving like snails. I've made many friends in the unit.

On one of these boring and everlasting autumnal days, *he* appeared. Igor. He's also seventeen. He has leukaemia. His older sister is staying with him – she's twenty, a part-time student. His father is working and his mother is three months pregnant – they are going to give Igor the gift of life. On the face of it he's full of optimism and hope, but on the inside? I don't know, all I see is emptiness and despair. He's only seventeen, but already he's an old man, although I too am already an old lady. We became friends and spent all our time together. We have everything in common: the same problems, interests, ideas. We're both seventeen – young, but chained to the hospital and deprived of a future. We read the exact same books, watch the exact same films, think about the exact same things. In the end our intense friendship grew into something more – love. Not wild, all-consuming passion, mad deeds, and pledges of eternal fidelity. No. It was something innocent, delicate, and hospital-bound. The most we could do was sit beside one another and watch a film, holding hands; we could go for hours without talking, or spend half a day talking non-stop. In short, we felt good being together, and we didn't build any plans for the future. But, as you might expect, we wanted more than just platonic love. We wanted sex. Despite our weakened state, our hormones were raging.

We soon found our chance when there was an emergency operation in the middle of the night and all the medical personnel had gone to the operating room. Igor's sister was smart; she went to watch television. My grandmother was sleeping. I went to Igor's room, and it happened. It wasn't anything like the films. We played around a while, neither of us knowing how to approach the other. Igor was excited, and so was I, and I don't regret a thing. Later on, we had similar opportunities.

In November Igor's condition grew markedly worse. I would hold his hand while he was sleeping. We talked a lot; it wasn't possible for us to talk too much.

"I love you, you know," Igor said once.

I nearly choked on the apple I was eating, I was so surprised. No boy had ever told me he loved me.

"I love you too, Igor," I said.

"If something happens to me, tell my family that I love them, too."

"Igor! What are you talking about! Everything is going to be fine."

"Sunshine, I only found out what love is here in the hospital. Dying isn't so terrible anymore."

And Igor held me.

Two days later he died unexpectedly from a brain haemorrhage.

"Don't leave me, please don't leave me," I wept, kneeling beside his body. It was a long time before they could pull me away from him. Finally they injected me with a sedative and I fell asleep. Igor's body was taken to the morgue. As you might imagine, I wasn't allowed to go to his funeral. I passed on Igor's words to his mother.

Autumn. End of November

I'm in a lousy state of mind – in fact, I've never felt worse. I've had a diagnosis. Lymphoma. It's a very bad case. How I'd dreamt of getting out of this hospital. I'd go home and grandmother would make me real hamburgers – in the hospital they're inedible. The doctors don't explain a thing to me, as if I were a silly child. They only talk to Grandmother or Dad. He visits me periodically, but he won't tell me anything – he's afraid of upsetting me. "Everything will be all right, my sweetheart." That's all he has to say. It exasperates me to no end. Grandmother is always crying, someplace where I can't see her, in the toilet or in the shower room.

I understand even without an explanation. An operation is too expensive, and the chances that I'll live are very slim. Finding a donor is highly complicated and costly. But how I want to believe in happy endings! I madly want to believe that I'll live. It's just not happening that way.

I no longer believe in miracles. Since Igor died I've been living in a dream state. Like a zombie, or a robot. I merely carry out certain commands: sleep, eat, extend arm for blood tests. Life has lost its meaning. How long I can hold out in this state of mind and with this disease, I have no idea. I don't believe, I have no hope, and there's nothing I'm waiting for. I only love.

Winter. December

My condition has deteriorated sharply. Fluid has been found in my abdominal cavity. The doctors have made several punctures and pumped out litres of fluid. My test results are very bad. There are hardly any cells left in my bone marrow. Life is slowly draining out of me, but I'm holding on to it all the same.

I nearly died in December. It was a very near thing, Grandmother told me. They were performing paracentesis to drain off the fluid when I suddenly began to bleed. They had to operate as a matter of urgency. In short, they cut me open and removed a tumour from my spleen. My pancreas was failing. I was between life and death, but closer to death. For several days I was kept in intensive care with the critically ill children.

I'm in a terrible way.

Winter. 31 December

The smell of pine, tangerines and potato salad. Champagne glasses clinking. It does not feel like a holiday. I'm dying.

Winter. 3 January

I've got up onto my feet and begun to walk. Slowly, but I am walking. I've even sat down a few times.

Winter. 7 January

Today is Orthodox Christmas. But Igor isn't here. I've been wandering the corridors; they're empty, as it's only 5 a.m. I just couldn't sleep. I kept walking, hands to the cold walls and solitary armchairs. I felt dreadful, as if my very being had been scraped out of me and nothing left in its place. My joy and happiness had been taken away, my communion with those around me, everything; I'd been left nothing but emptiness and disappointment. I couldn't even bring myself to weep. Suddenly I had an idea. I went into the ward, switched on the nightlight and, to the peaceful accompaniment of Grandmother's snoring, I sat down to write.

"Hello there, Igor. How are you? Don't laugh, I know you understand. Yes, I'm writing you a letter. A letter to the other world. It will never reach you, but I'm sure that you'll read it anyway. I'm certain there is life in that world, and that you are living there and you'll help me. After you died, life lost its meaning for me. It's hard, painful, cruel... I love you, Igor. Perhaps we only acknowledged our feelings once, and in some confusion at that, but all the same you knew I loved you. Maybe it wasn't the kind of love you see in films, but it was love. When you died, I wanted to follow right behind you; I feel the same even today, as I sit here writing this letter to you. Please, please help me to survive. I need to live for both you and myself. You know, if I get better, I feel you'll send me someone, someone I'll spend the rest of my life with. He won't be the same as you. But you must know I'll always be with you. My heart will always belong to you and no one else. Although it's actually possible to love several men without giving any of them short shrift. But perhaps not everyone would agree. And so be it. It's a personal matter.

"It's incredibly difficult for me right now. Every day I can see you – having your lunch, walking along the corridor, watching television. Igor, remember the funny way you used to sit in the armchair? In the lotus position? And the remarks the nurses used to make? And do you remember how we used to argue about happiness? I said it was impossible to be completely happy, and you disagreed. How we argued, yelling and gesticulating wildly, and in the end, you took me in your arms and said, "We're both right. Let's not fight about it!" I appreciated that. You were different from the rest. You know, your absence becomes more and more pronounced every day. I thought it would pass, but I was wrong. It's Christmas today, a big holiday, and I hope you'll read my letter. We were good together. You found the one you wanted, and so did I.

"You may find this annoying, but it would have been easier for me if you'd simply disappeared from my life. If you'd got better and just forgot about me. Then I would know that you were still alive. But you've gone forever. You died and left me alone with my love. Without any explanation. Igor, I want to tell you one more time that I love you. I love you across time and space. You're there, I know you are. Somewhere far away. Please, forgive me. Forgive me, and help me. Igor, I beg you, please give me life."

I put down the pen and looked out the window. In the faintly brightening sky I saw Igor's smiling face and I began to weep.

Winter. January

Understand and forgive – whom? for what? Everyone for everything. First and foremost, to forgive myself for attempting to destroy my true inner nature. For lying to myself and being afraid of the truth. I'd tried to be aware only of what I found advantageous and agreeable. I heard what I wanted to hear, saw only what I wanted to see. I only felt feelings that I found pleasant and enjoyable. I felt shy about showing emotions. I'd always had to force myself to pay someone a compliment – I thought they would either laugh at me or suspect me of brown-nosing. To forgive myself for being afraid of criticism, ridicule and rejection. I hurt other people because I was afraid they would hurt me. I deceived myself so often I became confused. I'd only ever thought about myself – my own needs, feelings, and desires. I didn't give a damn about anyone else, although I wanted other people to give a damn about me. I wanted them to help me. But everything in life has a price. And sometimes the price is too high.

We're all responsible for our own lives and must make our own choices. We each have our own destiny. We must pursue that destiny, without adding anything or drawing in the destiny of someone else; otherwise the consequences will be unpleasant and unpredictable. Life, after all, is relative. You can't pigeonhole someone and judge him on the basis of today alone. In life, all things come to pass, and sometimes what happens can't be foreseen in the most dreadful of nightmares. Someone might come along and bash you on the head with a sledgehammer and you'll never regain consciousness. You won't get the chance to say the most important words of your life, those words you always kept to yourself, waiting for the right moment. Right moments all have something in common – they never arrive. And you'll never get to say those important words. Either you'll have gone, or the other person will have gone. The only thing of any real value in life is our relationships with one another. All the rest is incidental – it comes and goes, but relationships are always there. The people involved may change, but relationships are everywhere, always. You have to understand and appreciate the people around you. Then, and only then, can they appreciate and understand you. Everything in the world has its own logic. All your words and all your feelings will, without fail, come back to you.

You have to be grateful for each passing day – grateful for your own two arms and legs. You can walk, breathe, look up at the sky, sit at the window. You can talk to people; after all, we're conscious, intelligent beings. There, then, I've philosophised a bit. The main thing now is to observe these principles. Although I should think that the person who could write these principles could also observe them.

At least in part. Is that megalomania? Yes. I'm enjoying it. Just kidding.

Winter. 18 January

On the eighteenth, at around 11 in the morning, Dad rang. He was excited and keyed up. He had something on his mind.

"Listen, sweetie!" he yelled into the phone, "Igor's mother... I mean, her daughter ... that is, I mean, she's going to be your donor! Do you hear!?"

Everything swam before my eyes. In a fog, I made my way into the corridor. I leaned against the wall, and lowered myself along its icy surface to the ground. I covered my face with my hands and began to weep. I now knew that I was going to live.

Ahead of me was life.

THE PIPE

Translated by Anne Marie Jackson

I'm creeping inside a narrow pipe. Its smooth walls press against me, so I'm advancing slowly. I can't even get down on my hands and knees. I'm lying with my arms stretched out in front of me.

I've lost track of time. I may have been in this pipe for a day, or a week, or half a century. My phone has gone dead. I can't call anyone or even send a text. And, anyway, what's the use? Sometimes I'll flick my lighter on, but all I can see is the eerie inside of this pipe, and the lighter gripped by my pale hands. Here it's neither cold nor hot. Because the air is stale, it's getting hard to breathe. I haven't lost hope. The pipe can't be endless. And the presence of darkness doesn't mean the absence of light. I really want to believe that it's all just a hallucination, a dream, a state of delirium; and that at some point I'll suddenly wake up, greedily breathe in the apartment air, and realize that it's all over. I pinch my arm a couple of times, but I don't wake up. This pipe has become my reality. And there's only one means of escape: creeping ahead.

How did I end up here? Perhaps I've been here since birth? I feel like it's in this pipe that my life began. But no, it's not so.

Once there was another life. I was five years old, playing with some kids in a sandbox. We were building an enormous town for good magicians to live in. From morning until lunch, the five of us worked painstakingly, completely absorbed. I had dug out a deep grotto and laid straight roads to it. Then a tall woman came along and said sternly, "You've gone and got sand all over yourselves again. Where's your shame? Now you'll get it from your parents. Well, hop along! Go home for lunch!"

We had to go our different ways. Because the town was all but built, we decided to come back after lunch and start playing. But when we returned, someone had gone and thoroughly demolished all of our grand buildings and grottoes. And the tall woman who had shooed us off came along again and warned us:

"You can't play in the sand – the sand is cold, it could make you ill. That would upset your parents. And you always get dirty! You mustn't do that!"

The tall woman plucked her whimpering son away. Streaming tears, he trailed reluctantly behind her.

As a small child I had already begun crawling into my pipe. Adults taught us what we could do, and what we couldn't. They handed us their fears, their complexes, their rules and their delusions. If only they had taught us to love and create.

Inside the pipe it's the same as before, it's dark and the air is stale. I try to make out some kind of light ahead of me, some faint glimmers, but I can't see a thing. Only darkness. Wearily I turn over onto my back. I try to lift my arms; immediately they come up against a solid wall. I begin banging with all my might. Pounding with my fists. This must be what it's like inside a zinc-lined coffin.

"Save me! Somebody save me! Can anyone hear me?" I begin to sob.

In response there is nothing but silence. It's all in vain. These walls are impenetrable. Hot blood trickles down my hands. My stomach grumbles, treacherously, as if it's beginning to consume its very self. I'm hungry, thirsty, sleepy... In my head I understand that at some point there will be light. I'm falling asleep. How strange. And frightening. I do not dream any dreams.

I was in the second grade. We were in the middle of our PE class. I couldn't throw the ball into the basketball hoop. My arms weren't strong enough; I was the smallest kid in the class. We'd been divided into opposing teams for a competition. The team winning the most points would get As and the losers would get Bs. Our PE teacher didn't pay any attention to the talents of individual students. I could run quickly and jump high, but I couldn't get the ball into the basket. The score was ten all. Our final task had begun. We had to throw the ball into the hoop! For ten minutes I threw the ball again and again. It either didn't go far enough, or else it flew over the hoop, but no way would it go where it needed to go. My team began yelling at me: "We're going to lose. Get it in the hoop! It's easy!"

We lost. The whole team got a B. In the changing room I burst into tears.

"It's all your fault!" said one of my classmates harshly. "If only you had made the hoop, we'd have won!"

I wake up. I'm creeping ahead. The pipe seems to make a little bend. It's getting really hard to breathe. I stop and begin hammering again with my shredded fists against the galvanized foundation of my prison.

"Damn it all... Come on, somebody, help me! Get me out of here!" I'm yelling for all I'm worth, choking on my tears. Around me there is silence... it's deserted... I'm all alone.

I reach into my pocket for the lighter. I want some light ... But the lighter is gone! Evidently it's fallen out of my pocket. I search carefully through all my clothing, but I can't find it. I've now lost even that poor spot of light. The main thing is not to go blind in the utter darkness of the pipe. At some point it will come to an end. I'm creeping on…

I was in the ninth grade – the top student, the pride of all the teachers. I didn't yet realize, then, that top-student syndrome borders on the mediocrity complex. We were in the last geometry class of the term. Alla Nikolaevna, a large, flabby woman, was checking our homework. We were supposed to have come to grips with sines and cosines on our own, but, expectedly, no one had bothered. Who's going to study a new topic for the end of term class? But Alla Nikolaevna had other ideas. She wrote out several problems involving sines and cosines.

"Valera, come here," she said in a sepulchral voice.

Valera quickly went to the board and eyed the problem.

"What are you looking at? Solve the problem!"

4*

"I can't. I don't understand," he answered meekly.

"Go figure it out... Solve it however you see fit." Alla Nikolaevna primped her short curls.

Another five classmates were summoned to the board. They, too, were unable to solve the problem.

"Vika, come to the board. Show the others how it's done!" said the teacher.

"I don't know how to solve the problem, either," I said. "I didn't understand the new topic." I went red. My top-student complex showed itself.

"From you I wouldn't have expected it, Vika! You ought to be ashamed... I'm disappointed in you."

I didn't deserve the proud title of top student. I was ashamed. I cried my eyes out for half a day. I spent two hours studying the new topic and learning how to solve irrelevant problems. Stock geometry problems. Stock behaviour. We were circus bears, and they were systematically training us how to dance to their tune. The pipe, composed of prejudices and doubts, was beginning to crush me.

Again I am creeping ... I'm moving ahead slowly, whispering prayers. I'm going over every memory that comes into my head. I have no tears left. The bleeding has stopped; a light film, slightly sour to the taste, has formed over the scratches on my hands.

Again I sense a strange bend in the pipe. Is this some kind of labyrinth? I don't understand. I'm neither hungry nor sleepy any more. My energy is consistently low. Perhaps my body has passed to another materiality. Or I've died without noticing it. Probably several lifetimes have passed since I first found myself in this pipe. Thoughts are whirling in my head. The first problems give way to the second problems, and then the second give way to the first again. When I creep out of this pipe, without fail I'll get down to solving them. I believe I'll succeed. Yet ahead of me there still isn't any light.

It's at my alma mater that I made more mistakes than anywhere else. Yes, it's a place where you can really learn what not to do. My mistakes have always made me miserable. They're punishable. And resurrecting the reputation of a bright student is a long and arduous process. The stains do not entirely wash away. I became a half-baked specialist.

"Who knows the answer? Raise your hand," said the elderly lecturer.

Several hands went up. I, too, answered as I saw fit.

"Incorrect. You're wrong. If you don't know the answer, then you shouldn't answer at all," said the lecturer.

In the evening, a classmate and I were having tea and chatting. In the kitchen the refrigerator hummed cosily. Cup after cup of tea. My landlady was watching television.

"Listen," said my friend, "why do you have to draw attention to yourself? I've got ideas of my own too, but I just keep them to myself. The teachers will make a monkey of you anyway and everyone will hoot with laughter," she said with conviction.

"I don't know why," I said honestly.

"No one gives a damn. What really matters is getting a diploma. That's the only reason I'm even going to university. All those assignments and all that blah blah blah... None of it does me any good. But I'll come up with something to say on the exam!"

"I'm already afraid of saying what I think. And what's worse, I've stopped thinking altogether!"

"But no one cares what you think! It would be a different story if you were taking private lessons from the dean... Or you already had a really cool job... Or your parents had bags of money! But as it is," my friend snorted disparagingly, "just let it go!"

A year later, I wrote what I really thought once again on a graded assignment. Once again it was the wrong thing to do. And once again I got the response:

"You're out of place here! It pains me to have to say it, but at this stage of your work I see that you haven't achieved anything and you haven't made any progress. You've just stayed in the same place, Vika! You need to do some thinking."

I touch the smooth, cold interior of the pipe as I keep on creeping ahead. Here my hands come upon some object. I run my hand over it. It's my lighter! Slowly I flick it on. What does this mean? It can only be that this is a never-ending circle. I'm creeping inside a circular pipe. No one can see me and no one can hear me. No one is going to save me. I begin laughing, bleakly and hysterically. The lighter twitches in my hands, trying to jump free. I feel how its heart is beating. As a child I'd carefully squeezed a chicken in the same way, and I could feel how its life was beating inside of it. The pipe is beginning to expand and contract by turns. I'm gasping. I understand, consciously, that I'll be inside this pipe forever. Such a cruel word – forever!

Often I've wondered what hell is really like. Well, here I am, and it turns out that it isn't all fire and demons in tar. I'm crying and laughing. It's not fear. Only hysterics. And suddenly I wildly want to live, to do something, to have my say. I want to turn the whole world upside down. To fix my mistakes. Only how can you dream of change on a large scale when you can't even turn around inside a pipe?

"Help me!" I wail, the sound breaking free of my throat and resounding throughout the circle of the pipe. "I'm trapped in here, but I want to live... Let me out..."

I worked as a sales assistant in a mobile phone shop. I hated it. I was poorly paid and worked awkward hours. I was afraid to leave... What would the people around me say? What would the management think? Every morning I dragged myself to this bloody salesroom. I swabbed the floors, put merchandise on display, sold phones, and flogged SIM cards that nobody wanted. I spent days on end sitting in a chair and looking out the window. To dull my grief I began swearing and smoking cigarettes. I was losing everything. My house of cards was collapsing. My dreams were buried in the jungle of my subconscious. I was trying to win people over. But they were going away, going away...

"No one cares about your dreams and ideas... Welcome to the real world. Now get your head out of the clouds!" said my boss. "We need to fulfil the sales plan. Pull yourself together and get to work!"

"How am I going to sell seven phones a day? You can see for yourself that we don't have enough customers!"

"You're the salesperson – that's your problem," she said. She left the salesroom and lit up a cigarette outside the door.

The New Year was drawing near. We had dissatisfied customers coming into the shop. They told us what we should do and how we should do it. They said that we didn't know our jobs and that we sold low-grade merchandise. The people around me always knew everything. It was just me who didn't understand. I swore, smoked and slowly went out of my mind.

"Vika," said my boss, "We have to fulfil the plan. Two hundred and fifty phones by the end of December! Find a way to sell them like cupcakes!" she laughed.

I was practically living at work. I failed the term. The company halved my pay. Before the New Year they'd needed to scale back wages. At the end of December I gave my notice and collected my final pay. Where was I to go? What should I do next? I had no idea. There followed rounds of other hateful jobs, other hateful people I'd rather avoided. And so it went, round and round and round! One took the place of the other over and again. And every time I left, it was like quitting a drug. I said I'd go my own way. But it would all begin again, right from the beginning.

The more you tell yourself you're beginning a new life, the more you end up failing to start it and just lulling yourself with promises. You put off the moment of transition to your new life, which never begins. Life simply goes on.

I continue lying inside the pipe. Sometimes I creep a little just so that I can stretch out my body. From time to time I flick the lighter on. I observe my shadow and the walls of my dwelling. Strangely I'm getting enough air. I'm neither sleepy nor hungry. At times I fall into a dreamless sleep. Memory, desire, emotion – they no longer exist. I don't know whether I'm alive or dead.

I'm enveloped in silence. My hands are becoming white and bony. My ribs protrude. My skin is drying out. I'd like to know how long I've been lying here. Although does the relationship between "how long" and "forever" really mean anything? It's weird. Dark. Quiet. Time no longer plays a role of any kind. Time no longer exists.

I've quit creeping. I'm simply lying here, holding the lighter in my hands, feeling its shape and its temperature. Even its colour. Then I begin feeling all of my body. It belongs to me and to no one else, however terrible or wonderful it may or may not be. Slowly I penetrate to the centre of myself. I feel my kidneys, liver, lungs, even my veins and the blood circulating through my body. Slowly, deeply, and with enjoyment, I breathe in and breathe out the heavy air. I feel the rise and fall of my chest, my ribs, my abdomen. There's nothing more that I want.

Peace. Quiet all around. It's good. Deserted. I'm alone. I exist. There's no way out. And no need to find one. How strange that I exist, but there's no way out. And there's no need to worry about anything, there is no need for pointless illusions or ambitions. There is no longer any need to bang my head against the wall and make my fists bleed. I don't need a thing. At this point the pipe cracks and collapses heaping me with chunks of broken zinc. With my thin, pale hands, I slowly brush the fragments away from my face and body.

Anna Lavrinenko

TALES OF THE OLD THEATRE

Translated by Amanda Love Darragh

The Tale of the Architect and the Unknown Actor

Once upon a time the walls of the old Theatre had been painted yellow; now they were dull and worn, and most of the paint had peeled off. Cracks ran like wrinkles in different directions, and graffiti scrawls were still visible despite the feeble attempts to paint over them. The building wasn't actually that old, but its pitiful state made it look as though it had been there since time immemorial.

The Theatre was tucked away in a quiet spot in the centre of town, flanked by a city bank on one side and a shopping centre on the other. A lane lined with poplars and narrow yellow benches led away from the back of the Theatre. In spring the flowerbeds there were full of purple irises, pansies and wild roses; amorous young couples came here to stroll, and the benches were colonized by groups of teenagers swigging beer from large plastic bottles. In winter it was deserted, used only by actors and solitary pedestrians on their way home.

The Theatre's architecture combined features of neoclassicism and modernism. The building was modestly decorated but undeniably imposing, rather like a bashful maiden whose ignorance of her own beauty serves to enhance it. There was nothing ostentatious in the harmonious appearance of the Theatre, in its classical proportions and regard for the traditions of antiquity – just a great love of art, architecture and the theatre.

The façade and side walls were adorned with sculptures crafted from marble and stone and executed with reference to motifs from Ancient Greek tragedy. The portico featured a niche containing a group sculpture: in the centre, wearing a laurel wreath and holding a lyre, was Apollo, protector of the arts. To his right was Thalia, muse of comedy, and to his left was Melpomene, muse of tragedy. Both were pensive, melancholy and magnificent in their draped robes, which emphasised their breasts and thighs.

Inside the building, the foyer was cool and quiet; the floors were covered with coloured tiles, and the main staircase leading to the first floor was made of marble. The auditorium was decorated with a painted frieze depicting an ancient ritual procession: the muses, half-naked goddesses and long-legged, muscular deities danced and drank wine to the rustle of a red velvet curtain with a white tasselled fringe.

The Theatre was built in 19—. It was designed by a German architect who had been invited to the city of N by the Mayor. The architect was a modest and cultured man. Having suffered from a slight stammer since childhood he was not particularly at ease in social gatherings, but nevertheless he was well liked in the city of N. He had a sparse beard and wore a morning coat embroidered with roses, together with a pair of laced ankle boots. Although his personal style was considered highly eccentric at the time, it did not in any way detract from his artistic achievements.

While the Architect was working on the construction of the Theatre he inadvertently fell in love with a certain Actor, who was exceptionally good-looking in a classically Slavic way. The Actor's physical appearance made people assume that he was an honourable, strong and noble man. In actual fact he was capricious, egotistical and, as is often the case with beautiful people, exceedingly dull.

Occasionally, feigning reciprocal interest, the Actor would join the Architect for dinner or a walk. At the slightest encouragement from the Actor – a look, a word, a smile – the Architect would tremble and ask almost pleadingly, "D-d-do I h-h-have any c-c-cause to h-h-hope…?" The Actor would appear to nod his assent, but the very next day he would withdraw his affections, becoming cold and distant. He would go drinking in taverns and flirt with young actresses, but he always returned to the Architect a few days later. Again he would look at him with fluttering eyelashes, bashfully lowering his eyes as though he were passionately in love and blushing when the Architect touched his hand. He was playing at being in love out of boredom, for his own entertainment, not fully understanding that the Architect, who was accustomed to sincerity and openness, believed the whole charade.

In an attempt to sublimate his emotions the Architect devoted himself wholly to his work, but still he could not forget the Actor. Ultimately, he poured all of his suffering, his passion and his tenderness into the creation of the Theatre, and although his love for the Actor remained unrequited, and his work brought him neither fame nor fortune, he felt no regret.

As soon as the Architect's work was done he left for his homeland and never returned to the city of N. He left his heart in the Theatre, in an unfeeling edifice of stone, plaster and paint, which was destined to become not only his masterpiece but also one of the country's most renowned works of art.

The Actor's fate was less illustrious: a few years down the line he took to drink, stopped getting work and was soon forgotten. According to the gossipmongers it was no great loss to the Theatre, because as an actor he had been distinctly average.

The Theatre was also subject to the vicissitudes of fate. It thrived in the early years, thanks to the patronage of the Mayor and the local administration. Attending a performance at the Theatre was considered to be worldly and fashionable; the repertoire included plays by Shakespeare, Ibsen and Chekhov. On some occasions demand was so high that extra chairs were placed in the auditorium. The company went on tour to other cities and other countries, and the Theatre hosted visiting troupes who came with their best productions.

Unfortunately, just before the elections, the Mayor died quite suddenly. His successors, who were not renowned for their integrity or any particular fondness for the arts, failed to allocate any funds for the maintenance and upkeep of the Theatre.

First the roof began to leak, then whole chunks of plaster began to fall from the walls. The curtain, once so luxurious, was reduced to rags – in some places burned, in others ripped. There was no money to replace the light-bulbs, so the corridors between the stage and the dressing room, the administrative offices and the other rooms backstage were dim and gloomy. New costumes were sewn from old, and the same props were used for three different plays. The Theatre was in dire need of renovation and had been for some time, but there was no one to take on the task and so a few years later it came to the end of its natural life.

Like many other buildings that fall out of use and into disrepair, at some point it will inevitably be declared a monument of cultural significance and awarded protected status. In fact, all that will happen is that the windows and the stage entrance will be boarded up and a heavy padlock will be hung on the front doors. A few years after that it will be turned into a hotel. By then no one will remember the cultural significance of this monument.

The Tale of the Artistic Director

Many years ago, Roman Nikolaevich – the Theatre's Artistic Director – had set up his office in a small room on the ground floor of the Theatre, next to the dressing rooms, and he had been there ever since. The middle of the room was occupied by a large desk, which was piled high with paperwork and figurines made out of papier-mâché. To the right of the desk, in the corner, was a cupboard full of documents; on top of this cupboard stood a plaster bust, nicknamed Van Gogh on account of its missing nose and right ear. To the left, next to the window, was a sofa, which was littered with newspapers, stage props, printouts of plays and discarded sweet wrappers. Roman Nikolaevich never tidied his office. He didn't have a secretary to do it for him, and the cleaner only dusted the surfaces and mopped the floors. In former times people had put the state of his office down to the idiosyncrasies of his creative, intellectual personality, but latterly his occasional visitors had begun to view it more as simply slovenliness.

There was a knock at the door and Ivan Timofeyich came into the room, without waiting for an answer. The Artistic Director abruptly shut the desk drawer and pretended to be writing something in a thick exercise book.

"Just a minute," he said, without raising his head.

Ivan sat down on a chair to wait. Roman Nikolaevich finally put his pen down and looked up. His chin was trembling and his face and eyes were red.

"Would you like some brandy?" he asked.

Ivan shook his head.

"Well, I'm going to have one, if you don't mind," said Roman Nikolaevich, taking a small bottle of cheap brandy from the top drawer of the desk. He drank straight from the bottle, pulling a face – there were no snacks to chase it with. "So tell me," he continued, "what's the matter this time?"

"Oh, the usual. We need new light-bulbs, we need plaster and paint... We need money, Roma."

"I see, and where am I supposed to get it from? You know as well as I do how much we made last month. It's barely enough to cover the salaries."

"We have to get it from somewhere. Maybe we could increase ticket prices, or ask the mayor's office? Surely it's in their interest to prevent the Theatre falling apart!"

"Oh, come on... Nothing would give the mayor greater pleasure! Imagine a plot of land this size becoming available, right in the centre of town – the perfect spot for another shopping centre! No, the mayor won't give us a penny."

"But you haven't even tried!"

"True. What's the point?"

"What's the point of anything?" asked Ivan, mimicking the Artistic Director.

"What do you want me to do, Ivan?" cried Roman Nikolaevich, raising his voice in a fit of temper. "You know better than anyone that I'm already doing all I can! Absolutely everything that is within my power! I've given my entire life to this Theatre, for God's sake! My wife left me, my grandchildren don't want anything to do with me, I'm half starving... But why am I telling you all this? What do you honestly think I can change? I can't force people to go to the Theatre! They don't need it any more."

Ivan Timofeyich couldn't argue with this. He had seen it with his own eyes – the stalls growing emptier by the day, groups of schoolchildren and students larking about in the boxes and the balcony, drinking hard spirits and cracking sunflower seeds. It would be better for everyone if they didn't bother coming at all, but educational establishments required their students to make a certain number of visits to the theatre.

Ivan Timofeyich could still remember a time when people came to the Theatre in evening gowns and smoking jackets, when nobody chewed nuts or swigged brandy from hip flasks during the performance. Back then the Theatre itself, as well as its Artistic Director, had been different.

Success had come easily to Roman Nikolaevich in his youth. Earnest and driven, he was barely in his thirties when he was appointed director of the new Theatre. The appointment was essentially a whim of the Mayor at the time, who had seen something in him – a passion, a kind of fire that seemed as though it would never go out. Roman Nikolaevich adored the Theatre; he adored the stage and the art of the theatre. He somehow always managed to select the right plays for the repertoire and had an infallible knack for hiring the most talented actors. He was also greatly respected for his ability to get on with everyone – not only the actors and directors but also the front of house team, the usherettes, the cafeteria staff and even the audience.

On New Year's Eve Roman Nikolaevich would dress up as Father Christmas and give the entire company gifts: sweets, chocolates and handkerchiefs. There was always a big party in the Theatre, and a lavish buffet with champagne and canapés.

But time began to take its toll. Fewer and fewer spectators

meant less and less money. The troupe was reduced to a minimum, and the shortage of actors inevitably meant that the repertoire was pared down too. Roman Nikolaevich still dressed up as Father Christmas at the New Year's Eve parties but he no longer handed out gifts, and they weren't really parties – there were just a couple of bottles of champagne, bought by the staff themselves, who stood around listening to a drunken Father Christmas promising that things would definitely get better, and that next year everything would be fine.

Either out of the goodness of his heart, in recognition of their old friendship or as an acknowledgment of his eternal gratitude, Ivan Timofeyich followed the Artistic Director like a silent shadow – hiding the unfinished bottles, trying to pick the right moment to send him home and covering for him in front of the actors. The difference was that he no longer looked up to the Artistic Director.

He thought Roman Nikolaevich would cope, that he would manage to put a brave face on it and persevere against the odds, but then all of a sudden he seemed to grow old almost overnight and stopped caring about anything.

It happened later that week, perhaps on Thursday – the Artistic Director went outside and spent the entire day standing in front of the Theatre. The sky was overcast and it was drizzling. The passersby, as gloomy as the weather, were preoccupied with their daily concerns and walked straight past him. Roman Nikolaevich observed them closely, but not one person so much as glanced either at the Theatre or at the posters advertising the performances. The flow of people thinned out as the morning wore on – he saw a couple of schoolchildren, a group of students, two or three unemployed men... None of them looked in his direction either, although the students could easily have done so. One of the unemployed men was clearly not in any kind of hurry and even stopped next to one of the posters to light a cigarette. Lunchtime was busier. By then the rain had stopped and the sky had cleared, but people still walked past the Theatre without looking at it. They looked straight ahead, at the road, at their feet, at their watches, at their companions – everywhere they possibly could except at the Theatre! It was as though it simply didn't exist. Several times Roman Nikolaevich actually shuddered and turned round to check the yellow building was still there. He ate nothing all day and got soaked to the skin but continued to stand there until twilight came, until he finally understood that his time was over.

Raisa the wardrobe mistress walked into his office without knocking.

"The mice have been eating the sets again," she told him, calmly and impassively, in the same tone she would have used to tell him that the curtains needed washing or that it was raining.

The director reacted equally impassively to the news.

"Which sets?"

"The ones for *The Storm*."

"Well, the little blighters might as well enjoy them! We haven't staged *The Storm* for ten years anyway, and we probably never will again."

"Roman Nikolaevich..."

"Yes?"

Ivan could tell that another argument was about to start – the kind that would end up humiliating the Artistic Director, although he never seemed to realize it himself – and he leapt to his feet.

"I'll give you a hand, Raisa. Come on!"

Raisa stood there staring at Roman Nikolaevich for a little while longer, but she didn't finish whatever it was she was going to say. Instead she turned and left the office, with Ivan Timofeyich close behind her.

The Artistic Director put his head in his hands. He might even have shed a few tears. He knew that his colleagues couldn't stand him, but there was nothing he could do about that. He knew that his beloved Theatre was dying, but he couldn't do anything about that either.

Right now, more than anything in the world, he wished he were in one of the plays that he used to put on. Then he could have been sitting at his desk with a loaded revolver in the top drawer, like the one they had in the props – with a long metal barrel and a heavy black handle. Although this gun would be real. He would open the drawer, take out the gun, put it in his mouth and... BANG!

The Tale of the Wardrobe Mistress

Raisa was in her fifties, but from behind she could easily have been mistaken for a much younger woman, what with her narrow waist, her slender ankles, her long, thick plait of lovely fair hair and the way she dressed. Raisa loved to wear patterned gypsy skirts, brightly coloured blouses and wide-legged trousers. Her arms were always adorned with multicoloured bracelets or bangles, depending on her mood, and around her neck she wore strings of beads, eye-catching pendants and long chains. Her ears were decorated with enormous hoops, clip-on costume jewellery, or clusters of multicoloured stones that fell to her shoulders. Full of exceptional optimism and sincerity, Raisa was one of those extraordinary women you find yourself instinctively drawn to. Within minutes of meeting her you were desperate to make a good impression, hardly daring to hope that you might become friends.

Raisa's extraordinary spirit was evident also in the world she had created in the wardrobe room. Pink stockings trailed from hats with feathers and wigs of all kind (auburn, blond, curly), topknots and false moustaches sat directly on top of shoes, instead of mannequins. Scattered amongst the chaos, which appeared to be out of control but was in fact perfectly well organized, were the costumes – all mixed together, historical and contemporary alike. The walls were hung with black and white photographs of famous actresses and scenes from various performances, and there was a little table with vases full of fresh flowers, from the garden of her dacha. Over by the window, in the lightest part of the room, once you managed to make your way through the ever-encroaching thickets of costumes and accessories you would find the most important item in the wardrobe room – Raisa's old sewing machine, which she had inherited from her mother. With the help of this instrument, she was able to create and effect extraordinary transformations.

Raisa and Ivan Timofeyich had been good friends for many years and might well have become lovers – both had failed marriages behind them, but their friendship meant so much to both of them that neither wished to jeopardize it. Even so, when he followed her to the storeroom where the stage sets and props were kept, Ivan Timofeyich fell back a step so that he could admire Raisa without her noticing – her beauty was so simple, so natural and obvious.

The stage sets for Ostrovsky's tragedy *The Storm* – bushes, a fence and a gate – were made out of cardboard and papier-mâché. They were already quite old and had been used for several other plays too, not one of which had been in the repertoire for some time. Ivan Timofeyich and Raisa had grown accustomed to doing things together, and so they worked instinctively and harmoniously as a team. He carefully held the sets while she applied glue and superimposed a new piece of cardboard, cut to size, then pressed gently to help it stick. They waited a while for the glue to dry, then found the right colour paint and diligently painted the new piece of cardboard until it matched its surroundings and looked almost as good as new.

Usually they worked in silence, but this time Raisa was strangely agitated and kept calling him by his diminutive name, Vanechka, which she never normally used. She talked about one thing after another – her dacha, work, the rain.

"What's the matter with you today?" asked Ivan Timofeyich, laughing gently at her bustling activity.

"Oh, I don't know. It must be these sets!"

"Why have they got you in such a flap? It's not as though it's the first time we've fixed them."

Raisa said nothing at first, then the words came tumbling out, as though she were afraid that if she didn't speak her mind now then she never would.

"I tried to act the part of Katerina in *The Storm*, you know... It was a bad choice. Tragedy is not my genre! Whatever possessed me?"

"What are you talking about?" asked Ivan Timofeyich, confused.

Raisa smiled.

"I applied to drama school once."

"When? You've never told me this before!"

"There's nothing to tell. I didn't get in." Raisa sighed and was silent for a while. "I'm nothing like Katerina. I wasn't then, and I'm not now. Of course I had no idea at the time – I was young, I had my whole life ahead of me, and the dream seemed so noble, so attainable... But what did I know about anguish and suffering? How could I possibly understand heartbreak and a ruinous obsession with flight?"

As Ivan Timofeyich listened he imagined her as a young girl, tall and beautiful, walking into the main hall of the Theatre Institute. He saw two men and a woman sitting at a long table, sipping their water, making notes, calling "Next!" and looking up with interest when this cheerful, rosy-cheeked girl breezed in, because there was something special about her, something that caught your attention and made you look twice. She would have made a magnificent Governor's daughter in Gogol's *Government Inspector* but instead she read the part of Katerina, a character so alien to her, both physically and spiritually, that she convinced no one. No sooner had she begun the monologue about people not flying like birds than they said to her, "Thank you, that will do."

Raisa often thought of that hall when she lay in bed at night, unable to sleep. She imagined herself walking in and doing it all over again, but reciting something different this time, something joyful and impassioned. Her audience consisted of just three people, but they were the three most important people in her life at that moment, and when the hall rang with their applause she knew she'd been accepted.

"So that's what happened, Vanechka," she concluded. "As for the rest – how I became a dressmaker, how I married the wrong man – well, you already know all that."

Ivan Timofeyich couldn't find the words to comfort her. What could he possibly say? He took her hand and squeezed it. Just at that moment, a butterfly flew into the wardrobe room. Its wings were iridescent, a shimmering spectrum of bright blue, purple and turquoise. The colour of the sea. Neither Ivan Timofeyich nor Raisa knew that it was a *morpho rhetenor* – a rare species of butterfly found only in South America. Neither of them knew where it had come from or how it had found its way into this dusty room. Neither of them knew how long they sat there watching the butterfly in complete silence, captivated and entranced, until one of the usherettes ran into the room and the spell was broken.

"Ivan Timofeyich, there you are!" she cried from the door. "I've been looking all over the Theatre for you. Go to the hall, quickly, Lilya Viktorovna wants you – they need you on stage! I was supposed to fetch you straight away, but I've already spent half an hour looking for you. She's going to be furious!"

Smiling goodbye at Raisa, Ivan left the wardrobe room. The usherette ran after him, leaving Raisa alone with the beautiful butterfly.

The Tale of the Young Playwright

The actor who played the main part – the part of the Man – was late, and Ivan Timofeyich agreed to stand in for him in the rehearsal. All he had to do was read his lines from the script, although he already knew the part off by heart.

The play *Being Overruled*, which had been in the Theatre's repertoire for a number of years, was one of Ivan Timofeyich's favourites. It was a simple and touching love story about a middle-aged couple, who seemed to have grown apart. The husband spent all day languishing in bed, apparently suffering from "love-sickness", while the wife harboured a secret desire to sign up for acting classes and spent her time memorising Bernard Shaw's play *Overruled*. In reality, the husband had been jilted by his lover and the wife was too old to become an actress, but by force of habit they continued to play their respective roles. This play, by a Young Playwright whose name had long been forgotten, ran exclusively at the Theatre. The Playwright had refused to allow it to be staged in other theatres, having signed over all staging rights to Roman Nikolaevich.

This short summary of its contents would probably suffice, but the Young Playwright has his own tale, which is somewhat extraneous to our story but nevertheless deserves to be acknowledged.

The Playwright started writing plays at a young age and was convinced that this was his true vocation. However, his endeavours brought him neither fame nor fortune so he also worked in a firm selling men's shirts. From time to time amateur or student theatres would put on his plays, but this did not bring any tangible benefit and he continued to dream of seeing his plays performed at a real theatre.

"Writing a great play takes time," he would say. "A lot of time!" But he was able to find it only in short bursts – either in the bus on the way to work, or while he was taking a bath, or during his lunch break. Time was passing, but success remained elusive. His girlfriend was keen to get married, and she continually reproached him for his idleness and lack of commitment.

One day, having made the decision to take his future into his own hands, he announced to his friends and his girlfriend that he was going to lock himself up in his apartment for a whole year to work on a play.

"I'm handing in my notice, taking out all my savings and shutting myself up at home for a year. I'm not going to set foot outside, except to go to the shop or into the yard for some fresh air. I won't see anyone, not even my mother! I'll spend this time writing something – not just 'something', but something great! I'll sell it for a fortune, and then I'll finally be able to get married!"

This gave his girlfriend pause for thought. She couldn't wait to get married – she had her heart set on a big white dress, a pair of doves, a toast-master, a photographer and a reception after the ceremony at Canteen No.9. Everyone said the food there was excellent, particularly on special occasions. But on the other hand, if she waited just a little she could marry a genius! How her girlfriends would envy her then! So she agreed to wait for the Young Playwright.

After handing in his notice and settling a few other administrative issues, the Young Playwright was ready to embark upon his period of voluntary isolation. Not everyone is capable of tolerating loneliness, but the Young Playwright was actually looking forward to it. He anticipated the following schedule: he would get up at 8 a.m., go for a run, take a shower, have coffee and a fried egg for breakfast, then work on his play until lunchtime, after which he would permit himself a short nap. After his nap he would continue working, editing what he had written that morning, and then it wouldn't hurt to take a little light exercise. Finally supper, which would consist of chicken breast baked in cream, aubergine braised with mushrooms, salmon baked in sauce, fried potatoes with wild mushrooms or seafood spaghetti. He would permit himself a glass of wine with dinner, maybe two, and while he was eating he would listen to music. After dinner, of course, he would relax by watching a film or reading a book.

However, when he woke up on the first day of his new life, he felt like staying in bed a little longer. Why shouldn't he? He had the time, after all – a whole year's worth! And he'd been working so hard recently, he hadn't been getting nearly enough sleep. He eventually got up at around midday and sat down in front of the television. He wasn't in the mood to work – a filling lunch of meat dumplings had sapped his energy. When the infomercial he was watching ended (after he had given in and ordered a self-cleaning mop), the Playwright took *The Adventures of Sherlock Holmes* from his bookshelf and read it late into the night, snacking on sandwiches and sweet tea. On the second day, when his alarm clock woke him at 9 a.m., he remembered that he had stayed up quite late the night before and decided that he could probably permit himself a little lie-in. Again he slept until midday.

The third day was just like the second, as was the fourth, and so the weeks went by. The Young Playwright stopped shaving and no longer bothered to change out of his dressing gown, which by this point was in dire need of a good wash. When his food ran out, he would go to the nearest shop and stock up on dumplings, instant noodles and sandwiches, but apart from these rare excursions he never left the apartment. He put on weight and acquired an unhealthy pallor, but he neither noticed nor cared. At first the Playwright was in heaven – spending his days loafing about, drinking beer, watching television, reading interesting books, sleeping, eating, doing whatever he liked – but as time went on, little clouds began to drift into the clear blue sky of his existence, and these little clouds soon became storm clouds. He was almost out of time, and the play still wasn't written. Occasionally he would sit down at the computer and force himself to write a couple of lines, but lack of inspiration meant that he always ended up back on the sofa again. Every day he promised himself that tomorrow – yes, definitely tomorrow – he would be strict with himself; yet every day, when his alarm clock woke him at 9 a.m., he turned it off and slept until lunchtime. The storm clouds were growing larger and more ominous with every day that passed, and the Young Playwright wept at his own helplessness.

Then one day he came across the play *Overruled*. What was it about this particular play? What distinguished it from the hundreds of other plays that he had read that year? It is impossible to say. But whatever it was, as soon as he'd finished reading it he sat down at the computer and neither the television nor the self-cleaning mop could distract him from his work. Maybe his time had simply come. The play was written in about a fortnight, and the year was up ahead of time. It was not a great play, of course, but it was a good play – the best he had ever written.

The Young Playwright had a shave, put on a clean shirt and trousers, printed out the play on twenty-five sheets of paper and went round to see his girlfriend.

"Oh!" she exclaimed when she saw the Playwright on her doorstep. "I didn't think you were coming!"

"Why not? We agreed to meet in a year's time, so here I am. Ahead of time, in fact! What's the matter? Aren't you pleased to see me?"

"But... I didn't think you meant it."

The Playwright turned pale.

"Didn't think I meant what? What are you saying?"

"Well, I decided that I wasn't destined to marry a genius... So I married an electrician instead."

"But I'm not a genius," the Playwright said sadly.

There was a bench in the yard. The Young Playwright sat down on it, placing the pages of text on his knees. From that moment, the play that he'd been so proud of just five minutes previously ceased to hold any meaning for him. He glanced through it indifferently. Yes, it was good; yes, it was the best thing he'd ever written; yes, a real theatre might even stage it – but he no longer cared about any of it. Leaving the pile of paper on the bench, he stood up and walked away.

Five minutes later Ivan Timofeyich, who was on his way to work that day in good spirits, found some pages of printed text blowing about in the wind near his house and gathered them up.

The Tale of the Old Actress

She usually finished work at 9 p.m. It took her until about 9.30 p.m. to get changed and then she would spend anywhere from a few minutes to half an hour chatting with those who were still at work, stretching the time out as much as she could to avoid going home. She left the Theatre between 10 p.m. and 10.15 p.m. and was home by 10.30 p.m. Without eating any dinner, the first thing she did was to take a shower. She would tie her hair up in a knot on top of her head, put a shower cap over it, climb under the hot streaming water and just stand there for several minutes with her eyes closed, not thinking about anything. Then she would take the citrus gel from the little shelf, squeeze it generously onto a sponge and rub it over her whole body – her chest, her arms, her legs, her stomach. She couldn't reach her back. After she'd rinsed off the soap she would dry herself with a large terry towel and then wrap herself up in it. She would rub cream into her face, take the shower cap off, let her hair down and comb it out. She would take an aspirin (or a glass of brandy, to help her sleep) and then lie in bed, flicking through the television channels and eating ice cream or chocolate-covered nuts. She would fall asleep to the sound of the television.

She was one of those ordinary, unremarkable women you can walk past in the street without even noticing. Something might catch your eye, a ridiculous coat or a shapeless lilac bag, but you don't bother turning round and a moment later you've already forgotten the coat and the bag, and as for the face – you never even noticed it in the first place. No one ever recognized her as the actress who spent years portraying the ravishing Nora in *The Doll's House*, the romantic Juliet in *Romeo and Juliet*, the loyal Lady Chiltern in *An Ideal Husband* and the enigmatic Woman in *Being Overruled*. All her ordinariness disappeared as soon as she stepped out on stage. It was the only place she could truly experience joy, suffering and death, and everyone believed in her.

Despite the popularity it had enjoyed during its heyday, the Theatre had always remained provincial in essence; consequently there was a high turnover of actors, particularly as far as the leading ladies were concerned. Actresses came and they went, in search of recognition and fame – some to bigger towns, some even to the capital – but they merely went from being stars in a small town to being anonymous and superfluous elsewhere. If they ever came back, life had worn them down to the extent that they were no longer suitable for the role of Juliet. Others got married and had children, and all of a sudden these charming leading ladies were transformed into ordinary housewives, with domestic concerns and family matters replacing the stage as the focus of their attention. Many promised themselves that they would return to the Theatre, but they never did.

Lilya was the only actress who stayed at the Theatre. She wasn't like the others. People advised her to leave – she could become famous, they said, maybe even a film star! But Lilya had no desire to leave.

Time passed too quickly. Without even being aware of it herself, she had stopped playing young girls in love and started playing their mothers. It was a strange feeling – the same plays, the same stage, but different roles. It wasn't that she'd made a conscious decision to devote her life to the Theatre, that was simply the way it had turned out. She had so many vivid, dramatic experiences on stage that real life seemed more like a series of rehearsals for a good play. The simple fact was that she belonged to a peculiar minority of individuals who don't strive for fame or fortune, and she was one of the lucky few who manage to find their place in life.

If she ever regretted not having a family or thought wistfully about the fact that she could have been a grandmother by now, then her memories of the roles she had played and all the emotions she had experienced on stage were on hand to comfort her, to stop her losing heart. The Theatre was her home and her family.

Moreover, she wasn't quite alone. She had a Devoted Admirer, who met her after every performance as he had in the past, in their youth. She hadn't found him attractive thirty years ago – he had seemed too young, too naive, too ardent – but the men she had favoured were now conspicuous by their absence. They had all disappeared. Her Devoted Admirer was the only one who had stayed, but by the time she realized that love and kindness are more important than certain other qualities it was too late. Back then she had been too young to value his devotion; now she was too old to make any changes in her life. Her face had become too wrinkled, and so had her heart. Or so it seemed.

But she did enjoy their evening walks. He was good company. And when she was with him, she felt that she became interesting and beautiful. She really had no idea why, but that was definitely how it felt. Yes, she could hold forth on any subject! She could keep up any conversation going! She was irresistible!

They could talk about anything and everything, with one exception – they never spoke about the future. It had already been decided for them. He mentioned it only once, when he had said to her that if he ever failed to meet her after the performance, if that day should ever come, it would mean only one thing – that he had departed this life. Although she didn't admit it to him, or even to herself, Lilya Viktorovna feared this day above all else.

* * *

She led the rehearsal as though she were the director of the Theatre – it wasn't the first time it had happened, and it didn't occur to anyone to contradict her. Even so the actors, relaxed by the absence of the leading man, were less than enthusiastic and began asking after just half an hour if they could make a phone call, or go for lunch, or run to the shops because there was a mid-season sale on. It didn't really matter... At the end of the day they all knew their parts, and in any case the prospect of stumbling over their lines in front of a dozen audience members, who probably wouldn't even notice, was not particularly terrifying. Lilya reluctantly let them go, one by one, until she remained alone with Ivan Timofeyich.

"The youth of today," she said suddenly, in the tone of Lady Macbeth, as she turned to face the empty auditorium. "They can't do anything! Just three hours of rehearsals! In my day," she continued, her voice trembling like Juliet's, "I could spend twenty-four hours a day on stage – the afternoon learning new parts, and the evenings performing. Where have those times gone?" she lamented, as doomed and despairing as Hamlet.

The actress froze, either lost in her thoughts or possibly playing a role, then she snapped out of her reverie and looked at Ivan Timofeyich.

"Are you still here? That's strange... You should have been the first to go."

"I can stay, if you like."

"No, you can go. Run along and get on with whatever it is that you do. I don't need you. Apparently there's a sale on in the shops."

"You shouldn't think of me like that," said Ivan.

The actress looked at him closely.

"I don't think of you at all. As I said, you may go."

He left, and Lilya Viktorovna stayed on stage, muttering her part under her breath. Though it might already have been a different role.

The Old Actress was not well liked in the Theatre. She was too arrogant, too bossy, and frequently sharp tongued. Only Ivan Timofeyich knew what she was really like. About a year ago he had been held up at work one night, and by the time he had finished the cleaning and his other jobs it was nearly 1 a.m. He left by the stage entrance, carefully closing the door behind him. Then, as he turned round, he saw Lilya Viktorovna. She was standing under a street lamp with her back to the Theatre. He could have slipped away unnoticed, but for some reason he couldn't bring himself to leave her standing outside in the cold. In any case he was curious to know what she was still doing there, when the performance had finished over three hours ago. He went up to the actress and touched her shoulder. She turned round, startled and somehow relieved, as though she had been waiting for this all evening... but when she saw who it was, her face took on its usual haughty expression.

"Oh, it's you."

"What on earth are you doing out here? You must be freezing! It's so cold. Can I walk you home?"

"No, thank you," replied Lilya Viktorovna, trying unsuccessfully to smile. "I'm just waiting..."

She clenched her fists, and Ivan Timofeyich looked at her as though he were expecting her to continue, to tell him who or what she was waiting for, but the Actress merely repeated, "I'm just waiting. Go home. I'll be fine. Don't worry."

Ivan Timofeyich, being the kind of person he was, couldn't help worrying about her. It was very late, after all.

"I can't leave you here like this," he said.

"Oh, what a gentleman," said the Old Actress, her voice

dripping with sarcasm. She hoped that her tone would offend Ivan Timofeyich and that he would leave, but he ignored the jibe. She was a middle-aged woman, frozen and alone, and he had no intention of leaving her there on her own. She'd only spoken to him like that because she was feeling confused and emotional about something. It wasn't worth getting upset about.

"Can I wait with you?" he asked.

Lilya Viktorovna looked at him strangely and nodded. She had realized that there was no point trying to get rid of him. They stood there for a little while, with Ivan Timofeyich blowing on his hands and stamping his feet. He envied the actress and her endurance – she was standing perfectly still, without moving! Suddenly, more for his sake than her own (she knew that he would stay with her, however tired and hungry he was), she said, "Let's go home. It's late, and there's probably no point in waiting any longer. My place is not far from here. I'm quite capable of walking there myself, but if your chivalrous nature will not permit you to leave me here then you may accompany me."

Ivan Timofeyich nodded, and together they set out towards her house. He fell back a few steps behind her and didn't ask any more questions. He wasn't to know it, but that was the day that the Tale of the Old Actress came to an end.

The Tale of the Leading Man

Although he wasn't hungry, Ivan Timofeyich went out to get something to eat. It was snowing, but the snow was melting away as soon as it hit the ground. No slush or dirty snowdrifts to worry about yet... But then, it was only the second time it had snowed that year. Ivan Timofeyich hadn't even got around to changing out of his autumn boots. In the shop next door to the Theatre he bought a bread roll and a packet of kefir, which he ate right there, in a sheltered spot called the Cafeteria, amongst the tall metal tables that were covered with breadcrumbs and spilled tea. There were no chairs in places like this, so he stood by the window and looked at the Theatre. The way the snow was falling on it reminded him of one of those glass balls with Christmas scenes inside, which you could shake and it would fill with snow.

Ivan Timofeyich seemed like an insignificant individual, but in fact in many respects he was indispensable. He had worked at the Theatre for many years, during which time he had learned how to do most things, such as cleaning the dark red velvet curtain, clearing the stage after every performance, changing lightbulbs and helping the wardrobe mistress mend ripped dresses. Neither he nor the Artistic Director who had taken him on could remember his original job description.

He hadn't been particularly popular with the girls when he was younger, and as he got older he became even less attractive. Being rather tall he had a noticeable stoop, which grew more and more pronounced with every passing year. His skin was so pale that it looked transparent and his hair, once dark and lustrous, had become lank and greasy. He had it cut every three months by an incompetent hairdresser. Unfortunately, neither of them seemed to be aware that the fashion for ruler-straight fringes had long since passed. Ivan Timofeyich wore the same suit to work every day, although the dark blue, double-breasted jacket with large black buttons was slightly too small for him, as were the matching trousers, which rose up to reveal black socks emerging from the tops of his brown pointed shoes. In the winter, the jacket did its best to conceal a heavily pilled, dull grey woollen sweater with an indistinct pattern; when it was warmer, this was replaced by one of three shirts – either white with a dark blue stripe, lemon yellow for special occasions, or dark grey, which was the one he wore most often.

The first time Ivan Timofeyich went to the Theatre, he was taken by his mother – a strict, taciturn woman, of whom he was rather afraid. Ivan Timofeyich's mother considered herself to be a woman of culture. She went to concerts at the Philharmonic, although she didn't know a thing about classical music; she visited art galleries, but she knew little about painting; she pretended to read the Russian classics, yet she always had a paperback novel near at hand.

The sun hadn't yet set, but there was an early autumnal feel to the evening. From a distance it looked as though the Theatre had been dipped in gold. There were people milling about the front entrance wearing suits, snow-white shirts, bow ties, long dresses and high heels, their hair smooth and sleek. Some of them held flowers to give to the actors. Still just a boy, Ivan was completely charmed by the Theatre – he'd never seen anything like it.

He gazed in wonder at the mahogany railings surrounding the balcony and the dress circle, the chandeliers that were shaped like flowers, the painted frieze... He glanced secretly at the curtain and glimpsed a flutter of red velvet, a face peering around the edge, but then it immediately disappeared.

The second bell sounded, then the third. The lights gradually dimmed and then went out altogether. The noise gradually died down too, and finally the auditorium was silent. The curtain rose with a rustle.

His mother spent the first act looking forward to the interval – she decided that she would treat herself to a slice of sponge cake in the cafeteria, and perhaps even a double

5*

brandy. Being naturally insensitive and slow-witted, she couldn't comprehend her son's delicate spiritual constitution and didn't even notice the way he watched the stage, wide-eyed with awe. During the interval, while he was animatedly discussing the performance, she barely even listened. Tucking into a sausage roll, Ivan was saying how wonderful it must be to be an actor.

"Nonsense," declared his mother. "There's nothing wonderful about it at all. They spend every evening weeping and wailing, they don't have any personal life to speak of, they get paid peanuts and spend the whole year living hand to mouth!"

"But Mama..."

His mother didn't want to hear any more about it.

The idea of transformation – that was what he liked most about the theatre. You could be a beggar one night and a king the next. He could live a thousand different lives in that way. He could love beautiful women, the kind he could never dream of loving in real life. He could open himself up and lay bare his soul, but instead of contempt and derision it would be met with applause.

Every day after school he rehearsed different roles in front of his bedroom mirror. He read long monologues and poems, and he spent all his pocket money on going to the Theatre. Ivan's dream took him there every day, but real life conspired to hold him back. Although he knew that his mother would never approve of such an impractical choice of profession, he still approached her several times with the firm intention of telling her that he had decided to apply to the Theatre Institute. However, his resolve always weakened under her glare. "I'll tell her later," he thought. But he never did. After school he studied at the Industrial College, and when he graduated he went to work in a factory. Deep down he already knew that he would never study at the Theatre Institute; not only that, but he wouldn't even try. He stopped going to the Theatre and began to avoid it altogether, so strong was his disappointment in himself, so great his envy of the actors. He decided to simply forget about the Theatre once and for all.

But some things are meant to be! It appears that people really do have a destiny to follow – their place in life is predetermined, and whatever they do, whatever challenges they may have to overcome, they find their own way there in the end. This is how it happened: they started laying people off at the factory where Ivan Timofeyich worked, and he lost his job. The day he received his final pay packet he walked through the checkpoint as he usually did, the heavy door closing behind him. He walked out through the main gates at exactly 5 p.m., as he had done for years, and suddenly he was overcome with a feeling of relief. Something had changed inside him. He didn't yet know that this was simply how it felt to be free. He didn't have a job or any money, but he was happy. The following day Ivan left the house, telling his mother that he was going to look for a job. He knew that he had a long road ahead of him. Up to this point in his life he had drifted along, doing what other people told him to, and even if he wasn't happy it had never occurred to him to do things differently. But now he was free to do whatever he liked, and his only fear was that he might not make the right decision.

It was no accident that he ended up at the Theatre that day, and it wasn't even fate – he knew exactly where he was going right from the start. Perhaps he had just wanted to prolong the suspense, to savour the anticipation of change. After all, the feeling of expectation before a special occasion can be more enjoyable than the occasion itself.

Ivan Timofeyich joined the Theatre when he was twenty-five, and this story takes place when he was sixty-two. After working in the Theatre all that time, he could no longer remember being anyone else. Even his dream about the stage nearly came true.

He loved being at the Theatre late at night, when there was nobody else in the building and the main entrance was bolted shut. At night the Theatre's ghosts, all its stories and legends, came alive. Ivan Timofeyich knew them like his own and carefully safeguarded them, even when they were no longer any use to anyone. It was the only time he ever stepped out onto the stage and acted in front of a nonexistent audience, with a nonexistent cast. He had been doing it for many years and could no longer remember when it had started. At first he couldn't relax because of the feeling that someone was watching him; he was terrified of being caught, but after a while he lost himself in the role and forgot his nerves. Then he got used to it, and once he had established that he really was the only one in the Theatre that late at night his confidence grew. He would spend at least two hours on stage – the length of an average performance, excluding the interval and applause. Then he would finish his cleaning and go home.

* * *

Coming in through the stage door, he shook the swiftly melting snow from his boots and went straight to the auditorium, in the hope that they would have started rehearsing again. But there was no one on stage. So Ivan Timofeyich started dressing the set. The sofa he dragged out from the wings was old and ripped in places, with springs sticking out. Raisa had recently covered it with a throw, which was someone's old shawl. He added two cushions that had been decorated with appliqué work, apparently to brighten them up a bit but in actual fact to cover up the holes. Next to the sofa he placed a side table and a standard lamp. Ivan Timofeyich made a point of putting a new light-bulb in – the old one had gone out at the most inconvenient moment, in the middle of a performance. The only thing left was a tall, decorative mirror with several drawers in the base, but he couldn't manage that alone. Someone would come and help him sooner or later, but for the time being he had other jobs to be getting on with. All the little things he did – such as changing the light-bulbs, sweeping the floor in the cafeteria, emptying out the ashtrays in the men's toilet, putting bottles of water in the dressing rooms – might have gone unnoticed, but if Ivan Timofeyich hadn't taken care of them all every day, so thoughtfully and diligently, it is hard to imagine what might have become of the Theatre.

At around 6 p.m. the actors started drifting back to the stage. Ivan Timofeyich also happened to be there – he was cleaning the curtain and waiting for something, although even he didn't know exactly what.

"Something" appeared at 5.55 p.m. in the form of Roman Nikolaevich, out of breath and in despair. He reeked of brandy and bewilderment.

"I'm sorry everyone, it looks like we're going to have to cancel the performance after all. It's nearly six, and there's still no sign of Lev. If we hurry up, we might be able to find the money to refund the tickets."

Wearily, having reconciled himself to fate some time ago, he sank into a chair and covered his eyes with one hand.

"What are you talking about, Roma?" asked Lilya, her voice harsh and strident. "Why can't we just replace him? He'll do," she said, prodding a young actor, who had only joined the Theatre two years previously and hadn't yet been given a lead role. "He's a bit young for the part, but we can make him up to look older... The audience aren't exactly going to notice. They never usually do."

"But I don't know the part!" said the young actor.

"What do you mean, you don't know it? Who's Lev's understudy?"

"He doesn't have one," the Artistic Director said quietly. "He's never missed a performance. So there didn't seem any point—"

"Nonsense! How can you not have an understudy? Roma, what's the matter with you? That's completely..." Lilya trailed off, without finishing her sentence. "Do any of you know the part?" she asked, appealing to the actors, who had somehow instinctively huddled together in a group. No one spoke. The silence was saturated with the Artistic Director's dismay, the young actor's humiliation and Lilya's contempt, which further heightened the tension, but suddenly it was broken by the voice of Ivan Timofeyich. He heard it and thought it sounded strange – it must have been someone else, someone nearby, because surely it can't have been him speaking in such a high-pitched, squeaky voice. The voice said, "I know the part. I know it off by heart."

The Artistic Director, Lilya and the other actors stared at him in silence, as though a bedside table had suddenly announced that it wished to be an actor. People aren't generally given to conversing with bedside tables, so nobody spoke – not even Lilya, who usually had something to say.

The first person to speak was the young actor, who was motivated not by the desire to come to Ivan Timofeyich's rescue but by the desire to save himself from the sharp tongue of Lilya Viktorovna.

"Actually, it's not a bad idea... He often helps me rehearse, and he reads quite well, almost professionally! He'll be fine. You heard him yourself, today at rehearsals. Not bad, is he?"

No one else said anything. The other actors, all of whom had worked at the Theatre for a long time, found the idea strange and incomprehensible. They just couldn't imagine sharing the stage with someone who had no experience and was completely unprepared. How could he possibly know the part? It would be easier just to cancel the performance! Sensing a way out, the Artistic Director was delighted at the turn of events but refrained from expressing his thoughts aloud – the others might not agree with him, and he was too mild and indecisive to champion his own cause.

In the end Lilya Viktorovna decided on behalf of everyone, including the Artistic Director. "Go and get changed," she commanded. "If the costume's too big, ask Raisa to adjust it. Just do it quickly! We'll have to have a quick rehearsal."

Ivan Timofeyich hurried to the dressing room, unable to feel his legs under him. Everything around him was spreading and blurring like fog. He could no longer feel his own body and cursed his tongue for blurting out such nonsense. He was bound to bring shame on the Theatre! He didn't know how to act and had certainly never done it for real. "You fool, you fool," he muttered to himself, over and over again.

The first thing he noticed when he found himself on stage was that he couldn't see the audience at all – he was blinded by the stage lights, and the auditorium looked completely dark. In fact, he preferred it that way as it helped to calm his nerves. Gradually his eyes got used to the bright lights and he could see the audience, but as a single, communal entity rather than individual figures or faces. Suddenly his fear evaporated and he was no longer Ivan Timofeyich, but a lovesick middle-aged man.

* * *

When it was over, he felt like himself again. He stood there, surrounded by his favourite people, and he could finally see into the auditorium: it was full of people giving him a standing ovation, and his mother was sitting in the front row. He was sharing the stage with Roman Nikolaevich, Lilya, Raisa and the young actor, and they were all smiling. He was no longer a middle-aged man but seventeen years old, the age he had been when he wanted to leave home and become an actor, and everything still lay ahead of him – a whole life on stage, and so many parts to play.

The Last Tale about the Theater

A man wearing overalls and carrying a toolkit stopped in front of the old Theatre. He'd never been inside, although he'd heard a lot about the Theatre and the shows they put on. He hadn't heard so much about it lately, come to think of it, and he probably would have forgotten about it altogether if it hadn't been for this job.

The man went in and found himself in a cool, quiet foyer with posters on the wall. The ticket office was closed. The little number tags in the cloakroom were hanging on their pegs – all except one, which had been replaced by a man's overcoat. The whole place was deserted.

He walked down the corridor towards a door marked Staff Only, but the door was locked. He looked into the cafeteria and the toilets, but there was no one there either.

"Hello! Did someone call an electrician?" he called, feeling extremely self-conscious.

It was dark and quiet in the auditorium, but the man sensed that there was someone on stage.

"Hello," he began. "You called an electrician yesterday... I'm afraid we got held up, couldn't come any earlier... It was quite late when you called, to be honest, as we told your director..."

But apart from the indistinct echoes of his own voice, there was no reply. The man walked up to the stage... and then he stopped.

On stage, surrounded by props and sets, lay a man. His body was twisted in an unnatural pose, his eyes were staring out into the auditorium and his lips were frozen in a smile.

The post mortem revealed that Ivan Timofeyich had died of a heart attack. His heart had simply stopped beating, and there is a good chance that at least in his last moments he was happy.

Following this event the Theatre closed down, initially for an unspecified period of time and then for good. Like many other buildings that fall out of use and into disrepair, it might have been taken over by tramps and local teenagers, but before this could happen it was declared a monument of cultural significance and awarded protected status. In practical terms, this simply meant that the windows and the stage entrance were boarded up and a heavy padlock was hung on the front doors.

For a long time, everything inside the Theatre stayed the way it had been left. Organized chaos reigned in the wardrobe room: pink tights still trailed from hats with feathers, curly wigs still sat on top of shoes, costumes were still strewn about the room.

The Artistic Director's office remained home to official documents and diplomas, although they were covered with so much dust that it was no longer possible to make out the names of the recipients and what they had done to deserve them. A newspaper lay on the desk amongst all the papers and second-rate plays, open at the last article ever written about the Theatre.

On stage the curtain was still up, as though the perform-ance were about to start. A pair of opera glasses lay abandoned in the fourteenth row of the stalls, seat number seven. Portraits of actors and actresses lined the foyer. All the little number tags were hanging in the cloakroom on the right hooks – except one, which had been replaced by a man's overcoat.

The posters near the ticket office in the foyer advertised *Decameron* on Wednesday, *The Honest Adventurer* on Thursday, *Two Funny Stories about Love* on Friday, and *Being Overruled* on Saturday. Unsold tickets for these performances lay in the ticket office. It was as though the Theatre were simply waiting for the audience to come back, for the actors to take to the stage, for the three bells to ring, the lights to go down and the performance to begin...

Several years later the Theatre was turned into a hotel. It's hard to imagine a Theatre being turned into a hotel, but that's exactly what happened. No one even remembered that the Theatre had been declared a monument of cultural significance. All that remained of this renowned work of art was the façade, and these tales... Tales that will never die but will in time become legends, like the Old Theatre itself, the memory of which will remain forever in the hearts of those who worked there and its audience.

The Artistic Director took to drink, and no one ever knew what became of him. Raisa carried on sewing, though no longer for the Theatre, and she raised two lovely granddaughters, hoping that one of them would become an actress. Lilya moved to another town to act in another small theatre, and she was never really happy about anything.

No one ever found out who called the electrician. As it turned out, there was nothing wrong with the electricity in the Theatre that day.

Ksenia Zhukova

Twenty Letters from the Twentieth

Written, projected, received, not sent...

Translated by John Dewey

1

November 1920

My dear Olya, I've no idea how things are going to turn out. I'm on a train, which is a huge relief as they said there wouldn't be any more trains. This one was put on this morning. You should have seen the scramble to get on, it was simply indescribable. May God speed us as far as the frontier, and then I hope we shall be together again. We've been apart now for a hundred and four days, four hours and thirty-five... no, thirty-six minutes. By the time I've finished this letter that calculation will of course have changed. I cling to the hope that this could mean a speedy reunion, because what would be the point without? Yalta turned out to be far from sunny. I still remember our trip there. You should see it now. I stood there waving at the last ship, swearing like a trooper. But what was the use? Nobody was going to stop it for some officer who'd turned up late, and in any case they told me it was packed so tight an insect couldn't have squeezed on board. I might have managed if it hadn't been for the rain. Everything's soaked. The roads all covered in mud. My boots too, not to mention the rest of me. You wouldn't recognize me. I'm so glad you and Zhenya are far away. Yes, can you imagine that, glad, because otherwise my heart would be troubled. As things are it's just sad that I can't talk to you and hug you both. The train has come under fire twice, but we're making steady progress. For two days now we've had nothing to eat but cabbage. But all that's neither here nor there. Later on, you see, all these moments taken together will be booked to our credit. Yes, and I know how things will turn out. You'll come to meet me in that lemon-yellow hat. Although what am I on about, it got left behind at our last address, didn't it. It really didn't suit you. On top of which you said it made you look like a schoolgirl and asked if I didn't think you looked ten years younger in it. And then I swore and said who it made you look like. I reproach myself so for that outburst. And for the piece of ice that cut your nose at the skating rink, although you won't remember that. That was more than ten years ago, more like twenty. Memories. We're slowing down. Could we have arrived? Or is it just another forced stop? The rain is just bucketing down all the time.

Forever yours, Gleb. May God preserve us.

2

13 August 1981

Dear Mum, it's raining all the time here. I don't know what else to tell you and Dad. Be sure to give Torrens a kiss on the snout for me. And please let him go in my room. I promise I'll wash his paws every day. Yesterday we had cabbage for dinner and supper. Yuck! And we had volleyball. We came second. That's not bad, Mum, considering there are seventeen teams in all. And just try beating the team of the eldest boys. We had a go, but bombed against them. My nose hardly hurts any more. And anyway, the ball didn't do much damage. Cabbage is really yucky. I don't want to go to chess club any more, photography club is much more fun. We changed a film inside a sort of black sleeve, and then we dried some prints. The mosquitoes are a pest. Everyone in our dorm joins in swatting them. Tomorrow we're going to play funny football. That's when we play against the girls. They dress up like us, in shorts and everything, and caps, and do pigtails in our hair for a laugh. They give us skirts too. Albina brought me her green one to wear. It'll be a hoot. Specially as we'll beat them hollow anyway. What else? Next time you and Dad come, don't bring any more rissoles. I couldn't eat them all, so I kept some in my pillow-case and they started to really pong. Our group leader bawled me out and mentioned it at line-up too. It's a pity Albina heard everything. Mum, don't ask who she is. I pointed her out last time. She has a red hair-slide and a grazed knee. I did that. Well, it was an accident. Albina's not bothered. I'm so bored. It's what they call 'dead hour' here. Still raining. They said if it doesn't stop we'll have football in the sports hall. Oh, and something else. Bring me a book to read, the library here is closed. The other boys say it's been closed all summer. What else is there to do during 'dead hour'? We've already had a garlic chewing contest. We've played 'sifak'[1]. You won't know that. Once we sneaked out

---

[1]A kind of 'tag', a game which became popular with school pupils in the 1980s. It consists of someone throwing the 'sifa'(any convenient object to hand such as a board rubber, rag or piece of crumpled paper) at the other players. Whoever is hit becomes the 'sifak' and must attempt to find a new target. The name is believed to derive from 'syphilis', the original idea being that anyone coming into contact with the 'sifa' is 'infected' by it.

of the grounds. Only mind you don't tell anyone here. There's nothing outside but fields and a main road. Anyway, Genka and me found a cemetery. It was different. Genka said it's called a mass grave. I told Albina and she wanted to go too, but they'd mended the hole in the fence and she wouldn't climb over. But mainly it's boring here. On parents' visiting day they're going to have a concert. And I'm going to sing in it. Me! Can you imagine! Isn't that weird? Bring me some sci-fi, only not too long, otherwise I won't get through it here. And I won't read it at home. Genka sneaked out again and went to the cemetery and said there's a monument there to people shot in the war. He said it had been put there literally a few days ago, because everything was new, even the writing on it. He even showed me where he'd got dirt on his sleeve. He said there was a list. Lots of children, babies even. Weird. I expect he got it all mixed up as usual. I know there was a war 'cos my granddad fought in it, but what have babies got to do with it? According to Genka they're still lying there in their prams. No, I definitely think he's a liar and made it all up. Albina thinks so too. This rain is awful, what else can you do during rest hour? Well, I'm writing home to you. I suppose I miss you. For tomorrow we've all agreed to have a go at eating soap from the washroom and a wax candle. Nobody in Albina's family fought in the war, or so she says. But that can't be right. She doesn't remember when the war began anyway, 'cos she's in the next class down. I suppose they haven't done the war yet. That's what she says, anyway. On the whole it's very boring here, and rainy. Come and visit as soon as you can. Last night we had a hedgehog here. We fed it curd fritters. Mum, bring my binoculars too. Dad knows where they are, in the cupboard. See you at the weekend, Gleb. Oh, and bring lots of chewing gum too, otherwise what else is there to do after lights out? Anyway, Albina's stupid, and her skirt too. And Genka. I mean, Albina's not actually stupid, just a pain. I'm really fed up with all this rain and cabbage.

3

21 June 1941

My dear, darling Mum. I'd so like to climb on your back and let you rock me like you always used to. When I was small, I mean. About my certificate: you know, I put it in a book, only the funny thing is I can't remember which one. But it's on my shelf over the desk. It's nice here at Grandma's. She gives me milk to drink before I go to bed. She says it's full of goodness. She's really funny. Of course, I drink it so as not to upset her. She's jumpy enough all the time as it is. She says things are tense and I have to go back. Well, that's our Grandma for you. Gleb and I have just got here and already she's had enough. I expect we're too much for her. Gleb gets overexcited. He's already killed a sparrow with his catapult and managed to break some rare plant in the neighbours' garden. I don't think they mind, though, they're good fun. And they don't make their children drink milk. Gleb drinks it too. Just imagine, Grandma told him if he didn't drink his milk he wouldn't be able to start school in the autumn. What rubbish. But Gleb believes her and drinks it. It's really horrible stuff, not like what we have at home, all gooey and tasteless.

The neighbours are good fun, though. Grandma says they haven't been here long and that they're refugees. The father, who we call Uncle Matvey, has a red moustache. His son Levka has made friends with our Gleb. They escaped from the Germans and tell stories of horrible things done by them, but I don't think it's like that. All right, they've had a bad time, but now they're with us. Although some of them are sowing panic, as the collective farm chairman said at a meeting. Gleb and I were there too: we hid on the roof and heard everything.

I'd really like a bit of adventure, but Grandma says she's going nowhere because this is where she was born. Tomorrow she's packing us off home. You'll get a real surprise! We're going with Uncle Matvey's family. Levka says they've been on the run like this for three years now since they've been refugees. Anyway, I expect my letter will reach you after we arrive. You'll get a real surprise! The holidays have just begun and already it's back to the city again. Never mind, I'll do some studying so I can get a certificate of merit next year too. Gleb says there's no way he'll do anything like that. You know, Levka says he hasn't been to school for a year now. It's been ten days since I last saw you, Mummy. I really feel how much I miss you. Never mind the country, I want to go home. Although there's such a nice little river here, and tomorrow morning we have to leave.

Now I'll finish my letter and go and say goodbye to the river. See you soon. Your dear daughter Olga.

4

30 March 1977

My darling Gleb, how I miss you. I realize how banal all this sounds. Here I am in the plane, writing to you. Soon we'll reach the sea, and already I can just imagine Simferopol in all its glory. I've never been there. In fact I have to confess that I've never seen the sea. I won't send the letter – after all, where can you post a letter in a plane? Especially as we'll be landing in two hours' time. But Gleb, I'll definitely post it to our address back home. This is how I imagine it: you'll meet me, we'll walk past a letter-box, and I'll drop the letter in. You'll ask, what's that? I'll come up with some facetious answer and then, yes, we'll head straight for the sea. And you'll tell me all about how you spent these two days without me. What a thing to happen. But never mind, there'll be times when we have to suffer the pain of separation for longer, and how much happier these two days apart will make everything afterwards, when we'll have all the happiness of life together to look forward to. I can scarcely believe we've been married for two weeks already. And here's our first journey as a couple having to start with us apart. Still, there's nothing we can do about it, it's just the way things are. After visiting the sea just long enough for us to grow tired of it, and it of us, we'll go back home again. And when we get home you'll run to the letter-box. No, first you'll wash your hands, and I'll make supper – just throw something together. At least, that's what I'll tell you, but in fact it'll be a meal fit for a king. I've just been staying with Mum, and studied her cookbook from cover to cover. So her illness has turned out to be my making as a culinary expert, although one shouldn't put it like that. Aunt Olga says that during her attacks Mum starts remembering her time as an evacuee, but otherwise not at all. I only know it was somewhere the other side of Samarkand. But why talk about that. I remember how I was walking along the road and you suddenly appeared from behind and said you were clairvoyant and could for instance guess my surname. And you did. Now we have one surname for the two of us. Perhaps even for three. I'm not sure, but I think it'll soon be so. What a stroke of luck I went down that road! And later, when you used to come to meet me at the school and wait for me to finish teaching… Gleb, darling, how I wanted to run off with you, run off anywhere. But I pretended I had to work with pupils who needed extra tuition. And you stood all that time under a tree, waiting for me. In fact I just sat on the windowsill and looked at you. Yes, can you believe that? I told myself off for being such a fool, but I couldn't help it. I'm such a coward. Anything scares me, even flying in this plane. Although I know nothing will happen, because you're waiting for me and we're going to the sea together, end of story. I'll look surprised and turn up my nose as if to say: So that's the sea, big deal! Yet inside I shall be ecstatic. There's a whole mini-volcano of ecstasy inside me, you know. And a whole ocean of panic. In fact I feel like panicking now, it's a bit misty. Well, it's all in my head, as usual, you know what I'm like. For some reason I'm really dreaming of marrow fritters. When I get there I'll make some straight away, a whole bowlful.

5

31 December 1937

Dear Grandfather Frost, we were told we had to write letters to you, so I'm writing one. I don't believe in you, because you don't exist. We were told to write down our wishes. My wish is to be with Mum and Dad. But you could include Olya too. I haven't seen her for a long time, but I don't really miss her. She's little. I'm lying here with my eyes shut, writing this letter to you. And when we wake up we'll write our letters on paper. They'll give us pencils. Most of the time I feel hungry. It's all right for you and Dad, you're goodness knows where, but for some reason I'm here. There are no books here at all. I wouldn't even mind staying with Aunt Albina. I haven't even got a bed. Could I ask you for one? Yes? Although no, I'd really prefer to have Olya here with us. Even though she tore my exercise book that time. But you can't blame her for that, she's only little. I sometimes think none of you ever existed. And Dad didn't say, 'Don't worry, I'll come tomorrow, they'll have sorted it out by then.' But the next day the caretaker made us leave. And took my satchel. And Mum didn't even say anything to him, only kept thanking him for some reason. After that there are lots of shadows. Lots and lots. I don't even remember where they sent Olya. Mum said she went to stay with Aunt Albina, but that we weren't to breathe a word to anyone. But I'm telling you. It's only a letter made up in my head. And I wouldn't write so much anyway. I think I'll only be able to do that next year, when I start school again. And when Dad comes back. I was told that Mum went to join Dad, but not to breathe a word of that either. That's what Aunt Albina said. But here they said I haven't got a Mum and Dad, and that my surname's Snegiryov, not Yevtishin. Nobody plays football here, and yesterday they knocked out one of my teeth. It's a good job it was a milk tooth and already loose. Grandfather Frost, I don't mind if it's not Mum and Dad or even staying at Aunt Albina's, just let me be anywhere but here. Please come and take me away. I wouldn't even mind staying with you. I'll help you carry the gingerbread biscuits. In a packet. We got them last year round the New Year's tree. I brought one back for Olya, and Mum laughed because she didn't have any teeth yet and told me to eat it myself. Grandfather Frost, nobody gave us pencils or asked us to write letters, it was last year we wrote them, at school. When we were still living in Moscow, not here in Kazakhstan. I can't even remember any more what those gingerbread biscuits looked like. I can't remember anything. Please, Grandfather Frost. Gleb. (I'm in second grade.)

6

6 September 1957

Dear Albina, or Alya if I may call you that. I know Gleb has always had a dodgy heart, which is why I'm writing to you and not to him. I think or at least assume that you must be a nice kind person, otherwise Gleb wouldn't be with you. You know, Alya, it's been fifteen years and three months since Gleb Ivanovich and I were separated by the war. I even had official notification of his death, sent in error. But my heart told me otherwise. It was all such a rush back then. Little Olya was crying, and for some reason I can remember a pot standing in the middle of the room, still warm and with one handle broken off. That was Gleb, Gleb Ivanovich, he'd bumped into it in the dark some time before and broken the handle. I remembered that pot for a long time afterwards. Usually people write that their heart tells them otherwise, but I really did believe Gleb was dead. We were evacuated in a hurry back then together with our factory. Olya was ill for a long time. She's seriously ill now too, and all as a result of that. She is a good girl. She's studying at Medical School, or rather was until she was struck down with this illness at the end of her second year. Anyway, I discovered Gleb was still alive a long time ago. I'd searched for him through the address bureau. They'd refused to pay out a pension, saying he was listed as missing which didn't count as proof of death, so we weren't entitled to any benefits. And then there were problems with work. To be precise, I didn't have a job. And then I managed to find Gleb, but he was already married to you, Alya. What good would it have done for me to go poking my nose in? So many years had passed. It was two years before the war when we got married. So I would never have dreamt of bothering you if it weren't for Olya's illness. I remember that Gleb had heart trouble too back then, and still has. Don't be surprised, I have a friend who works as a nurse in the hospital where Gleb's having treatment. What I want to ask you is to break it to him gently that we're still alive. I expect he thinks we're dead, but we're not, we just changed our address. That was because of my brother, but that's another story. Please do that, Alya. We won't interfere in your life in any way. But please break the news to Gleb Ivanovich. I very much hope you can do this for me, my dear.

7

To my parents. If you read this letter you should know that you're to blame for all this. I never thought some lousy cigarettes could get in the way of understanding your own daughter. It's not even jeans! Or those green buckskin pants I was expecting for my birthday, but no chance. And you promised! After all, you're adults and have to keep your word. That's what we were taught in that rotten school of yours. We've got democracy now, so if you don't understand what I'm on about then don't make any promises. But you could let me have a cassette recorder. Everyone's got one, Mum, surely you must know that – everyone, even the dorks who don't have anything. The only one without is me, your daughter. I borrowed one from Olya to copy recordings and she really turned up her nose when she handed it over. Why are you like this, why? You're so square, you just don't get it. Everyone's got everything, apart from us. You just can't be bothered. What it comes down to is that you don't love your own daughter. And what was that you palmed me off with, Dad: a Proton! Why don't you walk around listening to it yourself! You certainly don't listen to your daughter. How could you do that to your own dear daughter? All this term I've been getting good grades, slaving away for what you promised. On top of which I took on political-news sessions with the fourth-year girls. Do you think I did that for fun? But I promised, and I keep to my word. Don't try to find me, I've gone away. A long way away. And there's no point ringing Natasha or Olya because they don't know anything. I'll only come back when you've done what you promised. And for now I'll live the way I want to. For the time being still your daughter Albina.

8

26 February 1987

My dearest son Gleb. How are you getting on in the army? Your Pa and I often think of you and your send-off day. Everyone was so jolly. You don't forget something like that. Your Pa has hardly been drinking since then. His ribs are still painful. That was after your friend sat him in the pail. It was a shame about the salad of course, but it was more than we could eat anyway. Apart from which we get more money now. He just lies there most of the time, potters about the yard a bit and then lies down again. He discharged himself from hospital because he said there was no point being there. Perhaps he's right. At least I've already managed to get myself a shawl and now I'm planning to buy some high boots, so perhaps I won't feel the cold too badly this winter. So far it's been a fairly mild one here. It's seven months now since you left. I think you wrote it was hot where you are. That's good, you won't freeze there. The winters here can be very cold, though. I have to say I found some of your letters a bit confusing. Do take pity on your poor old Ma and write more clearly. My eyesight's none too good, but I can still manage all right with reading. There are hold-ups in the post, too. I've not had a word from you in two months now. But it's good you're in the army, what with all that discipline and the uniform. Of course, Pa decided not to press charges against your friend after all. It's good that you're helping a friendly republic, although I didn't really get which one it is. It's good you've got the mountains there, that's nice. As to not much growing there, what do you boys care about that? It's a pity we can't send a parcel. Today I finally received our special food parcel. There was buckwheat in it. As for boots, people have told me they're easy to get hold of down where you are. Perhaps you could send me a pair? My size is 36, but take whatever they've got, 38 or 39 will do just as well. Only not light-coloured ones, they soon show the dirt here. Take black or brown, and make sure they're fur-lined. Although as you know boots aren't warm enough for our winters, and anyway where would I wear them to? No, son, don't bother after all, just do your job there and make sure you write to us. I must say you're full of yourself, all this talk about your international duty. Olya popped in yesterday. She says you've stopped writing to her too. She's waiting for you. Although between you and me, and I haven't mentioned this before, there's something not nice about her. Well, I don't like her, and that's all there is to it. Call it a mother's instinct. You'd do best to steer clear of her, she's a trap for the unwary, not some innocent young girl. Although otherwise she's a good girl, son, helping me round the house sometimes and so on. She took your Pa to hospital for some tests, for instance. But no, I just don't like her, and there's nothing I can do about it. I hope you haven't promised her anything? Good. Or have you? Mind you don't get into trouble there. But write to us anyway, we worry about you. Although what could happen to you there. The army's the same as school, son. When you come back everyone will look up to you. In your last letter you said you had a difficult day ahead of you. But I have faith in my son. Your Ma Albina.

9

2 March 1993

Dear Ma, I've suddenly remembered. Yesterday Albina brought me some chicken. In the night I had stomach cramps and everything began to sway. Then I saw you. In my dream you kept saying to me: 'Let's go to the dacha, quick, let's go to the dacha.' And I just couldn't work out what dacha you were on about. Although you could say I'm in the fresh air now. The chicken was tough, I kept it in my mouth for a while and then spat it out. I think that's all. In such situations it's usual to say how good it is that you don't have to see all this. Even how I'm writing this letter to you. I move my finger through the air and read the lines as they appear. I imagine that you'll be able to see them and read them. In the meantime I rummage through this rubbish tip of mine called memory. Is it really all because of the chicken? And that kitten you and I had. For some reason we called him Dima. In the country Dima was mauled by a cockerel, and we used your shawl to transport him in, with only his nose and whiskers sticking out. Strange I should think of that. There are cats here too, but they're scared of us. Perhaps because one of them got eaten, only not by us: they did it, the others. That's what Albina told me, I didn't see it myself. I had terrible pains in my legs, but they've gone now. Perhaps it was all because of the chicken. Albina brought me some trainers, but here's a thing. It must have been some time ago now, and they couldn't get the trainers off me however much they tried – it was so painful, as if they were pulling off the skin. Albina got hold of a coat for me too. Alright, it's a woman's coat, green, with a collar, but just the job for cold weather. My head aches all the time, but not like then, after I'd just come back. You told me yourself I was screaming constantly, every night. And in my dreams I kept wanting to get back to Jalalabad. Suddenly I've had this flashback to our first day there, as clear as I can see this crack in the wall. We've landed. Lots of orange trees around. That was my first impression. And then suddenly stones flying. Aimed at us. That was the least problematic day we had. And yes, Ma, it wasn't my head that ached then, but something else. And those pills, they made everything a blur and you didn't feel like doing anything. There was something else after you died, wasn't there? After your funeral I don't remember anything for what must be several months, and only hazily after that. My Red Star medal has gone. I think I must have sold it, like the apartment, but I'm not sure. These people came and said, what do you want with one this size? Look, here's good money for it. They didn't give me the money, or rather they did hand it over but next morning it was gone. They said I'd been on a bender and spent the lot, but I hadn't even gone out, they wouldn't let me. I was supposed to get another place in exchange, but I couldn't live there. I went there, and it wasn't even in the town. In the summer I didn't want to leave my old apartment, but then I went to take a look at the new place just as the cold weather was starting. They said it was part of the payment and I'd had everything owed me. This new place didn't even have a door, so I rigged up a curtain instead. But literally within days they started demolishing it, and somehow I didn't seem to have any papers proving ownership. Other people were offered somewhere to live, but I was told I wasn't registered to live anywhere. But Ma, I can't even remember where the cemetery is to come and visit you. Not that I'd make it there anyway thanks to these damned legs of mine. It's as if my head's aching but there's no pain in my legs at all. In fact I can't feel anything there any more. I'd be lost without Albina. I was scared of her to start with, she looked so old, a frightful scarecrow. But I've got used to her and couldn't do without her now. We thought up a name for me between us. I've just this moment remembered, I'm Gleb, aren't I, not Dima. Dima was the cat. And he didn't run away when I was doing my time in the army. I spat out that chicken. I realised she wanted to poison me. She came here from Tashkent where she belongs and now she's eating our chickens and cats. The bitch. How I wish I could get up. It's all their fault. But I can't feel a thing. Ma, I'm Gleb, Ma...

10

March 1999

Hello, Mum! We're all here reading your letter, the whole family. Or not so much your letter but what you dictated to the nurse. Unfortunately we can't possibly visit you right now. You write that everything's fine with you there. And that they give you a cream puff with your tea, but not always. We don't have cream puffs here either. But we have to put food on the table for the children. You're well off, cared for by the state. Only you shouldn't worry us with this stuff about people stealing your blanket. I ask you, who would pinch one from an invalid? I'm sure you've got things mixed up or got the wrong end of the stick. Of course, I'll ask the manager when I come, only I don't know when that'll be. You must see that it's all a holiday for you, like at a health resort. You get your treatment there, your injections. But I've got high blood pressure, and Gleb's taken to drink again. Every weekend now. As they say, no light at the end of the tunnel. And all you can do is throw accusations at us. Mum, nobody's forgotten you, darling. No, I can't send your granddaughter to you on her own. She's very sensitive, and it's a difficult year for her what with university entrance exams. You and Dad always drummed into us how important education is for our lives. So now she's studying for her exams. We've taken on two tutors for her, but she bunks off lessons, the stupid girl, and Gleb found the envelope with the fees. The upshot was that I had to take on extra work, so there's no way I can get away to see you. You say you can already hold a spoon with your left hand. That's very good. But your speech hasn't returned. So you see, how could I have you here? Olya needs to study. I suppose I could give Gleb his marching orders, I've done that twice already. Mum, darling, perhaps I could have you here after all? Olya would start university, I'd kick Gleb out, and we could start a new life together. I'd let you have my room. Olya could sit with you after her studies. Do you remember how you always used to read to her before bedtime? I could never find the time. Olya still talks sometimes of how you used to take her for walks and the two of you used to play some sort of game about fairytale countries...

Well, Mum, I definitely won't be able to make it there to see you this week. I'm sure you understand. I'm up to my neck in work. But we'll definitely come and visit, probably next week or failing that the week after. Write and let me know how you are. Look after yourself. Your daughter Albina.

11

October 1968, Lugansk

Dear Gleb, hello! I think there's some misunderstanding. So I've decided to write to you. I simply can't believe that you've actually written: 'Sorry, Olya, I didn't want it to happen'. And yet when we left you were asking me to come and live with you in Moscow and saying how they'd extended the metro almost to your front door, and how nice it was there with the metro and the embankment. Believe it or not, I've never been on the metro. If you don't want me to come there any more, why don't you come to us in Lugansk. It's still warm here, but I see from the TV that you've already got snow there. We watched it at the neighbours – they've got a Rubin 401, would you believe. Don't laugh, but we watch 'Good Night, Children' there too. They have a new character now, Filya. He's very much like our dog, the one we used to have as kids. Anyway, I expect you don't watch such childish stuff, although it's really quite funny, you know. I nearly passed up my chance for a holiday then. That September was my first trip to the seaside. For some reason I thought it would be cold. And then you were there. To begin with I didn't even notice you, for nearly half the holiday. And then you moved to our table, and you started walking me back from the dining room to our block. And then, do you remember, that time on the beach? And now you write that you didn't want it to happen. What was it all for, then? Why did you ask me to come, why did you give me your address? My Mum and Dad don't know anything, nor the people at work. They all think I had a good holiday. It was the first time I'd been that far on my own. Up to then I'd always been with my Mum or a girlfriend. But why am I writing this, it's neither here nor there. I expect you were in a bad mood when you wrote that, weren't you? We haven't seen each other for nearly two months. Perhaps you'll come here anyway. You could stay here at our place and get a job at our factory. They're looking for engineers at present. Perhaps they'd transfer you? I just have a feeling it's going to be a boy. A little boy, can you imagine that? I've walked to the post office and feel a bit calmer. Now I'm sitting here and writing this letter. Otherwise at home I just cry my eyes out and can't tell anyone why. I'll wait for a letter from you. If you'd rather send it for me to pick up at the post office, then do that, I'll be expecting it. Your Olya, who loves you and is waiting for you. For you and our child.

12

9 August 2000

Hi, Alya! How are you doing there? By my reckoning I've been in Moscow for two months now. Two months since I left dear old Volgodonsk. Do you know if anyone else has left? Have you found a job? Do you remember how we celebrated after our diploma finals? Everyone said there was no way you could outdrink young engineers. That was when you broke my sunglasses, too. I'll keep reminding you of that till the day I die, my friend. I've got a job here as a courier in a publishing house. I have to commute from Butovo, where Gleb's sister lives, to Begovaya. Those are the names of different places here. Then it's another ten minutes on foot from the Metro. I get to work, sit down and read whatever I've brought with me from home. Sometimes I do nothing else all day, but not often. Then I have to travel all over Moscow. It could be up to five journeys a day, but sometimes just one. I got lost a lot at first, but it's OK now, I print off a map before I set out. The trouble is that for some reason nobody here knows where anything is. Alya, whatever you do don't tell anyone how I came to be staying at Gleb's sister's. Do you remember how we got to know each other? I'd gone to stay with my family for the summer. He was visiting his relatives on some family business or other and it turned out to be almost next door. We decided to go to Moscow together. It was his suggestion. He even asked my parents. And since my Dad had got a job on a building site there they let me go too. I haven't seen Dad yet. The system he works to is thirty days on site and then twenty days off, and he went straight home after his work stint. For a week Gleb and I took time out. He showed me the sights and we visited his sister. She's married with two children. Anyway, then Gleb got a phone call from his ex and asked me to go back home. But you see I'd told Mum I'd gone to Moscow to stay. So please don't let on that Gleb and I have split up. Not to anyone, do you hear? Anyway, Gleb's sister took me in. First of all I looked after their little girls. They go to kindergarten. And I helped out round the house a bit too. Then they decided to find me a job, so here I am at the publishing house. His sister also suggested trying to get a job with the police. There's two months' training to start with, and then you get your uniform, salary and all the rest of it. Best of all, they give you a residence permit. I'm going for an interview tomorrow. It's very near where we live. Alya, can you imagine, when I used to fetch the girls from kindergarten there was this fantastic guy there, a security guard. Well, are you going to ask? Yes, we meet up. Only at the kindergarten though, because his work doesn't allow him to leave, even to go to the shops. He's from Ryazan. But tomorrow he has a day off at last, and he's going to come with me to the interview. Perhaps I'll manage to persuade him to get a job there too. Tell me all the news from home. Things here are just brilliant. Olya.

13

January 1948

Alya, my dear. Who could imagine when you came to visit us in Dushanbe that it would be for the last time. You remember our neighbours? Well, they're dead. They were stoned to death. Before that the locals were shouting for Russians to leave. But where could we go? We sat things out for a while but then decided to leave after all. Even before that Gleb had been sacked from his job. Do you remember our garden? I've no idea who's taken it over now. But everything seems to have worked out more or less. I wouldn't have believed it. Katya's gone with her family somewhere the other side of the Urals where her husband has relatives. So my granddaughters are a long way away now. Olya's here with us in Kupavna, which is not too far from Moscow. I have a job at the local school. Gleb hasn't found a job yet. It's a worry that we have to rent a place to live. And the money has a habit of running out. Where do we go from here? Just turn up unannounced at Katya's? But she writes that they haven't got room to swing a cat as it is, they're all in one room. We sold everything in such a mad rush, even our furniture. I've little idea what the future holds. We haven't even got a home to go back to, not that they'd let us anyway. Gleb was invited here by a friend who promised him work, but in fact there turned out to be nothing for him. He's become terribly depressed and just hangs around at home doing nothing. I don't know, perhaps I should divorce him. Olya attends the school where I'm working. There's a PE teacher there, a jolly sort of bold chap of about fifty. And do you know, I think he's got his eye on me. Though I've been told he's like that with all the newcomers. Twice now we've had tea together after school. He lives opposite the school with his mother, an old lady of eighty. I get on quite well with her. I'm seriously thinking of divorcing Gleb and moving in there with Olya. At least I wouldn't have to pay rent. So in a nutshell that's how things are with us. Later on I'll get round to writing in more detail. This was just a first attempt to start the ball rolling. There's just so much I need to tell you.

14

May 1992

Olya, dear friend! Your brother Gleb walks around all day in a daze doing nothing. It's all terribly upsetting. I think it'll all sort itself out once they get to the bottom of things. He asked me not to say or write anything about this to you. But yesterday they asked him to hand in his Party membership card. Do you understand? And that's on top of it being a week now since they dismissed him from the hospital. And while I was compiling the timetable and checking pupils' reports the director of studies came up and asked in front of everybody if it was true my husband had been expelled from the Party. I said of course not. Well, what else could I say? I've sent Albina to her grandma in Saratov just in case. And all because of that newspaper article. That sort of thing just can't be true. Or rather, no doubt it is, but Gleb has nothing to do with it. It's such a mistake, such a mistake. Anyway, I'll write again later with all... sounds like someone ringing at the door...

15

22 March 1943

Olga, I'm composing this letter to take my mind off things. I expect you'll wonder why it's to you. I've been meaning to write for a long time now. I'm lucky, I've got somewhere to sit. There's a tiny chink here, so it doesn't feel quite so suffocating. Or rather it's so suffocating that I just don't notice it any more. I can't see a thing through the chink, but I imagine the train is passing houses and trees and the sun's shining. That was such a stupid quarrel we had, and on that day of all days. But afterwards I had other things to think about. It's funny, we played together in the same yard throughout our childhood, sat next to each other at school for seven years, and never quarrelled once in all that time. How could that be? I well remember that poplar: do you remember how we used to climb straight off your window onto it? And our night-time excursions? When your grandma caught us, we covered up for each other. You said I used to go off sleepwalking and that you couldn't let me go on my own, so you went with me. And they believed us. Mum even took me to see the doctor. He said the girl's growing, and prescribed more walks and vitamins. And we gave the vitamins to the kitten to make him grow. Do you remember, you tried to persuade me that if they were for making you grow he'd turn into a big cat within a day, perhaps the size of a dog, and there'd be a new breed, a 'dogcat'. And how you cried when he stayed the same. But your grandma found the vitamins behind a cupboard, so he hadn't eaten them after all. But you kept threatening to repeat the experiment, so I swallowed them without telling you. Then you decided to measure how much I was growing and made me stand to be measured against the doorpost every morning. But then you soon got tired of that and got the bug for playing at being a famous pilot like Chkalov. Grandma said girls can't be pilots, but you and I built a plane in that poplar tree and then jumped out of it with an umbrella for a parachute. And you got it in the neck again, because the umbrella was Grandma's. I remember it well: a lacy, pink thing, more of a parasol really.

Yesterday that old woman stopped groaning. And yesterday, yes, I think it was yesterday, the woman with the child died. The child had kept screaming until it was blue in the face, with the woman joining in. Oh, how horrible that was. These sounds. This awful din. You remember how we used to blow into a tube to make a kind of booming sound? This is the same here. Unbearable. I've noticed the ones who scream are the first to break. They're the first to give up the ghost. I don't want to go like that. I know you wouldn't approve. You remember our only quarrel? You pushed me out of the barn. I remember how you grovelled to them and how I didn't want to go. And as they led me away you made a show of looking angry. Later I realized you'd pretended. But it was no use.

I think the train's stopping. They've opened the doors. I can hear music, and there's a sign: Auschwitz.

16

October 1991

For homework we've been asked to write an essay about a dream we have. My dream is to be a swimming champion. At the moment I'm sitting in the changing room. The hairdryer's broken again, so I'm writing this essay while I wait for my hair to dry, because I've got lessons at one o'clock anyway. That's when the afternoon session starts. We had swimming heats this morning, and I beat Snegiryova. Yeah! I took second place and was inside the time for youth grade one. She fluffed her start completely. I got a certificate and a can of Fanta and was selected for the district first team. Well, Snegiryova was too, but she only got a consolation prize, a Snickers bar.

I've been going to swimming for two years now. And our trainer says I've got good chances. He calls them 'prospects'. I like swimming, only it takes a long time to dry your hair. Either the sockets are not working or the hairdryer's fused. There's only the one here. On Thursday I saw a cockroach in the shower. Although that's nothing, at home I came across a cockroach in the stewed fruit. Mum fished it out with a ladle and then nearly burst into tears. I told her I didn't like stewed fruit anyway and that everyone has cockroaches these days. I was at Snegiryova's, and they were scurrying all over the windowsill there. But Mum wouldn't let it drop, and when I told her about the shower she really went ballistic, saying they can carry infection. And she made me take a broom and sweep through again, although I had homework to do. Hasn't she got anything better to think about than cockroaches? Our house is clean enough anyway. And stewed fruit really is yucky. When I was in year one I used to dream of those jars of fruit from Bulgaria. They'd disappeared from the shops, and I really missed them. And then I started going to swimming. One day a trainer came to our PE lesson at school and invited me to selection trials at the swimming pool. Mum kicked up a fuss because she didn't know who'd take me there. But I said it was only one bus stop and I could walk anyway. I told her everyone from my class was going but I'd have to stay at home again just because nobody could go with me, and it wasn't fair. And Mum let me go. I thought they'd get us into the water straight away, and I couldn't swim then. But they took us into the sports hall and made us do somersaults, jump over vaulting horses, climb ropes and run against the clock. Only after that did they let us in the water. A real crush built up in the changing room and we cracked on we were queuing for salami. That's a game we play during break, 'queuing for salami'. Our dream back then was to wake up in the morning and find two salami sausages as long as your arm under the New Year's tree. Wow, I'd have got stuck into that sausage then, skin and all. When they handed out humanitarian aid Snegiryova shouted there would be sausage in the packets, and a queue formed behind her just like in the shops in those days. But it turned out to be dried milk in a sort of package. Milk powder. And tins of ham, six each. I wrote a poem back then:

> People say that war is looming:
> There'll be ration cards, and gloom
> All throughout the former Union;
> Everywhere fierce passions fuelled
> By political conceit.
> People say that war is looming:
> With a start the soot-black raven
> Will arise and spread its wings
> Like black ash above the nation.
> Soap'll be severely rationed.
> By the time of reconstruction
> I shall be an aged woman.
> Still I live a life that's normal;
> War will stand all on its head.
> And when peace has been established
> Not for now but evermore

I can't think of any more. Otherwise I might have become a writer. But that's boring, you have to sit at a desk all day, and I have a job sitting through lessons. Now I'm waiting for my hair to dry. No, being a swimming champion is better. You get Snickers. Although I really prefer Milky Way.

17

June 1919, Ryazan Province

Dear Olya, I am deeply disappointed. You have shown yourself up as a run-of-the-mill petit bourgeois. Writing letters is bourgeois too, but I'm leaving and won't be back for about two months, so will leave this letter for you on your bedside table. Jealousy is something no Komsomol girl should permit herself. It's a relic of that past we are struggling to overcome, and people like you just drag us back again. Even Albina understands that: all the bourgeois petty-mindedness of your unworthy behaviour. I very much hope that by the time I return you will have understood all this and we shall be able to continue living as a true commune. As you know, Albina has only been in the city a short while and is not all that politically conscious herself. I thought you would have a positive influence on her. But not content with opposing her coming here in the first place, you then refused to admit to your own political short-sightedness. I'm not putting this very well, but that's not important. What's important is to realize where one's gone wrong and makeup for it before it's too late. I wanted to entrust Albina to you, and you spat on the trust I'd placed in you. That is behaviour unbefitting of a Komsomol member. I am extremely upset.

18

May 1935

Dear Ma, I expect Uncle Nikolay will read out this letter to you and Pa. Give him my regards. How is Pa? Sorry I haven't been for such a long time, but we're up to our necks in work here. Well, I've put in for a promotion. And a new uniform. I still miss our village sometimes, though. I suppose you're busy with the harvest now. My mate is writing this letter for me. I'm taking classes, and soon you'll get a note from me personally.

I had a job getting used to things at first. I get very tired sometimes, the work's interesting but very hard. And there are too many enemies. Which is why I'm fagged out at times. My commanding officer's alright, except he's very edgy. He's our new commanding officer. The old one turned out to be a class enemy and they had us on the carpet for failing to report him. Good job I'd only just joined up and didn't know him at all. I was let off, but the rest were expelled from the Party. Serves them right, too. There are loads of enemies here. Last time you wrote that there weren't any pigs left. I was really looking forward to some salted pork fat when winter comes. Can't you manage it somehow? What about class enemies, are you fighting against them there? The trouble is there are so many it's a job to keep track of them all. They're good at disguising themselves. Pyotr and I went to a flat yesterday and arrested another of the bastards. Bald-headed cove, he was, though he did have a bit of hair at the front. Pyotr says I shouldn't dictate that to him, he's not going to write it down anyway. But I can tell you that while we were there arresting that low-life our Pyotr turned the place over and pinched a figurine. He's not too happy about it himself, in fact he wonders why he did it. He's scared someone will find out. But you won't tell, will you? Pyotr misses his folks too and wants to go back to his village, same as me. But to be fair, it's not bad here. The food's good, you can stuff yourself and there's still plenty left over. Keep your chins up there, Ma. My work's pretty nerve-wracking too. Though Pyotr says we shouldn't write about that. But they scream so much. That's if the children wake up. Well, I suppose the kids aren't to blame for having parents like that, are they? I don't know what happens to the kids afterwards, that's not part of my job. I expect they're taken to be re-educated so their minds aren't poisoned by saboteurs and they can be part of our radiant future. But things here are really good. So good that sometimes it's scary. Only I haven't bought a pillow yet. I met this girl. She's a teacher, you'd like her, only she's a bit skinny. Her name's Olga. Pyotr can't take that figurine back again, because we sealed up the flat. There was a kid there, too, a little boy, left on the stairs in his pyjamas. I handed him over to the caretaker, but he ran off and sat down in front of the door. Stupid kid, he was too young to understand what was going on. That we'd saved him from being infected by harmful ideas. There are lots of people here who could be infected too. I'm going to tell about that figurine after all. Tomorrow.

Your son Gleb.

19

30 December 1999

Tomorrow is New Year's day. The end of the twentieth century. They said the twenty-first century would start in 2000, not 2001. But it's all the same to me. The main thing is, they're discharging me, and it's for good. Yesterday I asked Olga Innokentevna, 'I won't have to come back here any more, will I?' and she stroked my head and sighed. I expect she's got used to having me here and doesn't want to say goodbye. But I'm better now, and I'm going home. I'm fed up with being here anyway. They've disconnected all my tubes, and I have to swallow loads of tablets and be given these drops too. I'm glad I won't have them at home. Then there was that transplant. I felt so ill, not like before, but really ill. Even now I feel sick and find it uncomfortable to sit. But since I'm getting better, it must mean I'm... well, getting better. I'm writing this letter to myself to read later, some time in the twenty-first century. My hair will have grown back, too. For now I have to wear a bandana and my head itches all the time underneath. Mum and Dad haven't said anything about school. I expect I'll have to start again after the holidays, but I've forgotten everything by now, and I don't like school anyway. Everyone will laugh at me for sure for being fat and having no hair. And how can you explain to them that those are side effects, as Olga Innokentevna says? I can remember in the first year teasing one boy myself: "Fatty, Fatty!" He ran off crying and complained to the teacher, but I never got into trouble for it. What's more, everyone in the class started teasing him too. We'd take his food off him at lunch time, telling him he was fat enough already and didn't need it. He cried and said something about a deficient metabolism and diabetes. We taunted him so much that he was moved to another class, but the same thing went on there too. After that he stopped coming to our school altogether. But I never got in trouble or got told off for it. In the winter I started having lots of colds and didn't get better for a long time. Then the health centre referred me to a specialist, and we went to Moscow. Or no, first of all I had to stay in our local hospital. That was a real pain in the summer. We also went to Hanover by plane – really flew there, brilliant! Well, everything's quite different there. And for some reason everything's pink, even the walls. Then we came back here. No, to begin with I was at home, and after a while I started school again. But I fainted in maths and they brought me back here. That's why I don't want to go to school. Olga Innokentevna told me I don't have to go if I don't want to, and she's allowed me to eat whatever I want. At last. The trouble is I don't fancy anything. I feel so tired. I'm tired of writing too. I'll have a sleep.

20

27 March 1969

My dear and highly esteemed newspaper, this is already the twentieth letter I've sent you. My post is clearly being intercepted somewhere along the way by some extra-terrestrials, i.e. Martians. What's this you write: Today is the first anniversary of the death of Yuri Gagarin? You've got it all wrong, he didn't die, he was abducted by those aliens to be experimented on, perhaps not even on Mars but some other planet like it. They're keeping him locked up so he doesn't reveal their secrets. When Gagarin was in space he discovered something he wasn't supposed to, you know. He told me about it yesterday. How he did so is not for you to know, otherwise they'll come and get me too. But I'm not allowed to, I'm in receipt of a disability pension. I've also sent poems to your newspaper, but you never received them either. I read the paper every day but they're nowhere to be seen. That's why I'm sending them again. They're about space, as you might expect. Space is our future. I've already started collecting my things together. Publish what I've sent you without delay before they come to get me. I'm already picking up signals from there. And I have to complete my mission before it's too late. Your faithful reader and future specialist on cosmic intelligence of the twentieth century, Gleb.

Anna Babiashkina

AN ALMOST ENGLISH DETECTIVE STORY

Translated by Muireann Maguire

An Almost English Detective Story

With much wisdom comes much grief. Especially if you trust to the wise saws found in books rather than to plain old common sense.

Zhenya had a reputation among us as a notorious Anglo-maniac; and she deserved it completely. In the old days she would probably have been sent to Siberia for kowtowing to the West. Judge for yourself: she ate oatmeal porridge in the mornings, always sported English leather shoes, dressed in neatly tailored English-style suits and listened almost exclusively to the Beatles. Needless to say, the American Cinema was her favourite movie theatre, and at home, she had taken to watching only English films on DVD. She bought books during trips to foggy Albion and in the "Anglia" bookshop in Moscow. Zhenya even read Russian authors in English translation; she was convinced that if an author hadn't been translated into the language of Shakespeare, he wasn't worth reading. To complete the picture, let's add that among a small group of our friends, she demanded to be called Jenny Tailor; this was how she thought her name, Zhenya Portnova, translated into English. With this sort of personality, it's hardly surprising that she had had for the last two years a live-in American boyfriend called George, who was based in Moscow for business reasons. George chattered cheerfully away in a mixture of Moscow argot and Boston jargon with Zhenya's son "Basil" (Vasya, in Russian), sending Zhenya into ecstasies. Basil (who was intensely irritated by this version of his name) studied at a special English school, naturally. George and "Jenny" were doing well for themselves, and one fine day she came to the reasonable conclusion that it was no longer her place to push a damp mop over the floor, sweep up dust, prepare dinner and do other unappreciated labours. At a family council, Zhenya received full support and the very next day she started looking for "domestic help", as she put it in the best English idiom. Our mutual friend Lena, who was amusing herself with a part-time job as a course inspector in a third-rate college, set Mrs Tailor up with a non-Muscovite student, who was willing to tackle housework after her lectures for the sake of three hundred dollars a month. Zhenya met this girl, Anya, explained her requirements, and handed over a set of keys to the apartment. They agreed that on Tuesday, after her classes, the student would start work. All Monday evening Zhenya fretted: after all, someone she barely knew was about to come to her home and take over the housekeeping! "Just in case" Zhenya hauled over to a neighbour's, for temporary safekeeping, most of the household electronics, excepting the computer, the television, the washing machine and the dishwasher. All the money, valuables and documents were put away in Mrs Tailor's work briefcase. But the poor woman's heart still couldn't rest. In search of a solution, she took her *Guide to English Traditions* off the shelf. And as always, the British were able to suggest a simple and ingenious solution to the situation. Zhenya read with interest that in Olde England housewives, after hiring a housemaid, would give her an extremely simple test: they would place ten coins in hard-to-get-at places around the house. If, after cleaning up, the servant handed over all ten coins, she was proven to be completely orderly and honest. If some of the coins remained in their hiding-places, this meant that the housemaid was lazy. And if all the coins vanished from their places, but not all of them returned to the housewife's pocket – then the maid was plainly a thief.

"*Zis is great!*" Zhenya exclaimed in English, and searched her purse. She would have liked to scatter ten twenty-dollar notes through the flat; but, as luck would have it, all she could find in her purse were four fifty-dollar notes. "It'll do," she decided, and began feverishly figuring out the best places to distribute them within the apartment. After some consideration, Zhenya hit on the thought of using those corners which she was most reluctant to clean herself: the dust high up on the dresser, the floor behind the shower-stall in the bathroom, under the living-room carpet, and under her son's bed. In these places, on Tuesday morning, Zhenya placed the American notes, after her husband and son had already left for work and for school respectively. Meanwhile, she was astounded to find under her son's bed a packet of cigarettes and a copy of *Moulin Rouge* magazine. All day long, Zhenya found it impossible to concentrate on anything. She made an excuse to leave work early and rushed home. When Zhenya entered the apartment, Anya was already putting the freshly washed crockery back on the shelves.

"Very good, Annie", Zhenya praised her cautiously, looking suspiciously at the sparkling mirrors and glass-panelled cupboards, "and did everything else go OK?"

"Yep, everything went just fine", Anya answered cheerfully. "By the way, when I was cleaning, I found some money on the floor, and some more on the dresser. There it is, take it, please." And Anya held out a slender little stack of greenbacks.

Zhenya counted them: there was only one hundred and fifty dollars. "And where did you find them, dear?" the lady of the house asked in a somewhat brooding voice, studying the gleaming inlaid tiles.

"Under the rug in the big room, in the bathroom and on the dresser, can you imagine?" the girl babbled. "How ever did they get there? By the way, Elena Maksimovna says hi."

"Really?" Zhenya returned without the slightest interest, on her way to her son's room. Groping under the bed, she established that there was no dust there. But the fifty-dollar note wasn't there either. "This is just too much, *fackin' sheet*!" Mrs Tailor whispered feelingly, although another five-letter Russian word was on the tip of her tongue, and went into the hallway. There Anya was already putting on her cashmere coat, which Zhenya effortlessly recognized as an item from Lena's wardrobe last season.

"Well, mind if I head off then, auntie Zhenya?" the small-town girl chirped familiarly.

"Anya", the well-bred but baffled Zhenya asked in an embarrassed way, "did you happen to find any money under the bed in my son's room?"

"Nope, none at all," the girl drawled in surprise and chuckled suspiciously: "But if I find any the day after tomorrow – I'll hand it over straightaway!"

"So you're planning to find it the day after tomorrow?"

the lady of the house shrieked spitefully. "And where will the money come from – will you put it there?"

"We-ell, I... Well there's money all over the place in your house", Anya blurted nervously.

"Let's cut to the chase: where are the fifty bucks which were under my son's bed?" Zhenya asked her point-blank, realizing that this domestic help was not to her liking at all.

"It wasn't there, honest, there wasn't anything there," the frightened girl answered.

"Oh really? It wasn't there? Well I put it there with my own hands today!"

Anya began nervously and repulsively twisting her mittens between her fingers, muttering something about how she never would, not for anything, that she wasn't that sort, and more such nonsense.

Zhenya felt disgusted, and flung the door open: "Goodbye! I think the fifty dollars you took is quite enough payment for your visit today. I have no further need of your services."

Anya's chin was trembling, she produced her purse which she stuck under Zhenya's nose, along with her handkerchief and her college record-book, which somehow appeared in her hands. In a word, their parting was brief, but tearful.

Exhausted, Zhenya went into the kitchen, distractedly tossed back a whiskey for the sake of her nerves, and nibbled some of the beef stroganoff prepared – not so badly, either – by Anya. All that evening she felt shattered: never before had she encountered such cynicism and outright mendacity!

All week Zhenya felt agitated and uncomfortable, and she couldn't even do the vacuuming. As might have been expected, towards Sunday George inquired discontentedly why no-one had washed any laundry for four days? (He was becoming irrevocably assimilated; every month he became more like a typical Russian man. Sometimes Zhenya even thought that she would have to change her life partner for a more authentically foreign specimen. For instance, George had started preferring vodka and cola to Pepsi-Cola, and he drank it by the pint.)

Ultimately, Mrs Tailor had no choice but to emerge from her depression and pick up her mop – although it was precisely the obligation to wield a mop that had originally driven her into depression. When she had finished work in the living room and the master bedroom, she made her way into her son's room. Her son had no wish to clear off to allow his mother a chance to clean his room. "Just five more minutes!" he squeaked desperately, eyes fixed on his computer screen as he expertly steered his new joystick.

"Oh, that George! Haven't I told him not to spoil the child!" Zhenya grumbled quietly. "Where's the point in letting the boy sit for hours in front of his computer playing at driving and shooting; he'd be better off with a new book. No chance – yet again he buys him some electronic rubbish!" At last, Basil took himself off to the living room, and Zhenya sent her mop-head under the bed. As Zhenya pulled the mop forth yet again, about to plunge it into the suds-filled pail, suddenly money spilled out from under it – a hundred-rouble note, a fifty-rouble note and even some tens.

"What's this?" Mrs Tailor demanded firmly, waving the wet notes under her son's nose. "Did you take these from my purse? Out with it!" It emerged that, on Tuesday, her precious son had forgotten his school record-book at home. The strict schoolteacher had sent him straight home from the second lesson to fetch this important document. Vasya had searched for it everywhere, even under the bed – where he had discovered the fateful fifty-dollar note. Without thinking twice, this enterprising youth bought himself a joystick for his computer, which he had wanted for a long time, and only afterwards, realizing that the money was not precisely his to spend, had his conscience begun to torment him. Being basically a good boy, Basil had corrected his misdemeanour as best he could: he left the remaining change in the same place where he had found the money.

"Helen, is there any chance you could find another of your students to work as domestic help?" Zhenya asked our mutual friend the following day. "No, no way, there won't be any more tests!"

An Underground Entertainment

Everything fluctuates, everything changes. What doesn't fluctuate, doesn't change. But humans, alas, are not among these fluctuating substances.

Not long ago, many of my acquaintances started coming down with essential disillusionment, just like some sort of infectious disease. Perhaps the problem was that they'd all reached a certain age, or it was a case of some mass hypnosis. But facts are facts. For example, Katya, an old friend I hadn't heard from in four years, called me up for no particular reason. She started sighing down the line, just as if for all these years we'd been walking our Pomeranians together in the park and hers had just died.

"No, I don't want to work anymore. No way. I just wish I could do something creative! Something artistic that would set my imagination free!"

"Don't tell me you've left PR?" I inquired cautiously, recalling that four years ago Katya had been given a soft job as PR director of a very important telecommunications company.

"Not a chance!" she answered, with a touch of resentment.

"So explain to me why PR isn't creative work? You get to think up all sorts of unusual campaigns, strategies and slogans. You come up with new joint projects. You have a say in branding."

"You can have all that! I'm sick of it. Ultimately – it's just a job. The same thing day after day. I wish I could do something... inspiring!"

The next person to call was my thirty-seven-year-old friend Marina. She also complained about her hard life as a TV producer – boring and repetitive work, as she put it, which was draining all the juices out of her still-unmarried body.

"Yeah..." Marina sighed heavily, after recounting how somebody at work had, for the umpteenth time, rejected a pilot Marina herself had directed (her first time as a director). "I've finally realized that I'm never going to be a famous director, I'm never going to earn a million dollars. I need to send this job to hell and get married."

"Do you have someone in mind?" I was intrigued. All her life Marina had let romance take a back seat. At first, her priority had been getting a degree in economics, then learning English, next finishing a diploma in cinematography, then polishing her French, next learning to play the guitar. After all, you need all these skills if you want to have a career or earn a million dollars! But now she was prepared to throw these intellectual riches at someone's feet?

"Oh, it doesn't matter who," Marina was surprisingly undemanding. "The main thing is that he's got to be rich," she continued, unromantically. "You know, my ideal husband would turn up at my door once a month, stick two thousand dollars under the doormat, head back to his Lexus and call me from there: 'Darling, your money's arrived. Love and kisses, bye!' And then I wouldn't see or hear from him for another month."

"And what would you be doing all this time?"

"Well, I'd be doing something creative. For example, I'd like to take up painting. And by the time I'm fifty I'd be famous for something, like Frieda Kahlo!"

In short, I was utterly mistaken to assume that Marina had undergone some powerful spiritual transformation.

Next, my friend Lyuba, a purchasing manager for an options company trading in vodka and wine, also suddenly longed for creativity and started cursing figures, overheads and shares receipts. But she was a business-like individual: if she wanted something, she set about trying to make it happen in reality. After a troubled couple of months she called me, full of joy:

"I've found what I need!" Lyuba announced animatedly. "People who share my ideas! I've talked to lots of my friends. And Oksana, who's tired of being a housewife (but her husband won't let her get a job), came up with a brilliant idea. We'll have our own theatre! We'll be as inspired as we want! For the time being, we're going to meet at her place in Veshki once a week."

Just in case, I gave the phone number of the energetic purchasing manager to two other friends who were also in the throes of self-realization. And sure enough, before long Marina called me up again:

"Lena...." I could hear her smoking nervously down the line. "We really need a play straightaway. Any chance you'll write us one? After all, you're a writer, you work for a magazine. I can't find anything that's right for us."

It turned out that Marina had already been chosen as the play's director; thus, her education magically expedited her life once again. Now she urgently needed a play – one suitable for eight women of approximately the same age, with no training as actors. There mustn't be a single man in the play. The props had to be simple. And nobody should be cast as some kind of ugly old witch; they all had to have roles midway between Cinderella and Scarlett O'Hara. No-one could die in the middle of the action; all the women were remarkably superstitious and suggestible. Honestly, I tried to refuse, but Marina knew my weak point.

"You can do everything you try," she said. "You're a genius, after all!"

"You think so too?" I asked, trying to ignore the inner voice hinting that I was being crudely manipulated, that she was playing upon a vulnerable spot. I agonized deeply, but not for long. A couple of weeks later I submitted for Marina's judgement an opus for eight unjustly accused sacrificial lambs, all locked in one cell at a police detention facility. The plot, I admit, was rather artificial and amounted to the fact that one of them kept trying to hang herself out of a mixture of grief, lost honour, and disappointment. Four others were militant and stubborn; they all struggled to save her, insisting, "Once you get out of here, you'll have your revenge." Meanwhile the remaining three broadly agreed that death was the only possible response to this unfair world. They were delighted by her decisiveness and kept trying to distil poison for her, despite the primitive conditions. Naturally, at the end everyone was vindicated, and nobody wanted to die any more. Overall, it wasn't even funny. I knew this myself. After all, I wrote it in two weeks. Strange as it might seem, they accepted the play and started rehearsals. Now Marina called me more often and spun out our conversations even longer.

"No, this is a nightmare!" she complained. "It's completely impossible to work with these dumb chicks!" Straightaway she caught herself: "But this is just between us, OK? Don't breathe a word, all right?"

Later she called and said that the actresses demanded to

see the author. She invited me to Veshki for tea. I was also interested in meeting these women who had torn themselves away from their families for the sake of my play and their creative enjoyment. So I went. It turned out that the other four women, like Lyuba, were entering the world of art for the first time. One of them worked as a realtor and specialized in office space; another was a HR manager; and a third, as far as I gathered from the conversation, was some sort of sales director in a famous hotel, while the fourth was a marketer who did something in metallurgy. In a word, a rather imposing group. Marina introduced me and announced:

"So if anybody has any questions for our author, please go ahead."

"Lena, I just thought of something," Katya, the PR manager said, cutting the cake, "after all, we can't stage this play just for ourselves. Wouldn't it be cool if you were able to squeeze an ad into that journal of yours?"

I almost choked on my tea and asked snidely:

"So, are you planning to have the premiere at the Moscow Art Theatre?"

"PR is beside the point!" the realtor butted in. "We need to sort out the venue first of all. For example, an office will soon be vacated right on Leningrad St. It's not very big. But it would serve very well as a small theatre – there'd be room for fifty. And what do you think? Just 250 dollars per square metre – a special price for you!"

"The venue can wait!" Marina groaned. "The author's here!"

"True, there'll be time enough for the venue," the female marketer interrupted her. "There are more pressing issues. Here we've wasted so much time learning by heart this…" she broke off, evidently reading a threat to freedom of speech in my expression, "this… interesting text, and has anyone run a market study? Personally I would be more concerned about the play's commercial potential. People want to be amused, and here they've got a mix of melodrama and tragedy. It's true you can have good melodramas," she cast another glance in my direction, "but…"

Here Marina flung herself back in her chair and nervously sucked on her cigarette. "By the way," the HR woman interjected, "now that we've practically got the words off by heart, I think, it's time to invite a set designer to work on the props. I've brought along a pair of CVs – perhaps we could take a look at them? And here's some info on the music we'll need. By the way, once we've hired a venue, won't we need a ticket-seller and a cleaner? I can get this organized in a couple of days."

"What's the point of cleaners, if we haven't sorted out the location!" the realtor continued fretting. "We'll lose the opportunity! I can't hold it forever!"

"We can still have a theatre company without a location!" said the sales director meaningfully. "But without a systematic plan for ticket sales there's no point to anything." She started drafting something in her notebook.

"Once we've got our PR, distributors will queue up to get tickets for our show!" Katya interposed once again.

Only Oksana listened to everyone with interest, nodding and pouring tea. As she showed us to the door, she said with great satisfaction:

"Oh girls, we have such an interesting time together! You must definitely come next week!"

Marina and I waited until the "actresses" had driven off in their cars, and then got into her vehicle.

"Well, what do you think?" asked Marina, scattering ash around the ash-tray.

"Well…" I stammered.

"That's how it is at every rehearsal!" said Marina with pain in her voice; tears appeared in her eyes. "It's always about the venue, sales, structuring, marketing. How can anyone become a great director with that lot? Can anyone really make a million American dollars out of them?"

"Well, Marina, someone's already making millions of dollars out of them. But in a different way."

"Well, if they love their work so much that they can't talk about anything else, let them stay boring little saleswomen, marketers and PR officers for the rest of their lives!" sobbed Marina, wiping her tears away.

"Don't worry about them," I tried to cheer her up, "after all, you've become a real director!"

"Yeah, and you're a real playwright," she answered, with an unpleasant laugh.

The Sorrow of the Snow Maiden

Every parent wants their children to be happy. Strangely, sometimes children pull this off by themselves, in spite of adults' awkward efforts to enforce happiness.

All the girls in our class envied Masha Koroleva (even her surname meant 'a queen'). Her father, who was in the navy, brought back bright felt-tip pens and strawberry bubble-gum from abroad; the school uniform looked better on her than on anyone else; the boys carried her schoolbag to class for her; and teachers always gave her only A's and B's. All her life she always got the best of everything: when she went to college, she studied economics at Moscow University; when she got a job, they made her general director; when she married, her husband was a CEO. Even in school plays she had always been given the most appealing roles – always Princesses or Beauty Queens. Masha knew how to unobtrusively revel in her many achievements: framed photos in her home tastefully indicated to the highly-placed guests (no other kind were invited) how beautiful and charming their hostess had been in her barefoot girlhood. Unmarried gentlemen, after gazing at photographs of little Masha as the frail and innocent Snow Maiden in a school play, visualized the display cases in jewellers' shops, understanding that a woman like that deserves to be spoiled. Sometimes their dreams came true, and beautiful Masha would receive at New Year's or on International Women's Day, let's say, a little ring with an impressive stone. Her husband didn't object – he too had been persuaded long ago that a woman like his wife deserved luxury.

Masha's five-year-old daughter Tanya had started kindergarten the year before; Masha had wisely decided that her daughter needed to meet other children. That is, she needed to learn how to interact with a group of kids from different backgrounds. In the first days of December, Masha brought her little one to kindergarten herself, letting the nanny off delivery duty. Masha imagined that her score as a good mother would rise in the eyes of her husband and other admirers if she herself, in her thin-soled leather shoes, scrambled over damp snowdrifts in order to fetch their precious little girl from the den of noisy and infectious kids. As she was wrapping Tanya up in a cashmere scarf, the teacher materialized beside her, and murmured mysteriously:

"Maria Sergeyevna! Are you aware that New Year's is almost upon us?"

"Don't mention the word," said Masha, nodding. "Are you collecting money for presents?"

"Well, yes," the teacher brightened. "But besides that, we're going to put on a New Year's play. Little Tanya will need a costume. Who would you prefer her to be – a Rabbit or a Snowflake?"

Masha looked the teacher in the eye and said:

"The Snow Maiden!"

"We already have a Snow Maiden. Olya, you remember her, a very fair little girl with pigtails? And your little girl has red hair, and what's more it's short. It's very pretty, of course," the teacher caught herself. "But Grandfather Frost's granddaughter has to be fair, like snow."

"As I said already, my child can only be the Snow Maiden," snapped beautiful Masha. "Who is responsible for planning this event? May I speak with the headmistress?"

The next day, Mrs Koroleva, in all the businesslike splendour of her prosperity, was sitting in the headmistress's office. They discussed the details of the script as well as the scope of the charitable aid which Masha's firm could provide to the children's institution. They agreed that, over the vacation, Masha's firm would pay for double-glazing to be installed in the kindergarten. When the satisfied mama was already on her way to the door, the headmistress asked:

"And besides, why is it so important to you that little Tanya plays no-one but the Snow Maiden?"

"Oh! It's very important. When I was a little girl I always played either the Snow Maiden or a Princess. And this is my point: for more than six months after the show I remembered I was a princess. Even more than that, fifteen years later I remembered that I was the prettiest girl in the school. It was very helpful in later life – to feel that one is a character in a fairy tale, adored by everyone, able to do whatever she likes. And so, a little girl should know she is a Princess from childhood on."

Masha would have said much more; the headmistress gasped loudly, "Aha! I know what you mean, Maria Sergeyevna!" And she thrust her hands into the pockets of her washed-out, once-white coat.

Masha hurried to the shops: she needed to buy her daughter the most beautiful Snow Fairy costume. She also had to get hold of an artificial pigtail of red hair – the teachers had insisted that Grandfather Frost's granddaughter should have long hair.

After parking outside a boutique garnished with little lanterns, Masha suddenly realized just how happy she felt that her daughter was going to be the Snow Maiden. "Damn, it's hers by right of inheritance!" Masha whispered, as her foot sank into a muddy puddle. Next day, the happy mother had a small dinner with recitations of the Snow Maiden's songs, to which I was also invited. After her fifth Bailey's, Masha admitted that she had once, long ago, talked to a psychologist, who had let fall that girls who were cast as a Princess found it easier to survive their teenage years. They weren't prone to under-age sex, drinking or drug-taking, and they waited patiently for their Prince in his shiny Lexus, instead of flinging themselves at the first man to pass by on a bicycle. Masha, who had long sought an explanation for the phenomenon of her own prosperity, immediately put her faith in this theory.

And so the long-awaited day arrived. Mrs Koroleva sat in the front row on a child's chair with her video camera, recording the historic moment. Rabbits and Snowflakes positioned themselves around the Christmas tree. Now they were singing the New Year song and starting to summon Grandfather Frost and the Snow Maiden. Happy Masha pointed her camera towards the doorway where her daughter was about to appear, all in white and arm in arm with Grandfather Frost. And there they were: the nursery teacher, breathing heavily behind a false beard, and little Tanya in a spangly dress and a colourful tiara. Grandfather Frost went into ecstasies over the tree and trumpeted, somewhat nasally:

"All our guests I do invite, all my dearest friends tonight, let's take the floor for a round dance, and greet the New Year as we prance!"

The next part of the script was spoken by the Snow Maiden. Little Tanya loudly chanted: "Fly, Snowflakes, fly, round and round you're falling! Fly, my little friends – the Snow Maiden is calling!"

Masha surreptitiously wiped away a tear of contentment and kept on filming. The children awkwardly started to form a circle. Grandfather Frost pronounced forcefully:

"Take my wizard's staff, Snow Maiden, and see: gather all the Snowflakes in a circle under the tree!"

Little Tanya reached out for the tinsel-covered mop handle. She grasped it firmly and pulled it towards herself. It didn't come! A blonde-locked Snowflake – the former Snow Maiden – was hanging on to the other end of the staff. The demoted Snow Maiden had no intention of surrendering and hung on to the mop-handle with both hands. Grandfather Frost attempted to settle the question amicably.

"Snowflake! You don't need that staff! It's only for the Snow Maiden…" Grandfather Frost stumbled, trying to keep "his" song in tune.

"I am the Snow Maiden!" the Snowflake yelped loud enough for the whole kindergarten to hear. "I'm the real Snow Maiden! And she," she tilted her chin at Tanya, "is just a Snowflake! I even know all the songs! Listen! The tree's so fine we gaze and gaze, so pretty we are all amazed!"

"So many apples, nuts, and sweets/For our guests, so many treats!" Masha spiritedly interrupted her rival, also wrapping both hands around the staff.

The fathers, observing the children with faint interest

until now, brightened up noticeably. The children, who had almost formed a circle, now drew together in a knot around the trio with the staff.

"Tanya's the real one!" yelled some of the Rabbits.

"No, Olga was Snow Maiden first!" others shouted.

"They're both rubbish!" sneered the Snowflakes.

One of the Snowflakes didn't lose her head; she grabbed hold of the staff as well.

"I'm a Snow Maiden too!" she announced confidently, flinging a challenging glance at Grandfather Frost.

"So am I!" said someone on the right. "No, I am!" came a voice on the left. Within a few seconds all the Snowflakes, and even one of the Rabbits, were clinging onto the staff and bawling piteously. The teacher, suffocating under her heavy Grandfather costume, sighed heavily, and bellowed:

"Every Snowflake who can touch the staff is now a Snow Maiden! Now I have lots and lots of granddaughters. Come, children, let's dance!"

"No, I'm the only Snow Maiden!" a chubby Snowflake wailed heartrendingly, and flung herself into the arms of her grandmother, seated in the front row.

"Now, what's the matter, darling, don't cry," the grandmother comforted her red-faced grandchild. "You know you're the prettiest of them all. We'll get you something nice to eat right away," the old lady found the perfect solution.

The chubby Snow Maiden dramatically burst into hysterics. The other children swiftly figured out what to do. With convulsive wails, they threw themselves into their parents' embraces. One of the Rabbits, Vasya, knocked against the table, and all the biscuits the mothers had lovingly prepared crashed merrily onto the floor. Little Lena the Snowflake slipped on the cream from a cake and landed on the floor in all her white lace finery. The teacher tore off her suffocating beard. Sveta the Squirrel, who had been so nervous about the show that she had refused to eat for three days beforehand, was so startled by seeing Grandfather Frost's real face that she fainted. Parents leaped out of their seats and, tripping over tiaras and rabbit ears, rushed to rescue their children.

"I was Snow Maiden first!" the ex-Snow Maiden was still insisting, shaking the staff. "I was first," she yelled, and knocked the video camera off the chair where Masha had unwisely left it.

In a corner, Petya the Rabbit was steadily thumping Vladik the Squirrel because the other had stolen his toy the previous day. Fathers rushed to separate the boys. Auntie Nusya, the nurse, phoned for first aid. An hour later the children had been washed; scratched chins had been dosed with ointment; and everyone had been fed with the rescued cakes and sweets. As she wrapped little Tanya up in her cashmere scarf, Masha overheard a conversation behind her:

"I was always the Snow Maiden when I was a girl," one of the mammas was saying.

"And so was I," answered another. "I was opposed in principle to my daughter being a mere Snowflake. It somehow lowers one's self-esteem, don't you think?"

Lessons in Hysteria

Formulas for women's happiness are a bottomless well of human foolishness. If only because you never know which formulas for male happiness the object of your desire has studied.

Just a couple of months ago Lusya was convinced that sooner or later she would get married. For example, she might meet the man she was fated to marry in a cafe. Or in the office of the translation agecy where she worked and where she transposed texts from the language of Shakespeare into the language of Lenin, and the other way round. For some time, though, Lusya has been seriously alarmed about her future. No, Lusya hasn't become a cripple, lost her mind or even gone up a dress size. And if she still lived in that miraculous world which she had inhabited until her twenty-fifth birthday, she might still be waiting for her innocent maidenly desires to come true, convinced of her own inarguable virtues. She usually allowed herself at least three of these virtues. Two of them were common enough. In the first place, Lusya's shoe size was only four. Sometimes, in a burst of flirtatiousness, she even bought herself shoes in Moscow's biggest children's store. Secondly, Lusya was a decent cook. Her third virtue, in Lusya's own opinion, was unique and was certain to play a key role in determining her future. This virtue was tolerance.

"Essentially, a man is ready to fall in love with any woman who is the least bit attractive, provided she doesn't make him stop smoking, watch football, play computer games, or drink beer with his friends. Judge not, that ye be not judged," Lusya willingly explained the basic premises of her research in man-taming to her friends over Martinis. It should be noted that she had based her research findings on a single formula for personal happiness pronounced by Lily Brik, legendary lover of the no less legendary poet Vladimir Mayakovsky. "You must make a man believe," taught Brik, "that he is remarkable or even brilliant, and that other people don't understand him. And allow him to do what he isn't allowed to do at home. As for the rest, you'll get there by wearing classy shoes and silk underwear."

Six months ago, Lusya was presented with a chance to put the worldly-wise Lily Brik's advice into practice. She met a very suitable man. He wasn't Mayakovsky of course, but after all, this wasn't the revolution any more. As it happened, this suitable man was called Aleksey Solovyov. He was a good-natured fat man and he owned one of the capital's advertising agencies. The brief time when they shared an apartment could be described as living in perfect harmony. Lusya bought classy shoes and silk underwear in unlimited quantities, delighting Aleksey every evening with a new outfit. Aleksey, naturally, was allowed to smoke in all the rooms, watch football at full volume and drink beer with his pals. Aleksey was highly impressed by this permissive regime. Their happiness seemed so solid that Lusya made up her mind in favour of feminine genius and masculine gullibility. The storm broke completely unexpectedly. One Friday Aleksey called home around six o'clock in the evening to tell her he'd be home late, as he was off to drink beer with his partners in the firm. Lusya wasn't remotely surprised; on Fridays, Aleksey often went for beer with friends. Sometimes, these gatherings went on until the small hours, and he would leave his beloved Audi behind at whatever bar they'd been drinking in and come home in a taxi. Not forgetting, incidentally, to pull over at a flower stall in order to surprise his beloved; a woman who, unlike his former female partners, never demanded to know where he'd been, who he'd been with and what he'd been up to. In a word, Lusya treated his call like a weather report: "OK, honey, have a good time! Just remember, that your little kitten will be at home waiting for you," she purred. "I've made you something very tasty, and the Moscow-Yaroslavl match will be on TV soon. Do you want me to record it?"

"Thanks, honeybunny," Aleksey answered, "You're just the best ever. When I think of Vaska! He's afraid even to call his old lady, he says the bitch will start hollering down the phone at him to come home right away. But you're the most sensible and understanding woman in the world. I love you!"

A pleased and smug Lusya put the phone down and curled up to watch a TV serial or two. But right then all the channels seemed to be conspiring to show some stupid thrillers. Lusya switched off the television and went to bed with a romance novel. And just at the most exciting moment, when Tom was starting to stroke Mary's firm bosom under her dress, tears of happiness started to Lusya's eyes; she pressed the book passionately to her own breast, and her gaze rose dreamily to the ceiling. When this unexpected wave of sensation had washed away, Lusya glanced rapidly at the clock. It was already one in the morning! Good heavens! Aleksey still wasn't home.

"I ought to ring him," Lusya thought. "What if something's happened to him?"

She had just picked up the telephone when an unexpectedly wise thought made her hesitate. What if he decided that she was trying to control him? That she was infringing on his freedom? No, she had to call with some cunning excuse, to make sure he was alive without hinting that it was time for him to come home.

Lusya spent a quarter of an hour thinking deeply; finally, she tapped out her beloved's mobile number.

"Aleksey, honey! There's a word I can't figure out in the crossword!" Lusya cried cheerfully down the line. She felt happy because her loved one was clearly alive and, to judge by his voice, perfectly healthy. "Can you give me the name of a football team from the premier league, nine letters, beginning with 'L'?"

"Well, Lokomotiv," Solovyov answered, sounding puzzled.

"Perfect, Alexey, you're so clever!" She was about to put the phone down.

"Lusya, was there something else you wanted? Why did you call?" her normally polite Aleksey demanded with uncharacteristic abruptness.

"Just for the crossword," Lusya babbled, confused.

"And, like a fool, I thought you were about to tell me to get my ass home and threaten me with a divorce," Aleksey said in a strange tone.

"Of course I'm missing you, and it would be fantastic if you were here. But if you're still having a good time with the guys, of course I understand. No-one has the right to deprive a person of his pleasures!" the young woman said soothingly.

Slightly alarmed, Lusya went back in bed, holding her chick-lit novel, and soon fell asleep. She woke quite late, at half past ten next morning. Alexey still wasn't home. Forgetting about the proprieties and the complexities of relationships between the sexes, Lusya immediately rang her husband on his mobile. No-one picked up. Disdaining appropriate behaviour, Lusya started going through her husband's papers in search of his friends' phone numbers. At that moment the doorbell rang. Yes, it was him – Aleksey. Lusya tried to fling her arms around his neck, but he silently pushed her away. He stepped gloomily through the door, headed for the wardrobe and began riffling determinedly through the suitcases.

"Are you ashamed of your behaviour last night?" Lusya asked tactfully. "Don't worry, I don't have a problem with it. You have every right to spend your time on what you decide you need." Lusya's politically correct speech was interrupted by a telephone call, during which a nightclub manager informed her that Mr Solovyov had left his mobile and his papers behind. When Lusya got back to the hallway, an enormous suitcase had appeared.

"Are you going somewhere?" the soon-to-be-former Mrs Solovyova enquired timidly, feverishly trying to figure out how to act in a situation like this, without appearing hysterical and possessive.

"No, you're the one who's going," Solovyov answered laconically.

"Going where?" Lusya, who was prepared for anything, asked him tenderly.

"Wherever you like! I have no right to infringe upon your freedom, darling!" said Alexey acidly. "I don't want to live with you, because you don't give a damn about me! You don't go crazy when I'm not home at half past five in the morning! All the other men have proper wives who call them and worry about them. Vitka's Larisa calls his phone every five minutes to tell him she's broken another plate because he's not back yet. Dima's got a real beauty: his Tanya threw her wedding ring off the balcony! They both spent the whole morning crawling on the lawn looking for it. Now that's a woman for you! That's love! And what does my wife do? Snores all night like a gopher!"

Right then Lusya should probably have flung herself at Alexei and shrieked piercingly: "I hate it when you're not there! I can't cope without you! I didn't sleep a wink, I called up all the morgues!" And then she should have grabbed some old rag – the dirtiest one she had – and run around the apartment howling threateningly: "Just you treat me like that again! Just you go drinking with your pals again! And there'll be no football on television for a month!" But Lusya behaved like a fool, or, if you wish, like Lily Brik. Weeping modestly and quietly, she started to pack her bags, muttering some lines to herself from one of Lermontov's poems; something about having nobody to offer a friendly hand. She put her tiny little shoes in the suitcase last of all. Perhaps she was hoping that Solovyov wouldn't be able to withstand this soul-wrenching vision: pale, quiet Lusya and the enormous suitcase, into which one by one her cute, exquisite things were disappearing. But Solovyov withstood the test. He even helped to haul the suitcase down the stairs to the taxi he had ordered in advance. In parting, he snapped: "I just knew you didn't give a damn about me. You haven't even started howling like a real woman should." And he slammed the car door.

Then Lusya howled like a real woman. But it was too late. The world around her had changed irrevocably, proving in its mean-natured way that nobody appreciates tolerance in a woman any more. Now poor Lusya only has two inarguable virtues, and those, you have to agree, won't go far towards a happy marriage.

Olga Rimsha

STILL WATER

Translated by Dora O'Brien

I decided to throw a party to mark my resignation. I'd slaved away for three lousy years in a fading business and, admittedly, played my part in letting things get badly out of hand. I'd felt compelled to contribute towards the inevitable demise of that absurd City Insurance Agency. I'd long been fed up with every single one of its clients, not to mention its manager whose paunch I took an aversion to from the very first months. When the agency was already on the countdown to its collapse I firmly planted my resignation letter on the boss's desk.

"Andrei," he mumbled sadly, "so you're abandoning a sinking ship?"

"Are you calling me a rat?" I sniggered, grabbed my employment record book and left. I was a free rat now.

The party went well. It was not yet daybreak but one could say it had gone extremely well. The raucous crowd had finished off all the food in the house; chaotic heaps of bottles, broken crockery and what appeared to be the remnants of my favourite salad littered the floor. My temples were still throbbing from the music, my eardrums felt taut, my throat was on fire. My eyes hadn't yet recovered from the flickering lights, my ears from the noise, and my hands from warm handclasps. I was drifting towards a roaring abyss. Tomorrow would clearly be achingly boring and my head would spin just from remembering... but right now it was slowly shutting the world out with not even the tiniest chink of light allowed to sneak under the bedcover...

Morning smiled with a drizzle bursting through the open windows. I could hardly open my eyes which seemed glued shut; I shivered, turned round and caught sight of a girl's tired face on the pillow next to mine. She looked sweet. As I touched her shoulder I was aware of her warmth and I quietly whispered to her, smiling smugly:

"Not bad..."

The kitchen was a terrible mess. There was nowhere to put a plate down had there been any left. Barely restraining the impulse to hurl everything against the walls and turn a once cosy room into a battlefield, I grabbed a half-eaten sandwich from the table and went back to the bedroom. I noticed that the girl had changed position and had shifted closer to my pillow, which probably still retained my smell. I sat down quietly next to her and bent over her ear:

"What's your name?"

"Ira. Don't you remember me?" she said somewhat hoarsely, without opening her eyes as though in a dream, and she added: "That's a bit much..."

I spent a few minutes examining her ear with its intricate bends and twists. Then I sensed her warm breath and instinctively thought I should take a shower, yet really did not want to at all.

"Where did we meet?" I asked, not even thinking that this might sound offensive to her.

"Yesterday… here." She suddenly scrunched up her eyes and stretched. She smiled, showing her slightly yellow-tinged teeth.

"You seem to be making yourself at home here," I said, moving even closer to her.

"I'm not really interested in your opinion." She was still smiling and I began to resent this.

"Get dressed and get out," I said, without altering my tone and with no hint of pity. Yet I wouldn't move away from her warm body: it happens, you know, that your body and your words behave quite disconnectedly without the slightest chance of the situation being settled in a conventional way. At first her smile faded but when she noticed the genuine interest in my eyes, she beamed again and carefully placed her finger on my neck without a word.

"Are you deaf?" I continued, "I really need you to go."

"Are you afraid your girlfriend will find us?" She was so composed as she spoke that for a split second I actually believed in the existence of a girlfriend.

"What girlfriend? Don't make me laugh. I'm a free man…"

"Which means you can do anything that comes to mind," she interrupted. She seemed to be saying this with some regret, as though she'd have liked to be in my shoes. The shoes of a person with nothing holding him back so that he can move about at will.

I really wasn't tied to anything. Only a very short time ago I'd had to get up at seven in the morning, stick my legs, numb from sleep, into a pair of trousers and rub a stiff toothbrush against nicotine-stained teeth. Every single day I would stare at the computer, only to be faced with a big fat nothing. Every blessed day I would smile at clients – it wasn't their fault, of course – whose constant loathsome presence before my screen-weary eyes and whose legitimate if very annoying wish to find out the truth about the pitfalls of insurance drove me to distraction. Yesterday I'd shaken off that awful duty.

"Do you want something to eat?" I switched from anger to concern.

"If you're cooking," she said, screwing up her eyes and curling up again in the blanket. How could I not remember last night? No, something was coming back to me, but very dimly. Perhaps, in time, I'd be feeling her lips on my ear for real.

"OK," I said, no longer with any thoughts of saying no.

Fifteen minutes later I carried in a tray with scrambled eggs in a pan, two slices of bread, forks and a mug of tea for her. For myself I brought in a bottle of cold beer. I sat down in the armchair opposite her. After enjoying the fizz and the first sip, I suddenly felt the urge to examine her from head to toe. I must admit, nature had been kind to her, if not overly generous. The first thing that struck you was her shoulders. They were rounded – despite desperate attempts to rid herself of the habit – and this gave her an air of touching vulnerability. To straighten her spine, which she did from time to time, seemed to cause her a great deal of irritation. I can understand that working against your own nature must be extremely annoying. Her eyes… Her eyes would not stand out – when I think of all those eyes I've seen – were it not for the fact that they were always laughing, or more accurately, mocking. I wasn't able to make out their colour, something between brown, grey and green. Her features were regular rather than beautiful, her skin – not very smooth or rosy, but not bad. Just skin. Her figure – now that she could indeed be proud of and, judging by her occasional brash movements, she knew it. A not altogether flattering picture but she pleased me: beneath her rather commonplace appearance you could feel life and good sense. She clearly had stimulating thoughts in her head, usually a good indication of character. No, she wasn't a beauty, but she had something.

"Why are you looking at me like that?" she mumbled, her mouth full of egg, and she smiled again.

"I'm examining you," I said without the slightest embarrassment and still staring at her.

"And do you like what you see?"

"No." I know that I can be cruel at times but my unwarranted candour made no impact whatsoever on her expression. Only in her eyes did I notice a flash of contempt – as if to say that no self-respecting person would ever utter such a thing. So I added:

"At least I'm being honest. Why tell a lie? It'll be easier for you this way…"

"You're right. I should go," she suddenly said, and she jumped up from the bed and quickly slipped on her clothes. I didn't react. My head was spinning with lots of thoughts no longer related to Ira. I hadn't grown so used to her as to have her name forever linked with that smiling face. I'd already lost all thought of her when I suddenly heard her voice calling from the hall:

"Shut the door after me!"

"I will…"

"I'll leave you my number, just in case…" she said in a firm voice, although it betrayed a forced ease. When I went into the hall to shut the door she'd vanished but on the key ledge there was a scrap of paper. There was a number on it. I didn't even touch it.

"After all, anything is possible…"

* * *

Today, as I discarded my office worker's glum expression, I wanted to stretch the mask of freedom, and the happiness that freedom gave me, as far as it would go. But even freedom can stick in your throat. It makes your head spin so that it eventually loses its appeal. It had been sorely lacking in my life and even after losing everything from my time on a swivel chair, I didn't die, I didn't fall flat on my face; instead I suddenly began to dream. And dreams… they not only put us back on our feet, they even give us wings. And so I flew towards a miracle – towards the entrance to a grey building with cheerful signboards, smacking my lips in anticipation of the sweetness of what was to come. Yes, the place did look like a beehive, but I wasn't there to lick honey.

Having knocked as politely as possible on a door with a forbidding notice, I quietly walked into an office that smelled of expensive cigars. I sat down just as quietly in a nearby armchair and fixed my eyes on a man who was laboriously sorting out some documents with an air of self-importance.

"Who are you?" he muttered blandly without looking up and I didn't immediately catch on that he was addressing me.

"I rang you. I was given an appointment," I was trying not to use too many words, feeling, however, that my tone betrayed my anxiety. I took a deep breath to control my breathing.

"It's not me you want."

"Where should I go then?"

"What's your name?" the man continued without turning away from his papers.

"Andrei Tsarikov."

"What?"

"Tsarikov. Andrei."

He finally looked up. His eyes showed not the slightest interest beyond common politeness. I braced myself, tried to show a bold readiness for even the most complicated questions and unwittingly began to fiddle with the edge of my pocket.

"I'm ready for questions."

"It would be more appropriate if you did the questioning rather than the other way round. You're the one who wants to become a journalist." He smiled for the first time. "But first of all I need to understand what kind of a person you are. Therefore my first question to you will be rather a trite one by journalistic standards. Why do you want to be a journalist?"

"I've dreamt of being one since I was a child," I blurted out and it took me no time to understand that I was talking absolute rubbish. "Well, that's to say that even as a child I was writing… I wrote articles on a variety of subjects…"

"On what, for example?"

"As I said, a variety. Some at school, others at university. Many people liked reading them."

"Still, what's the point of it all?"

"Nature provided me with a critical mind. When I see something interesting or on the other hand, something terrible, I can't wait to comment on it, to expose, as they say, its good and bad sides. I can't work somewhere I have to keep quiet, you understand, where they shut me up. A journalist is someone who in my opinion can speak the truth and that suits me."

"Do you think the truth is always of interest to people?"

"Of course. What could be more interesting? To get to the root of the matter and to arrive at the corresponding conclusions – that's the most interesting thing in life."

"Some people think differently and there are plenty of journalists among them, successful ones, by the way."

"No," I retorted, sensing by now that I wouldn't get the job. "Those are not journalists, but storytellers, writers… I believe that a journalist is obliged to tell the truth."

"What are you prepared to sacrifice for it?" The man asked me as blandly as before without having yet got round to introducing himself.

"I don't know." I thought for a while. "I don't think everything… Is that what you wanted to hear?"

"Are you prepared to betray love? To use mean tricks?

To deceive everyone around you to uncover the truth which you so love?" He appeared to be shamelessly provoking me to come out into the open, to acknowledge my own greed for a truth that could be betrayed for another truth. And it does happen – it's like a woman, and when we say we love women it doesn't mean that we love every one of them. That's why I quickly admitted to being wrong.

"I am. I have no moral boundaries. As for love… I've been amazingly lucky. I know nothing about it, except of course that it can happen. It's never happened to me."

"I'd still like to know how far you'd go. Where you wouldn't be prepared to poke your nose for love or money?" He grinned slyly, as though groping for my weak spots.

"I'd never commit murder."

"So you do have moral principles!" He suddenly cheered up.

"As any sane person would," I said, shrugging my shoulders.

He lapsed into silence and became engrossed again in his important business. He had something of the look of my previous boss, which annoyed me. His measured movements betrayed a comfortable life, his eyes indolence, but he spoke clearly and his words could cut to the quick. It was good to know that you still had it in you. And I was hugely relieved by the absence of a fat paunch. It meant that he'd not lost everything in that labyrinthine brain of his, that he could still emerge from within and see his most unattractive side that everyone else observed. This led me to an amazing conclusion – he could put himself in my place if he wanted to. And when he turned what looked like an empty gaze back at me I understood that he'd give me a chance.

"What's your education?"

"Language and literature," I said realizing that this was

only education on paper. There wasn't even the slightest iota of it left in my head.

"Fine," he said indifferently. "Have you ever worked as a journalist?"

"At university," I faltered, "I worked on a newspaper... I can't recall its name."

"It doesn't matter even if you were just twiddling your thumbs," he said not unkindly, and he gathered from my averted eyes that he was right. To what extent had he sized me up – to the very core? Had I so trivially laid out before him everything there was to know about me that it was now impossible to ignore a niggling conscience?

I didn't respond.

"Well, it's not that important. You won't make the grade for a full-time position. I can't trust you, I can't rely on you as I would on a professional. But as a freelancer..."

"That's just what I was after," I interrupted, feeling really glad. He seemed to have sunk into a kind of lumbering impassivity. God knows, perhaps his nerves were dulled. I believe he wouldn't have screamed if he'd accidentally smashed his finger with a hammer. What's more, he would have remained silent if someone had done it to him. I could see he was genuinely good at what he did which was why he was so condescending. It's unpleasant to feel like a fledgling who's being offered a ledge to take off from and who's left with the problem of whether to fly or not.

"I've nothing more to ask," he said sedately. "I've no need to inquire about your life and your principles. That's just empty chat if you're no one, if you're not worth a penny."

He handed me his business card.

"As soon as I find you a suitable assignment, I'll call you. If you don't hear from me for a while, then call me: there's so much going on it's easy to forget. If you write something worthwhile – I'll let you in… No, you'd have to try again. I like hard-headed people, in the best sense of the word, and heads get hardened by being knocked about."

He stopped paying attention to me and buried himself again in his piles of paperwork.

I remained seated for another ten seconds in the armchair, worn out from its constantly changing occupants and I examined the attractive features of my intended future boss. Yes, women would definitely like him and he was not yet forty. It was with such thoughts that I made my way to the door, calling out "goodbye" into the silence, and rushed out of the office.

* * *

It was only once outside that I glanced at the business card. At the top it said *People and Events* in an attractive script and right underneath, in slightly smaller script, Konstantin Korpevsky, editor-in-chief. Why had that Korpevsky not introduced himself, shaken my hand, smiled politely and amicably, offering me a cup of coffee? Why had he not acted as I'd had to in my previous job? Because I was just a commodity, one who possibly but not necessarily would add some pennies to further line his pocket. But they'd hardly be noticeable among the heaps of banknotes. I'd hardly refuse to get them for him, as I was also hooked on the drug, a dose of which had been promised me. What was I to him? At best a pesky fly, which if it turned out to be a very rare one, would help him win credit as a famous collector.

This Korpevsky was probably an old hand. I'd spotted his watch – he'd not bought it in a market stall, nor even in an ordinary shop; how much it cost him I couldn't tell, nor do I like the thought of such huge sums. His jacket was rumpled but expensive, his tie of an expensive brand was carelessly worn. But the main thing that gave away the rich man was the way he looked at you. He had everything he wanted, wasn't interested in talking to anyone beneath him, he'd fulfilled himself and wanted to see how others would manage – this actually spoke in his favour. He was talented and not afraid to take a gamble. And how I would have loved to get the upper hand some time.

I put the card in the inside pocket of my jacket for fear of losing it. This could be a chance in a million – it would be crazy not to grab it. This newspaper had a huge circulation and was sold out in town within one day. And how incredible it would be to see, on those crisp pages with their distinctive smell of print, letters that made up my name. My name which that man or that young girl who were rushing past were not yet familiar with but might be one day.

I glanced up at the sky and saw birds. They were swirling low over the land in a chaotic dance. Glancing down at the pavement I discovered them there too. Had they taken over?

I had nowhere to go to in a hurry today so I decided to take a stroll and gather my thoughts, particularly because the sight of birds always drew me to movement and reflection. Just then I caught sight of a former colleague, Slava Pliukhin. He was walking quickly, constantly glancing back, and he was carefully holding some kind of bundle. I decided not to catch his eye, as I had nothing to brag about yet, but to my annoyance he spotted me and hurried towards me.

"Andrei, how good to see you!" He seemed genuinely pleased and grabbed me by the sleeve.

"Hey, steady on! What are you so happy about?"

"We haven't met in a long time!"

"A week at the most." I thought that he would now ask me how my week had been, had I come up with something worthwhile, had I found a comfortable seat to park my bum on, so I hurriedly began to question him first:

"By the way, how are things at work?"

"At work…" he spoke indistinctly, and a bitter smile twisted his face. "Why this interest? Do you actually care?"

"Listen, Pliukhin, I don't care but I somehow get the feeling that you can't wait to tell me about it. How's our boss, has he put his head in a noose yet or is he still hoping to survive?"

"A noose…" he repeated after me in a startled tone. "No, he hasn't put his head in a noose, why should he?"

"Forget it, I was just joking," I was filled with an unpleasant feeling: things were in such a bad way that the poor lad had lost all sense. He was tongue-tied, his eyes were restless, his hands would start shaking any moment now. He looked unwell. No, it wasn't right to be so stuck to your work – so what if it went to hell?

"Listen, Pliukhin," I added a moment later, "don't you want to quit?"

"I already quit. Just a moment ago," he said, looking to one side.

"Well!" I was extremely surprised. Pliukhin respected the boss more than anyone, and he even liked to exchange pleasantries with the clients, which in itself is unthinkable. He seemed to hold the whole insurance thing in awe without any fear of such problems that might unexpectedly come our way. And now today even he'd run off – well, the smell of a decaying enterprise is an unpleasant one and drives away even the most dedicated employees.

"Yes, I quit." He kept glancing around him as though looking for someone. "If one can put it that way… In simple terms, I walked out and will somehow have to get hold of my employment record card later …"

"And what will you do now?" I said, though it didn't interest me at all. His behaviour seemed odd to me. He was usually composed, happy-go-lucky and cheerful. He'd been the only one who had occasionally brightened up those grey days, one you could chat with about any nonsense that made the day go by faster. He was only twenty-three and I found his groundless enthusiasm for his work in such a doleful place inexplicable. I was just glad that it didn't interfere with my slothfulness.

"I don't know," he said and he suddenly thrust his bundle at me. "Could you hold on to this for a while?"

"What?" I failed to understand.

"Could you hold on to this for a while?"

"For how long?"

"Just a few days," he said quickly, and shoving the bundle into my hands he turned to go.

I was utterly dumbfounded by what had just happened. Perhaps because he had so easily palmed off that bloody bundle on me and had so simply avoided any perfectly legitimate questions. I came to when his back was scarcely discernible in the crowd. I felt the paper parcel from all sides and recognized something hard wrapped in something soft. It wasn't difficult to guess that that was fabric. I was suddenly brimming with curiosity but I didn't dare open the parcel in broad daylight and in full view of everyone. I tucked it under my arm, looked all around me and spotted a small basement café not far from where I stood; it probably wouldn't have many people in it on such a morning. I quickly made my way there.

* * *

The café was gripped by loud music. In various corners people sat on settees in small groups, laughing and sipping coffee. The barman behind the bar seemed bored. I looked round and spotted the letter "M' I was after. I'd hardly get noticed going there. I know that when my own head is being pummelled by a resounding beat, I get distracted, and my thoughts retreat to the middle of my numbed brain. I find an abuse of decibels in some cafés greatly annoying.

The music was still booming within the tiled walls of the toilet. I got into one of the less smelly cubicles and sat down on the edge of the toilet after first checking if it was clean; then I shoved my hand into the bundle. What an absurd situation I was in! Here I was turning into a possessor of a terrible secret as my fingers groped in the packet and distinctly felt a large, still warm, well-greased pistol, something I'd never held in my hands till that moment.

"Not bad…" I whispered.

The old pistol – it had possibly seen WWII – stared at me with its black hollow muzzle. I don't know much about weapons but even a fool would recognize a revolver. There was a time when it was a great boon to one's honour to play Russian roulette. It was as though by letting death come so close and just escaping it you could respect yourself more than ever before. I was amused by where my thoughts were leading me. I wasn't even considering such crazy behaviour yet the tips of my fingers were strangely affected by that lethal piece of metal.

I twirled the heavy revolver in my hands and wondered how it could have found its way to Pliukhin. He was such a quiet and unremarkable man, you wouldn't suspect him of being a criminal, yet of course those are the ones who can turn out to be the most desperate thugs. I didn't imagine, however, that Pliukhin was capable of anything bad, he'd somehow got hold of the revolver by chance and become so frightened that he passed it on to someone else at the first opportunity. But by what kind of chance?

Twisting the barrel I suddenly felt that the revolver, from whose muzzle hundreds of bullets had probably flown, had begun to fascinate me. How many lives had it destroyed, how many deaths had it caused? In reality, there might be a discrepancy in the numbers. One innocent death could mean scores of people destroyed indiscriminately, a father, a mother, a lover or someone's child. But it could also be the case that one justified death would lead to hundreds of people being saved. There's no point in calculating ahead, it all boils down to Lady Luck in the end. But I doubt she's the one who pulls the trigger.

The barrel was worn – I don't know whether the same fingers or different fingers had touched it but the barrel had suffered their imprint. I too twisted it. It gave me an uncertain feeling, a kind of abstract indifference towards all those whose last moments of life it had counted off. I'd never imagined that an empty, soulless object could decide someone's fate, destroy or let live, but that day, right then, seated on the edge of a toilet bowl, I suddenly understood this. It was simple – so simple that it was hardly credible yet if you believed it, you could not let go of that truth, which could become an obsession.

Without knowing why, I placed my index finger on the trigger – my hand strained with a strange urge to press it right away. I gripped the revolver in my palm. When your heart beats rapidly, it's so odd that your body can feel deliciously calm, like a cat before it pounces. Another instant and my brain shut down completely. I forcefully bent my finger, pressed the trigger and, as if in slow motion, a deafening shot resounded only a few seconds later. I nearly fell back in a stunned heap into the toilet bowl.

Split seconds later, when the noise in my head had slightly abated, I discovered a hole in the wall on the right – not a very big one nor a particularly small one, molten and wrenched apart along its edge, emitting a pungent smell and an acrid wisp of smoke. As I touched the gaping hole with my finger I got burned. I looked at it – there was some kind of nasty sticky red blob... Taking another peek through the hole, I tried to focus elsewhere and was able to make out something strange, red and blurry. I'd never thought that your hair could literally stand on end, but in this instance I could distinctly feel a restless anthill stirring beneath my scalp. I felt my ribcage suddenly pumped up with hot air that set my insides on fire and I thought my chest would burst. My hand began to shake as if I were having a fit and I ran it across my cold forehead. A second later I bolted, quick as a flash but on legs like cotton wool, out of the cubicle and tugged at the door of the next one, which flew open with a bang. Slumped in the corner was a man with a hole in his left temple. Stunned by pain and exhaustion I closed my eyes.

* * *

The city kept spinning to the point of nausea, my eyes felt dry. The birds seemed to be glued to the sky while the road had suddenly come alive and slipped away beneath my feet. I walked as though drunk or exhausted after a 24-hour marathon or as one crippled by illness; walking was bewilderingly hard. I managed to drag my legs through inertia or innate habit. Somehow I made it home, threw the bundle with the pistol in a corner and collapsed on the bed, shoving my head under the pillow.

What had happened? I couldn't believe any of it. Yet I'd seen it all with my own eyes. I'd never wanted to kill and yet for some reason that pathetic revolver had cast me as a killer, a stupid, faint-hearted, mindless killer. I had no doubt that the guy was dead. As dead as I was presently alive. Amazing how fragile the dividing line is. Even more incredible is that I'd so absurdly, and without any forethought, smeared that line across a tiled wall forming a conspicuously red salty stain.

I remembered everything. I'd apparently not taken anything in at the time. I hadn't grasped even a fraction of the reality of it or been able to store it, in the slightest detail or as a whole picture, in my mind. But now, lying down at home with no one beside me, I suddenly felt a horrifying mosaic taking shape in my head.

He was in the right-hand corner and wasn't moving. One arm dangled freely, the other lay on his knee, as though holding on to his pulled-down trousers. On his face – aloofness, aloneness and self-sufficiency, nothing special, no fear, aggression or surprise. A face made of wax, not alive yet not quite dead, as though held up between sleep and a strange awakening. His eyes were open but empty, with sunken pupils whose glassy surface reflected the whole cubicle. The wall against which his head was resting, or more accurately was stuck to by the stray bullet, was unbearably red, even crimson or wine-red in places. His brains were a bloody mess. His temple had been pierced right through and was also reddish-black. His blue shirt was spattered with a wild pattern of blood. And the cheap watch on his wrist was probably still working as though nothing had happened. Indeed, time is indifferent to whether you're dead or still holding on.

He'd not reached forty but was over thirty. Some stubble on his cheeks but few hairs on his hands and chest. Short-cut dark hair, and had he lived he would have been nearly grey within three years. At the corners of his mouth some lines pleasantly disposed to chatting, and across his whole forehead a soft deep line – he must have enjoyed thinking. He was of average height, average size, rather thin and sinewy. He was so clearly and strongly embodied in my mind that I shivered instinctively – he would appear in my dreams and I wouldn't be able to do anything about it, even if I took to drinking vodka by the gallon.

How could I remember in such minute detail what I'd only seen for a few seconds? Three or four at the most. After five seconds I'd broken out of the basement window, got outside, and glanced round to make sure no one was in the inside courtyard. Then I'd wandered vacantly for a long time and now I was lolling about in a warm bed, the pillow over my head as though it could hide me from reality.

After some time of strange stillness I suddenly began to feel as if my feverish hot skin were being ripped from my muscles and, beside myself, I began to pull the sheet up over my head and body. I was overcome by fear, despair and the impossibility of what had happened to me. I inhaled deeply and was on the brink of throwing up. I badly wanted to and also felt like hitting my head against the wall until I'd smashed it to smithereens. But I didn't utter a sound. However horrifying this all was, I decided to keep it inside me. I'd never before felt so choked up. What was crushing me was actually only frustration, but a huge, awful, unbearable frustration, which made me want to cry for as long as I had tears and until my face muscles ached from exhaustion.

I dozed off but my sleep was so troubled I woke up five minutes later. I don't know how long I'd been home, but through the window the sun was suspended as a ghastly red-orange ball, which meant it would soon vanish on this side of the planet. I rubbed my eyebrows, ears and cheeks and breathed out with a shudder. Then I convulsively began to shake up my bed, rummage in my pockets and throw away various odds and ends from the shelves: finally I found my mobile phone. I tried to calm down and find one number among hundreds of unwanted ones, Pliukhin's. He didn't pick up for a long time but I stubbornly kept on ringing until I heard his muffled sleepy voice as though from far away:

"Hello."

"Pliukhin!" I shouted and then stopped. What could I say to him?

"Yes, Andrei, I'm here…" he hesitated. I felt my head

spinning mindlessly and couldn't wait to put the phone down as there was seemingly nothing to say. "Are you going to remain silent for long?"

"Pliukhin, where did you get that pistol?" I blurted out.

"The revolver?" He seemed to be expecting this stupid question.

"I don't see the difference!"

"Well... a friend gave it to me to hold on to for a while..."

"What the hell did you give it to me for? What kind of a revolver is it that it's being contracted out like some sort of badge of honour? What are you up to?"

"Me? Nothing. And what's happened to you?" he said quietly. I decided I shouldn't be making such a show of myself.

"Come and collect it," I threw at him after a moment's idiotic silence.

"I did ask you to keep it for me for a while. I really need you to do that."

"If you don't come and get it today, I'll throw it away, do you understand?"

"OK..."he hesitated again and reluctantly agreed. "I'll come and collect it, but tomorrow. I can't make it today. But don't throw it away."

"I won't promise," I said dryly in a low voice and put down the phone.

There was a bitter lump in my throat. I flung the phone into the armchair. I refused to feel anything – outside or inside myself. I couldn't feel my skin at all. And I blamed Pliukhin for all of it. He was the one who'd landed me with the revolver, who'd whipped up my curiosity and got me into such a horrid mess. And now he was so composed and cold that I would have shaken him into action if I met him.

Hold on. I replayed our phone conversation in my head from beginning to end. I was done for – he wasn't going to collect the pistol and for me to chuck it out seemed dangerous. What made me think that? It was all quite straightforward. When he'd met me so inopportunely on the street he'd been restless and scared. I'd attached some importance to that fact and had noticed how his behaviour had changed since I'd last seen him at work, but there'd been nothing to support those observations. Yet now I could see: he'd had the revolver. And now I was just as shattered and upset and I couldn't wait to get rid of the thing. Meanwhile he was in great spirits, composed, still a bit subdued but sure of himself and of his actions. He was not about to take the revolver back, if only because he remembered how it had distressed him and thrown him into turmoil.

In the soft light of the bathroom I saw myself in the slightly steamed-up mirror. I didn't recognize myself. This was a different man – with my looks, my facial expressions and lines, yet completely different. As though what had been inside my skin had died and the new substance hadn't yet emerged. A moist film covered my eyes. I felt uneasy at the way they looked back at me. They had an empty, strangled, weary, nervy look. For no obvious reason my lips had suddenly become chapped and swollen. My skin had grown flabby, greyish and had lost its former freshness and youthfulness. I briskly splashed my face with cold water, again and again until the top of my head was soaked and the icy water trickled down my neck. I nervously took off my shirt and with all my might began rubbing my face, the nape, the neck and shoulders. The sudden onrush of blood made me turn red and I mussed up my hair. My face, staring back with a washed-out look, was repulsive to me and I made an effort not to spit at its reflection, but I did spit on it in the end. Then I smeared the saliva all over the mirror and just fell apart. I slipped down onto the cold bathroom floor and began to sob. It was only then that I realized how agonizingly alone I was. My bathroom was my only refuge in the world and even there I felt terrible. In a flash there was no one. And I imagined myself flying in infinite space, hidden away in a small dark cubicle, and if I went outside, I'd go deaf from the hollow sound of the desolate void.

* * *

Had I left any evidence? Anything at all that could be seized upon? So that I could be clutched in a deadly grip from which I'd never break loose? Had I left traces, had I remained in the mind of any of the visitors to that ill-starred café? Had the shot been heard instantly or had they only found the poor devil when someone needed to go to the toilet? I imagined how all of a sudden that person's heart would have nearly exploded. It would have thumped like crazy from a flurry of distaste and indignation, just as mine had done. I had no way of getting away from that endless succession of alarming thoughts, once they'd taken root in my muddled head.

I couldn't sleep. I had visions of the man whose life I had inadvertently cut short. But the strange thing was that I wasn't in a hurry to pity him or even repent. My fate hung in the balance – with every second of the night I became more and more absorbed in the brutal awareness that my life would never be the same again. And what lay ahead? What lot was God reserving for me?

Morning came and I got up from my very warm bed just to stretch my legs and wash my face. Just that, without looking in the mirror or using the towel. I don't know what I'd expected, but the cold water didn't refresh me nor did it clear my head. It was still very early, the sun had only just come into view and I was extremely surprised to hear the phone ring. Then I got scared. I grabbed the phone anyway and nervously pressed the button:

"Pliukhin?"

This was followed by a strained silence the other end.

"Andrei Tsarkov?" a voice finally said. "I imagine I've got the right number?"

"You have."

"This is Korpevsky speaking."

I almost choked. His strong voice pronounced those words so distinctly and calmly that I instantly pushed aside all thoughts of what had happened: Korpevsky must have found me a job and I got ready to rub my hands. I don't know what got into me but his voice, deliberately relaxed yet demanding at the same time, made me take the plunge:

"Good morning…" I was absurdly glad.

"Andrei, are you available today?"

"Yes, of course. More than."

"In other words, you're languishing in a pool of idleness, if one was to interpret your expression 'more than'?"

"No," I said, partly lying, "but then again, you're right." I lied again not knowing which of those truths to choose from.

"Well, that's not why I rang. There's been an incident: a man was shot not far from here, in a café near our office…"

"Near the office?" I blurted out nervously, once again transported along the interminable expanses of the universe, and succumbing to the hateful echo of deathlike silence. I was terrified. A moment later I gave a start and all of a sudden it all seemed irrelevant. Totally irrelevant.

"Yes, right nearby. Will you take it on? Write something about the victim. It's not that interesting but it'll help me get an idea of what you can do. Well, would you like to write about him or not?"

"I will," I said firmly, feeling an inexplicable anger rising up inside me.

"Well, you've been given a task, now get on with it. I don't recall the name of the café…"

"I know the place," I growled and by then that anger had crept up to my belly and was burning me up beyond belief.

"Well, that's fine then. I won't give you a deadline but don't drag it out. Bye for now."

"Goodbye," I almost grunted through my teeth as the anger had now fully taken hold of me. I flung the phone aside and clenched my teeth so hard that my jaw nearly cracked. And, without stepping away from that odious spot where I'd just agreed to undertake something despicable, I took the decision there and then not to deviate from the path I so craved the day before. And if everything went smoothly then life would again follow its usual course and I'd move on towards a bright future without any thoughts of the past. Not to allow circumstances to gain the upper hand and make me change my resolve – that was my plan of action.

I'd planned all this well but a few hours later, dressed and ready, as I stood in the hall about to open the door, my legs suddenly gave way. How to wipe off that beastly muck that had been smeared on my face the moment I saw the blood on the toilet wall? I could wash it till the cows came home, shave it till the skin was raw, but it wouldn't be the slightest bit cleaner. And it would give me away, betray my fear and feeling of impending doom, which I was trying to shake off but which was in no hurry to go away. There wasn't anywhere to retreat to – ahead lay the scary unknown but behind me was a roaring abyss. What choice did I have?

* * *

"OK if I smoke?"

"Please do."

With a swift movement I reached into my pocket for a

lighter and brought the flame close to the tip of his cheap cigarette. He began to puff happily and smiled.

"Strange why you muckrakers should be interested in this matter?" He slyly screwed up his eyes and held out his hand. "Pavel Minaev."

"Andrei Tsarikov," I introduced myself, smiling awkwardly and pressing his cold hand. I didn't expect an investigator, who'd of course see this hopeless case as a set-up, to be so polite and friendly towards me. He stood very straight and was amiable though at times there was a touch of insolence in his eyes.

"By the way, I can't remember, did you show me your identity card?" He suddenly asked me as though he'd just remembered. My ears started burning and I lied:

"Yes." Then, frightened by my own cheek, I added: "But if you've forgotten, I can get it out again..." I fished in my pocket where there was of course no such card. I now knew myself to be in the den of the enemy; although that young investigator, to whom clearly nothing of what had happened here was of any particular importance, was incredibly vague, I didn't relax but instead kept a very firm hold on myself.

"OK," he growled, tired of waiting, and I breathed a sigh of relief.

"I've got it somewhere..."

"Tell me, what's of interest to you here?" he wheezed, after inhaling.

"His personality," I blurted out.

"His personality?" Minaev smirked. "Whose personality? That poor wretch who was shot down in the smelly toilet? You think he's from the mafia? Or perhaps a local underworld boss?" He laughed insolently.

"And what's your reading of it?" I was still able to hide my agitation. "I've no feel for who that man was; I haven't even seen his body. My boss gave me a job to do and, like you, I'm here to do it. That's why I'm asking you what's required. So, what do you think? Is the matter worth the trouble?"

"I don't know," he went on, no longer smiling. "I've no concept of your line of work. But this incident is indeed a bit strange…"

"Why strange?"

"I, unlike you, have seen the body, and what's more, I've examined it very carefully. He's ordinary, so ordinary that you could meet a thousand such types in a crowd. So I assumed this wasn't a matter of a gangland shooting. He had no drugs, no gun, not even a gold chain or a wallet on him. On the other hand, he may have been robbed. According to the barman, he frequented this café, had a cup of cheap coffee and on the odd occasion he came with a girlfriend or some friends. He even bought himself a glass of dark beer at times. So tell me, where does such a man fit into gangland circles?" he smiled. "But that's the way it looks at first glance. It's very possible that the guy owed someone a substantial sum, or was blackmailing some moneybag… but in that case we would have found some physical signs of intimidation on his body, you see what I mean?"

"Sure."

"There remains another explanation: a drunken brawl, an altercation, a shot, a body. But the café staff deny this. Then perhaps he came here straight from where an incident occurred, the person holding a grudge followed him and in a fit of passion, blew the wretch's brains out. And those barmen didn't notice a thing."

"Well, yes, that's entirely plausible," I complimented him on this handy version of events.

"It's possible," he reflected, giving a big stretch. "Only I find it hard to believe."

"Why?"

"The killer shot from the neighbouring cubicle through the wall and besides, it hit him right through the temple. Would an enraged man in the throes of jealousy, for example, not have beaten the door down and shoved the wretch's head a couple of times into the toilet bowl? He did break the door down, but only after he'd shot him."

"He'd wanted to check that he was dead…"

"Yes, undoubtedly so," Minaev crushed his cigarette butt in the ashtray. "Got any cigarettes? I've finished mine."

"Of course, here you go." I handed him a packet and within a few minutes he was puffing away again. I wish he were not thinking this through so painstakingly. If he goes on this way, for all I know, he may get to the awful, idiotic truth.

He was sitting sideways to the window. The light fell on one of his stubbled cheeks with the other hidden in shadow, giving his face a twisted look. Every now and then he would guide his cigarette to his mouth, which sloped sideways. A slippery type – the thought sprang to mind. Minaev was not a good-looker and I guessed therefore that a firm character and sharp wit would be his main weapons in relations with women – and with men for that matter, of whom I was one. He spoke distinctly and correctly which meant he was well educated. But his old-fashioned hairstyle, unappealingly smoothed down with a long sleek fringe, revealed a man prone to habits possibly fostered in him by an old granddad. No, if he wasn't able to rid himself of what was clearly spoiling his appearance then he wasn't at ease with his inner self.

"I can't yet tell precisely who he was and what he did," he said. "It's still unknown. He lived and worked somewhere nearby because he often came to this café but as of yesterday morning we've yet to get anything specific."

"And when will anything be known?"

"Today, I hope," he got up and walked over to the window. "You can leave me your number. When I have something to tell you I can call you."

"Fine," I agreed and jotted down my number on a scrap of paper. "There you are."

"Only I won't promise anything," he said reluctantly.

"Goodbye." There was no reply from him, only a nod.

I left the office and was about to make my way to the exit when I noticed a young man hurrying down the corridor. I stopped and began to check the information boards on the wall. The young man shot past me towards Minaev's office. I decided to hang on a little longer as he might be just what I needed, bringing news of the victim. I turned out to be right. A moment later Minaev leapt out of his office, but stopped when he saw me.

"You've not gone yet?"

"No," I replied, and my knees began to shake. Why was he staring at me so?

"Come into my office, we can talk there."

"OK."

Minaev went briskly back into his office, flung himself into his old armchair, tapped his fingers restlessly on the table and finally turned to me with a very disgruntled look. I have to admit that I was on the brink of making a run for it without any explanations or questions. But I stayed. Most probably because my legs were just not obeying me.

"I don't know what to make of it." Minaev rolled his eyes.

"What do you mean?" I retorted, almost in a stutter.

"I never stop being astounded at the impudence of your kind! Not only are you after more blood, tears and injustice, but you also want to load it all on us foolish cops! And as for helping the investigation – there can be no question! By the way, were you yourself not interested in finding out more about criminal liability? In other words, in joining those who are loafing about in prison?"

"What?" I could hardly speak.

"Do you take me for a fool? You questioned me with the guise of an innocent lamb about that... man, meanwhile knowing full well who he was. Were you trying to find out how we operate? Because of the likes of you all sorts of maniacs are roaming the streets these days!"

* * *

I've always lived by my own rules. Even if those rules are dumb, at least it's good to feel that it's your own dumbness and no one else's, to know that I'll be dumb within my own boundaries, without going beyond them. I've always been aware of this dumbness, yet I kept on living by its rules. It seems that I've lived by them my whole life, ever since I was born.

On my forehead, right in the middle of my hair, I carry an absurd memento of my childhood. I don't remember how, where or when, but I clearly see, as though it were yesterday, a set of swings, with peeling dark red paint, flying straight into my face. Within an instant bright red blood was gushing out. So off I went to our good old doctor and he stitched up my wound with my granddad firmly holding my arms. The scar was in the middle of my forehead, I do remember that, but it's much higher today. That damned scar crept higher and higher under my hair with the aim of remaining hidden from sight forever. But my head couldn't go on growing endlessly and so my scar ended up millimetres from the hairline. Now no one can tell me that I had no childhood. It's been an eyesore ever since.

Also a pair of shabby child-size green slippers, in the shape of some short-eared drunken hare. I remember disliking wearing them, because my dog, who died a year after I got those unfortunate slippers, immediately pounced on them. I soon got fed up with having to pull her away, all fired up as she was, and I put my slippers back on the shelf in the hall. I still managed to wear them out after the dog left them alone – as did everyone else – when she went off to her own doggie paradise.

At school I always had a small bunch of friends I had fun fooling around with at break time or during boring lessons. They changed over the years: a new one would join us, another would fall by the wayside. I might be on equal terms with one, take advice from another or be the one in charge myself. We always sat together in one row and if we couldn't control our laughter, we'd all be chucked out, and our cheerful racket would sweep through the empty school corridors until the doctor with the odd hairdo darted out of her office and shut us up. Now, when I recall those friends' names, their faces convulsed with laughter, their knees smeared with green antiseptic, their dusty satchels, I understand them and myself less and less. The one who was studying biology and physics, and who squinted so badly when he cheated that his eyes ached, is there no longer. Nor the one who tore a girl's sleeve in a friendly squabble and whose thick literature exercise book she ripped to shreds in return. Nor the one who felt uncomfortable when playing truant and, if he did, would hide from the teachers who'd suddenly appear on his path. And when I think of all this, I feel sick at heart, not because I wish it all back. I simply no longer understand the person I was then.

I broke out of school as though it had been a prison. No, I wasn't beaten or humiliated, I was considered a decent, well brought-up boy. But if I happened to get a top mark, the teachers' eyes grew wide with astonishment. It's since then that I haven't been able to believe that I could be good at anything. I can come over as arrogant and self-assured but if someone tells me I'll be a success I'll pull a face meaning:

"Of course, I know that." But inside I'll be telling myself: "Why me, why not Vasya or Petya?"

Every summer I was taken to the country where all my cousins would gather together. I ate berries, watered the cucumbers and tomato plants and walked around barefoot. In the evenings I disappeared and only came back towards midnight. It was in the country that I had my first taste of vodka, my first kiss and that I dislocated my foot so that I couldn't walk for a week. I once upset my grandma, but I can't remember what it was about. I stayed in my room having a really hard time of it. I remember I didn't even go out to play football with my friends. In the end, in floods of tears, I wrote my grandma a note to apologize. My cousin returned the note, laughing away and saying that grandma had found five mistakes in it. I've never apologized since, particularly when I'm really in the wrong.

Sometimes my parents sent me to some summer camp or other and I'd begin to pack my bag a week ahead, but when I arrived there I'd discover that I'd forgotten some vital thing such as a toothbrush or a windcheater. The whole time I'd go round in the same shorts and tee-shirt, I rarely combed my hair, and washed my feet every other day. My bed was forever littered with sand or crumbs. Mum didn't recognize me when I got back. In camp I fell in love with an older girl, beautiful and inaccessible. Our whole group had a crush on her. When that camp ended and we all went our separate ways I even shed a few tears, yet now I don't remember her name or her face. The day the photographer came, her mother had taken her away to town for her dad's birthday. Now when I think back on those days, what first comes to mind are the damp clothes and bedding and also the sound of pop music in the evening twilight and swarms of huge mosquitoes. Those were probably my happiest days and now when in some marketplace I hear an old song they used to play at discos in my childhood, I stop and travel back there where, in battered flip-flops and with bitten nails, I was free.

Then I went to university, joining the language and literature department. In the first year I studied diligently, went to all the seminars and prepared for the exams like crazy. I very much wanted to become a journalist. In my fifth year I just managed to complete my thesis but when I brought home my diploma I quite forgot why I'd so desperately wanted to go to university, a place it had been so hard to get away from, even if I did have something to show for it. I completely lost my head. I had no money, no experience, no steady girlfriend. After some binging episode my mum looked up a job vacancy in the paper, which she shoved into my hands announcing that she no longer intended to feed me. I didn't believe her, but out of curiosity I found myself within two weeks sitting at a computer in a stuffy office, issuing insurance policies, having watched how others went about it for a few days at first and learning on the job. I soon got fed up with it but I wanted to eat and was loath to trouble my mother. I was twenty-seven. Imagining that I'd have to spend my whole life that way, I decided that I was still young enough to change things. To go back to what I'd studied for, when I still remembered about freedom, when I still understood the person I no longer am.

* * *

Evgeny Skvortsov. Aged 34. Unmarried. Never was and never will be now. No record of any offspring. I somehow wished that he'd had a son, somewhere far away, who was living with his mother, who'd have nothing to do with this Skvortsov, but that the son's features and body and perhaps character were like his father's – a man who no longer existed. It would have meant that he wasn't altogether dead. And that I wasn't altogether a murderer. And therefore not very guilty.

He came to our town five years ago, having before that several times changed localities, lodgings, women maybe, so that my wish wouldn't be that far-fetched after all. I didn't get hold of a list of his addresses, jobs and activities and there was no need for that. Everything that had happened to him at one time had now been transferred to a strange world, to my memory. How could I remember that which hadn't happened to me, which I simply hadn't known or seen or experienced? Somehow without having the slightest notion about his life, only having seen his death, I suddenly began to see what had happened before but didn't take in what had happened in front of my very eyes. What hadn't existed in my head now appeared unexpectedly, but what had been, vanished. Or was that how I wanted it to be?

He'd worked as a journalist for five years. Small fry, with little success, he'd made no name for himself and only after his death did he make others write about him, pay attention to him, mention him with big letters in a headline. In the past his name only rarely got placed somewhere below a small item in equally tiny script. Now my name was to appear under an article, a rather short one too, about him. My first article. My debut.

Minaev scared me when he said I knew that poor wretch who was murdered in the café. I actually hadn't known him but in the inspector's mind I must have. He worked for that same paper I so badly wanted to work for. Korpevsky must have known him. But I didn't. I suspect that Korpevsky hadn't been informed that the young man whose brains had been spattered across the toilet's plastic wall had worked earlier that day in his office and had perhaps dashed off the usual banalities, tormented by lack of money and boredom. There was no doubt about that; I heard about it from two of his colleagues. And if that were so, then I was in luck. Excited, I imagined the editor's astonishment when he found out from my article that the man who'd died in strange circumstances was someone who'd worked for him. Then my labour wouldn't be so shallow and uninteresting. I wrote with inspiration. All night. While the revolver, hidden in its paper wrapping, lay quietly in the corner.

I'd found out so little about him that I couldn't find the words at first. He had no family, didn't like making friends, had no reputation as a professional, he didn't have a girlfriend, or if he did, it would have been somewhere else. Having spoken for a few minutes with his colleagues, who I found smoking and chatting near Korpevsky's office, I suddenly understood that Skvortsov was the sort of man you sometimes think of as being a square peg in a round hole. I didn't write that. Who was I indeed to judge his mission in life? Who was I? I would have been comparing myself to his mother who gave him life, which I then took away.

I only wrote about who he was, who he worked with, giving no opinions, and that he was found dead in the men's room of a basement café with a hole in his head and seated on a toilet. Suddenly the awful meaning of this popped up willy-nilly in my mind, though that was not my intention: his death turned out to be the only interesting part of his life. Interesting for others, because neither I nor anyone else knew anything about his life.

A murder – what can be more momentous or appealing to readers? Enigmatic and irrevocable. That's what I thought, and to sound even more alarming I threw up a few scenarios, which could fully pass for the truth. They were prompted by Minaev. Skvortsov might have been killed because he knew too much, or out of jealousy, or because of debts or blackmail – just conjectures but perfectly plausible. After much wavering and repeatedly deleting black letters from the white screen, I attempted to write a less plausible version. It was only by daybreak, with the light and silence outside giving the impression that there was no one there besides myself, that I squeezed out a couple of lines to the effect that the murder could have been accidental – improbable yet accidental – and therefore almost divine, not of this world. I saved it and clicked the cross in the corner of the screen. I turned off the computer by pressing the red button at the mains with my foot. I knew that it could damage it but I was out of energy. I closed my eyes and switched off. I hadn't slept so soundly for a long time. And I had no dreams.

* * *

Korpevsky didn't call me for three days. Meanwhile the article was lying on his desk, collecting dust and losing its relevance. It tormented me and while occasionally glancing at the phone I tried to convince myself not to despair. No one had told me that my article would be published, but I so wanted it to be that every day began with a pleasant detachment from a reality where I so far counted for nothing. Korpevsky still hadn't rung and I was forced to hold back from reminding him of my existence. He'd strongly warned me not to bother him with phone calls. And I, strangely, during those three days forgot about Skvortsov. That article had only to do with me now.

It finally happened. I lifted up the receiver and took some deep breaths, then put it down again, rushed to the coat rack, grabbed my jacket and sped off. I had an appointment – Korpevsky himself was expecting me in his office, puffing on his usual expensive cigar. I still think that he had an extra source of income or else he wouldn't have had such refined tastes.

He was sitting surrounded by smoke that gave out a pleasant, aromatic rather than an acrid smell. I adore it; I myself smoke low-quality cigarettes, but even those I love. He was holding my article in his hands, running his eyes over it, as though he'd only then decided to look at those few lines, which had landed on his desk three days before. He finally looked at me, as I nervously sat in the chair opposite him, fiddling with the lighter in my jacket pocket.

"The article is so-so..." Korpevsky said grudgingly, flinging the piece of paper back on his desk. I said nothing – I had no time to think of anything, nor feel a sense of failure before he added perfectly calmly, "but I'll take you on, I have a place."

"I'm glad, thank you," I replied, relieved. "Very glad."

"Naturally."

"And the article?"

"What about it?"

"Will you still publish it?"

"No," Korpevsky snapped back. "It's of no interest. Well written, I grant you, but of no interest."

"Why are you taking me on?" I'd got to really liking the article, but Korpevsky was right somehow. It could only be of interest to me, after all I knew a tiny bit more than anyone else. Having just realized this I felt as though I was harbouring a massive bar of gold, very valuable and attractive, but also red-hot and weighty, in my chest.

"I can also not take you on," Korpevsky shrugged his shoulders.

"No, no, I accept..."

"I need someone. You wrote the article and must know that my journalist... one of my journalists died. I'll take you on for a trial period and can throw you out any time. What do I have to worry about? You write competently, even if somewhat boringly. You've got a couple of months to make good. I understand that writing about Sinitsin is rather lame… Try something better, look for it yourself…"

"What Sinitsin?"

"I mean Skvortsov. I hardly knew him…and didn't like him."

"Why?"

"Why? …What does it matter?" He suddenly fixed his eyes on me, looked me all over, then added: "I don't think much of you either at the moment; I hope you won't be like all those Skvortsovs who makeup some rubbish and then with a sour face submit it to me to look at…"

"You didn't know him at all…" I muttered, not pleased with myself and with such a bitter taste in my mouth that I felt the need for a big glass of water right there and then.

"You knew him?" Korpevsky looked surprised.

"No."

"But you look so offended as though Skvortsov was your brother!" He laughed.

"You're replacing him with me?" I said, still distressed.

"Yes, it's no longer his position. From tomorrow you'll be sitting in his chair."

"His chair?"

"What's the matter with you, Tsarkov? You're not yourself." Korpevsky crossly put out his cigar in the ashtray and looked mockingly at me through a haze of smoke.

"Nothing's wrong. I'm just sorry about the article going to waste; I liked it… But it's no big deal, I'll write another one. So, I'm to come here tomorrow?" I prattled on without looking him in the eye and oblivious to the fact that he'd mispronounced my name. I wished the earth could have swallowed me up because I was ashamed and angry with myself. I should not accept. I shouldn't but I did.

"Yes, tomorrow. And you'll have to write another article, lots of other articles..."

I hope they won't be as hard to write as the first one...

I walked along the corridor past offices and rooms where people were sitting in comfortable chairs, chatting, laughing, making tea or staring knowledgeably at their computer screens. I stopped by one of those rooms and took a closer look at a desk shoved into a corner, by the radiator and the window. By it stood a chair facing the door, just as if the person who'd sat there last had got up and gone out for a moment. A young girl sat at the neighbouring desk, chatting on the phone. I walked up to her and leant against the corner of her desk, and she looked up at me expectantly, covering the receiver with her palm.

"Is that Skvortsov's place?" I said, still looking towards that corner.

"Yes. Are you the new employee?"

"Yes," I replied casually. His computer had been switched off, notes in various colours were stuck to the wall unit alongside it and next to piles of papers and folders lay a pencil with its end showing traces of tooth marks. I frowned. It was unbearable to look at it and I began to feel awfully sorry for myself: every day from now on I'd be strangely tormented with a memory that I did not actually have and never could have. I'd be imagining him sitting there daydreaming, hoping for someone's love and thinking about the future... He may indeed have been a completely hopeless case who'd just wanted to die but I'd never find out.

* * *

Water trickled down the window pane. Through it you could make out blurred shadows of houses, trees and bustling passers-by. In my tiny bedroom there was just enough room for the bed to be pushed against the window. By sitting on it and pressing my knees against the radiator, I could then place a pillow beneath my elbows and rest them on the windowsill; I leant my forehead against the glass and peered down at the street awash with rain. Autumn was drawing in through the window. I shivered and pulled the blanket up over me. Outside there was the soft steady drip of rain. I always feel sad when I see water. They say that it stores people's memories.

On such days you recall those you once loved and the awareness that the link has been irredeemably lost brings on incredible sadness. And the main point is that that link is no longer of any consequence to anyone, least of all to you. Time is like water – you won't get another look in. But I wasn't remembering loved ones, or former friends, or distant or close relatives. I was remembering a person who'd only briefly crossed my path.

For a few years I stored a text in my old mobile phone: "I can't write, people *slip* here☺" I moved it more than once from an old mobile to a new one but then it somehow disappeared. I'd been careless. But then, what did it matter, I still remember it as I do many others. Previously, when I happened to stumble on it, I'd return to that strange weak-kneed sensation aroused by a girl from faraway France with the common, affectionate name Natasha.

I don't know why she came to us, to the cold winter darkness, who or what she was after. How had the thought of self-imposed exile come into her sensible European head, why such punishment? I admit I was sorry for her. But mostly I was baffled at her absurdly candid and uncomprehending eyes. I didn't understand her either. We just knew something else about each other then, something that hasn't yet been given a name.

She'd literally flown in from another planet and when I saw her for the first time I was really shocked: foreigners' faces can sometimes be so unlike ours, in their expression and the gleam in their eyes. And over there on the other planet, people speak entirely differently, think differently, they have different dreams and aspirations, they think we should live in a different way and are amazed at the simple things that make up our daily lives, something we've long been accustomed to. It all really separates us, but only in the first moments of meeting. Six months went by and she had to leave. It was then I noticed how close we were and that her looks and speech no longer seemed alien.

I don't know what it was all about and why her or me. But after she left we became friends by correspondence. In every letter I told her about my life. It was to her I once confessed that I'd fallen in love, it was to her I entrusted my secret dream of being a great journalist. She was the one who gave me support, responding with her own aspirations. Is there such a thing as an 'informational' relationship? I now believe there is. But I lost her physically, I couldn't feel her presence and I sometimes imagined that my letters flew off into the dark and a phantom brought back the replies. When rain beats against the window I remember her, or perhaps not her exactly, but the feeling that she aroused in me. What that feeling really is I can't understand either, but I miss it badly and I doubt I'll ever find it again with anyone else. And when I see people asleep I often think that they don't sleep but "*slip*". And it leaves me feeling both amused and sad.

Sometimes I think that God brings us together with people who are entirely unlike us so that we learn to overcome boundaries. Once we've grasped that, we understand that basically there's not much difference, and if there is it's only a positive thing. I ran my finger across the steamed-up glass. For some reason we often walk past those He brings us into contact with. We don't linger, as if we're afraid to lose a tiny bit of our freedom. But here I was without it and I didn't feel free at all when there was no one by my side. For some reason God takes away from us those with whom we've found a connection we don't want to lose. I don't know whether it could have been kept up for another couple of years: after all it would have faded to nothing in the wind and snow. Even that teaches us something important, which can only be understood with the passing of years.

When I think of people and am afraid of being forgotten by them, I clearly feel that I may not exist at all, that I've simply invented myself, together with those who may have loved or remembered me. That's probably how it is. If everyone around me were to forget me, I'd burst like a soap bubble.

The rain went on beating against the windowpanes and although it did so gently they still rattled. As if the cold was blowing through the glass at me; my skin, particularly on my cheeks and the tip of my nose, was pleasantly cool and damned tears got stuck in my eyes. Having sat this way with the rain just out of reach for at least half an hour, I abruptly got up and on my way to the kitchen I suddenly stopped. There, on the little table in the hall, amongst all kinds of small useful and useless paraphernalia, lay, unnoticed for several days, a tiny scrap of paper. Only then did I really understand that anything is possible. I had to see her, the one whose name I had in fact forgotten.

* * *

Nothing like this had happened to me in a long time. I'd left that romantic feeling of trepidation behind me for a few months now. That feeling of flying when you're walking. And now I wasn't walking, I was flying to the place where we'd agreed to meet, filled to the brim with a pleasurable ache and bittersweet delight.

The rain had subsided an hour before. I took out a black, warm and expensive overcoat, or rather a long jacket, from the wardrobe. The most stylish one my almost empty wardrobe could provide. Blacker than the night. Then my autumn boots, more like long-toed slippers, made of thin black leather with thin soles – I'd polished them until they sparkled. Touching them seemed hazardous so I put them to one side and admired them from the corner of my eye while I pressed the creases on my trousers which were also black. Rummaging through my drawers and scouring every shelf in the cupboard, I discovered a jet-black shirt, never worn and therefore clean. Throwing any superstitions to the wind, I pulled all those things on and stood before the big mirror. Without looking at my face I sized up my outfit. When dressed all in black I always discovered the eastern look in me. But it also made my blue eyes appear brighter and more expressive, only I wasn't looking at them at all this time. I can't remember any other occasion when I'd got dressed up with such care.

My black umbrella beckoned from the table in the hall but I went past it and turned the squeaky door lock. It was only when the door banged shut behind me that it shot into my mind, together with the cold wet rain. But to go back would have been a bad omen. I believe in omens very selectively, or perhaps someone else makes that strange choice…

Outside, a surprisingly warm breeze stroked my cheeks and I was quick to rejoice. But within a few steps I became aware of it grabbing my sides and ears with a biting chill. Even the coat couldn't rescue me but that actually had nothing to do with the weather. The rain was softly dripping over the puddles without touching me. I didn't have the time to pay attention to all that nonsense; I was running late like a young girl who'd forgotten the time preening herself and toying with her heartstrings.

I sat down on a bench under a cumbersome awning, the third one from the park entrance, in the left row, next to the large oak. That's exactly where I should have got to ten minutes earlier. Catching my breath, I checked the time on my mobile: I was a little late but only by a couple of minutes after all. She wasn't there, she wasn't punctual either. I breathed a sigh of relief and began to watch the people coming under the arch that marked the park entrance.

There weren't that many. A man in a dark jacket holding a parcel was walking straight ahead with measured steps, his paunch sticking out. Next to him a playful little boy of about ten, a rucksack slung over one shoulder, a warm tilted cap on his head, was running through the puddles, and the man swore under his breath whenever he came near enough to almost spray his trousers. The rain stopped. I looked up at the grey sky – a little bird ruffled by the cold flew straight to a bare tree. Scanty grubby clouds hung in wisps above the houses. The feeble rays of a pale and tired sun struggled to break through to the earth, the passers-by and me – with little success. Suddenly from high above, from the sky's brightest and highest point where there was an almost imperceptible yellow gleam, huge white flakes began to fall and I just kept on looking and looking… When the first snowflake landed on my warm face I glanced again at the arch. And there I caught sight of the girl.

She was trying to walk in a straight line, placing each foot down rather clumsily and not managing to get it quite right. All because she wore stiletto heels. The snow clung in white impermanent blobs to her dark-brown coat. Yes, she too wore an overcoat. Double-breasted, with large buttons and an upright collar. Through the slit you could see her skirt, made of lightly ribbed dark grey fabric. I noticed that, when she came very close to me. She held both her gloves in one hand.

She slowed down and I was about to stand up to greet her as befits a gentleman. But suddenly a huge snowflake landed right in my eye and I blinked instinctively and a moment later when I opened my eyes I realized that the girl had walked past. As I watched her go I understood my mistake. The one who'd left me the scrap of paper with the phone number wasn't that tall. I did remember that much. Even stilettos wouldn't have brought her to my height.

All my attention was once more riveted on the arch and feelings of dejection were gradually compounded with a curious excitement. It had been a while since I'd been fishing. I subjected every person who appeared in the distance to a visual analysis. But time passed and I began to wish I had felt boots and a fur hat.

About forty minutes went by, my big toes were numb with cold and I'd already stopped wriggling them every so often. It made no difference. Other walkers hurried by without leaving footprints because the wet white snow covered those instantly. I abandoned all hope of detecting among the stream of faces one familiar one, the one I wanted to see though I no longer knew why. I reluctantly got up from the warm bench and the wind lashed at my sweaty back. I wanted to move away but my hand, of its own accord, dug into my pocket and pulled out the phone. I dialled the number and began to count the rings, feeling my heart madly pumping blood right down to my heels... one, two, three... the receiver was picked up on the sixth ring and before the person at the other end could say a word and to my own surprise, I unexpectedly bellowed:

"Where are you?"

"Andrei?"

"Yes, this is Andrei," I said, slightly calmer, tugging the coat sleeves over my frozen fingers.

"I'm sorry, I'm not well and it's so cold outside…"

"And you couldn't have warned me sooner?" I exploded. "I'm standing here like an idiot in the snow…"

"If you're going to shout I'll hang up," she calmly cut me short. "I've just said I'm sorry. It's the way it is…"

"It's always the way with you girls… And there's no need to lie that you've been taken ill; you were just seeking revenge, is that it?"

"What for?" I could hear a chuckle. "I've caught a cold, I've got a sore throat…"

"You have? It doesn't sound like it," I went on, angry of course at my own rudeness and today's unnecessary stress. Who was I to question her? She had every right not to turn up and not feel the slightest bit to blame. Every right, so much so that she could delete my number and never answer my calls. But I kept going, not having the strength to stop.

"Listen, what do you think you are, a doctor?"

"There's no need for a doctor here, it's all perfectly clear."

"No, you're not a doctor, you're a detective," she began to laugh. "Perhaps you'll invite yourself here to check that I'm not lying?"

"I will," I screamed at her without thinking and heard a sharp intake of breath at the other end. After a few seconds of uncomfortable silence she replied:

"Fine. Memorize this address…."

* * *

Irina, I remembered now, Irina was her name. Standing by the entrance to a grey clapboard house with a black door by which yellowish-red leaves were juggling with the wet snow, I smoked. As though it were my last cigarette. I seemed to inhale the smoke right down to the pit of my stomach and didn't exhale it at all. All that because in there, inside me, lodged a combination of fear and joy, a cruel and abject joy. I hated myself deeply at that moment, but what for and why?

About half a lifetime ago, at thirteen or fourteen, I'd prepared myself for death. For an absurd and agonizing death. I found out about it myself, reading up about various illnesses in scary books. The images in the section on venereal diseases made a particular impression on me, and the fact that you could become infected by syphilis in communal baths or swimming pools made the most sense to me. I once discovered, just below my stomach and even lower, a generous scattering of red spots. With time they spread, were sometimes itchy, and sometimes flared up causing a nasty pain. I told no one. It's a shameful disease after all, one that makes you think that hanging yourself might be simpler. Then the rash disappeared – which meant that I'd reached the third stage, having somehow avoided the primary one. Which meant that nothing would help, that I was doomed. To die of syphilis at the age of twelve. Days, weeks, months went by ... I knew all there was to know about syphilis. Fired up, I read about that terrible disease from which people had died in the old days in their hundreds and even thousands. About legs losing their balance, about noses falling off. I now checked every day that my nose was still intact. It seemed to be slipping lower and lower down my face. In such moments I was more terrified than I'd ever been before. It wasn't the pain, death, or even the shame that I feared, but the fact that I'd die without having lifted a finger to save myself. No one had diagnosed me – I'd come up with it myself, you see. Others might have envied this unconditional faith in my own ideas, but I tormented myself beyond belief. How could I not believe if I felt worse and worse over time? Now that death was at my door, I thought I should go to church. It was the first time that I'd gone there by myself. And when, looking across the dozens of lit candles, I turned my gaze to Jesus on the cross, my inner voice suddenly started repeating that it wanted to live. Tears ran down my cheeks and there was no point in wiping them away. To live, live, live, just live. I left the church convinced that I was completely healthy.

I changed, if not right away. I didn't come to love life senselessly. I didn't stop fearing death, I didn't understand its inevitability and therefore its ordinariness. I didn't go and see the doctor more often, didn't read up less about diseases. I'm a hypochondriac but that wasn't the issue. I just found it ridiculous to think back on those days. Just ridiculous, with not a drop of hurt or fear. But I do clearly remember how I hated myself back then for being unable to stand up to myself, for that strange reluctance to lose faith in the horror and believe in the better. I hated that feebleness in me. Though not immediately, I did learn to be strong, I learned to wrestle with myself, I learned to laugh at the past if that made me feel better... I thought that I'd learned all that but now as I stood at the door and watched the bright leaves juggling with the snow, I understood that I still had a lot to learn and over a long period of time. And cigarettes are bad companions. The difference is that now I couldn't conceive of Skvortsov suddenly being alive. And to laugh at those days in the past was wrong. Cigarettes... they're just so much smoke.

I finished my cigarette. I threw the butt in the leaves, spoiling their beauty. But no matter, a thick layer of snow would soon cover that puny thing and then everything would be whiter than white. I'd still be all in black. I suddenly felt my mobile buzzing in my pocket. I got hold of it and pressed the button.

"Andrei, are you going to be standing under the window much longer?"

"Can you see me?" I glanced up at the neighbouring window but couldn't see anything.

"I can. Come up. It's cold outside."

"I'm coming," I tugged at the door. "Open up, it's locked…"

"Of course it's locked. Press 112 on the intercom…"

* * *

"I'm having raspberry tea, do you want some?"

"Yes, thanks," I smiled and she left me alone in the empty room for a moment. Everything was soft and cosy in there, with fun pictures on the walls and dried flowers and branches in a bright vase on the chest of drawers. The colours didn't grate on the eye and your body wallowed in the profusion of cushions. She herself was like that. I stuck out like a black stain against the pastel tones.

In the hall, when she'd helped me hang up my coat in the closet I'd been sharply aware of this, having thrown a cursory glance in the large mirror opposite. Every single one of our features accentuated our differences. At first I saw the hair. Impossible to overlook – a mop of dark blonde hair with natural golden-red highlights, slightly dishevelled, probably deliberately so, gathered at the back in an untidy pony tail that casually slid down her right shoulder. And her fringe, scrunched up to one side, just touched her left eye. My hair – short black curls along the sides and forehead, with an uneven hairline, twice mildly dented by high temples. In the back the hair, recently cut, twisted spiral-fashion towards the top of the head, one spiral smoothly set next to the other, and it never got ruffled, even after a shower. If allowed to grow just slightly, it would settle into smooth waves. Then the eyes. Grey… no, light-green with brown speckles. Elongated like almonds but narrow because the lower lids crept up over them and gave her the look of only just having got up. Mine – light blue, without any tinge. Big, would be bulging had the upper lid with its soft folds not covered half the eye, giving me a veiled look. Next I examined the nose. Small, short and straight, neither wide nor narrow, without anything extra or pretentious. Mine, on the other hand, was rather long, but delicate and slightly hooked and pointed at the end, in other words, poking itself where it's not wanted. Lips – hers were light, shapely, with a prominent upper lip. Mine were dark with a prominent lower lip. Her face was oval-shaped, mine definitely triangular-shaped. And the body… as she hung my coat up she moved so naturally and simply that I couldn't help noticing her softness. Under her skin, which was fair, there was a definite, smooth, evenly spread layer of fat. Under mine, which was dark and sallow, there wouldn't have been much room left for fat. I'm lean and sinewy, with skinny, slightly bowed legs, big hands and a stuck-out chest. Of course we couldn't be alike. Irina was the complete opposite of me in everything. Even in what we wore. In the mirror opposite as I took off my boots and tried on some slippers, I gave a silly smile when I saw how that one splash of yellow cheered up my whole sombre look. I noticed that she wore lilac tracksuit bottoms and top, with a kangaroo pouch on the tummy, made of warm brushed fabric. We didn't once catch each other's eye in the mirror – I continued to stare at it but she wasn't looking. I looked at myself quite casually as though I'd forgotten about my recent fears. I understood something curiously significant – for some reason I didn't feel tormented alongside her. A feeling to cherish so long as it warmed me, so long as autumn or even winter didn't get a look in.

"Here you are, only be careful." Smiling, she handed me a large mug.

"Ouch, it's hot…"

"I told you to be careful. Don't spill it. By the way, you've not yet caught anything?"

"No. But why 'not yet'?"

"The weather's turning bad, there's snow…No, just slush. Feet get soaked – simple as that. I've already caught something, I've just come in and my boots are wringing wet," she laughed.

"It's only begun to snow today, how have you managed that?"

"It doesn't take much. I've had chronic tonsillitis since I was a child. It only has to blow a little and my throat hurts, and then I start sniffling…" She spoke cheerfully, with a grin and she didn't seem to be holding anything back. "So don't mind me looking like this. I always let myself go at home. My scarf is somewhere, you've not sat down on it, by any chance?"

"This one?" I pulled an old red scarf, warm and soft to the touch, from under a cushion.

"That's the one. You don't mind if I put it on? You won't get scared?"

"Why should I get scared?"

"I look like a scarecrow in it," she sighed and wound the scarf round her neck, which made her appear even more touching. I smiled at her in response. Probably the first genuine smile since we met.

She sat down near me, tucking her right leg under her and resting her left arm on the back of the sofa. Smiling, she looked me straight in the eye and I didn't want to avert my gaze. This rarely happens to me. I prefer to look away before anyone manages to focus on me. That's because you often get the feeling that someone is trying to reach the very depths of your soul or even prize open your heart just for a bit of fun or out of foolish curiosity. But she was looking in an entirely different way. Her gaze hooked me – it took hold of me and I looked back at her without stopping as though I wanted to detect something of consequence that kept on eluding me.

Could it be that it was I who was fixed on her in an attempt to reach her soul? But she was smiling as though keeping herself from laughing. Only her eyes seemed to be hiding an entirely different meaning and I couldn't guess what it was while we looked at each other.

"Drink your tea," she grinned. "It'll get cold. And I've put in so many raspberries…"

"You'd be sorry to see them go to waste?"

"Very sorry. You can see for yourself that I can't get by without them." She gave a forced cough.

"Show me your throat…"

"What?"

"Show me your throat."

"Oh, so that's why you came by! And here I was thinking that you'd come to cheer me up or something but you're just checking…" She pretended to tell me off, holding back a smile. "All right then, have a look." She opened her mouth wide.

I carefully took hold of her throat, wrapped in the soft scarf, and looked straight into it.

"Yes, it's red but only a tiny bit."

I inadvertently, or perhaps on purpose (I didn't know myself), touched her chin with the ball of my thumb and softly stroked her skin.

"You feel hot."

"Of course, I'm not well…"

"You're as hot as you were then, remember?"

"When?"

"Well, when you were at my place. Do you remember how we met?"

"I remember," she burst out laughing and removed my hand. "That was terrible!"

"Why?"

"You don't remember any of it."

I felt confused at first then frowned and bit my lip. Me and my memory – were those two separate things? What did I really remember about our first meeting? About what had preceded the morning? Had she been so unremarkable that I'd forgotten about her straightaway? I'd even forgotten her name. In that case what the devil had dragged me here today? She must have got hold of me somehow. I could see that something had changed in her, and that something was bringing us together.

"I do indeed not remember how we met, you must forgive me. I don't recall the evening or the night, only the morning after. I've drawn a blank…Tell me about it?"

"Certainly not," she taunted me, looking me straight in the eye.

"Was it that bad?"

"No, not at all. Nothing happened. You fell asleep as soon as your head hit the pillow. We just slept next to each other, seriously."

"Really?"

"There'd be a case for lying but I don't lie."

"So nothing happened," I smiled happily, "which means it will."

* * *

This is all true, if succinct. Or, on the contrary, the feelings are there but it isn't at all obvious whether this is the way it really was. Having arrived in the office too early I sat down in the chair, alone in the silence…. Was I really there? The state I'm in when hurrying to a date was nothing compared to this; there was no tingling, no uplift, no niggling in the pit of my stomach. This weighed on me but didn't hold me down like some uncomplaining piece of meat: but it constricted my throat, heart, lungs, belly… and it felt as if all the living creatures would never be alive again.

I stared blindly at the screen – an unknown hand had created folders, sorted by size on a background with an elephant on it, but their names meant nothing to me. I'd seen that hand. Even now, if I close my eyes, I can see it. But I didn't want to picture it being able to bring that cold metal box to life. After all I'd been totally unlike him then. To think of that was upsetting and so, while only the darkness of the small hours came through the windows, I recalled the previous day. Then my head was able, more easily, to take in another person's life…

She liked to drink water. In big gulps, from an iron mug. Her summer childhood days also saw her banishment to the country, but a place where grass was scarce and sand plentiful, in a big Asian state with which less than twenty years ago we formed a large red blot on the multicoloured map of the world among lots of smaller specks. There in northern Kazakhstan, where, she told me, the sun was no stronger than ours, but where it felt twice as stifling and made you incredibly thirsty. So, especially after lunch or supper, her flush-faced family members invariably formed a queue by three water containers, two of them unopened. They drank greedily and with laughter, their teeth knocking against the big iron mugs. I don't know why they laughed, but the number of children with their all too artful ways must have been a reason. There were five of them, then six. When she spoke of that she laughed so wholeheartedly and warmly that I couldn't help but remember my days in the country.

Ira named three traits that characterized her family: a love of water and tea, loud voices and a love of eating often and a lot. That was it. They differed in other aspects, she said, and it wasn't at all interesting talking about that. Anyway, that roomy house, in a perpetual state of being built, rebuilt and nearing completion, was now someone else's and even the dogs who used to breed in the courtyard and live off table scraps, disappeared somewhere, giving up their night shelter under some unclaimed logs and in an old kennel to the new owner's dogs. The logs had gone rotten, the kennel had collapsed and been taken away to the dump together with other junk. Why, there'd been a time when she'd sat on those logs with her brothers and sisters, without a thought that they'd come to such an end. They were theirs and no one else's. No one would dare take them away. No one did, but the house was sold and they all moved here. It should have been cause for rejoicing but a little bit of childhood was now forever in someone else's care and no one would allow her to go back there now. Added to that, she said, lowering her gaze just a little and biting her lip, that was where her first love died and so her heart sometimes longed for that distant land where grass is scarce and prickly but sand is plentiful and in windy weather it can sprinkle over your head like a hot shower. But then the sky comes so close at night that it looks as if the stars are resting on the treetops where flocks of crows and jackdaws make a frightful din. And in the middle of the firmament there is the 'Huge' Dipper. She said that nowhere else does it hang so low.

Then she led the conversation to love. Having set aside her mug with the tea now grown cold, she also stopped telling me off for not drinking mine. I couldn't drink, I was all ears, for she seemed to be talking about me after all. She'd only a couple of times fallen seriously in love, the other times were suppressed by default or converted into a long-term memory, in other words, buried under new junk, new worries, problems, needs... Now and then one of those loves would suddenly rear its head, and after whimpering in her ear for a couple of days, it would fade away again. She wouldn't be able to tell whether it would survive or just die. That love, or infatuation…its hazy boundaries, its confused aim and the illusion of its actual availability annoyed her intensely which is why Ira declared that she would have preferred all those loves just to die, allowing her finally to clear her head. Then she gave a rather strange sigh and mumbled indistinctly that she was always forgetting to love. More precisely, that's what she wanted to think, because forcing yourself to remember about love was a pointless and basically impossible exercise. Because you'd always remember it if it really was there.

But the main thing that distinguished those brief episodes from the two real ones was that sudden nauseating feeling that struck you after a month or two of constant sensations. It's funny, she said, when love was more like the manic pursuit of another person's image and then suddenly turned into something completely the opposite. Finally you wanted to hide away your eyes, your ears and mainly your brain from that image. In those moments her soul somehow remained intact. I just thought that was very sad – when you want to love too much, the end result is almost invariably disastrous. This had happened to me more than once and so I understood her and didn't start accusing her of callousness. After all, she was looking, just looking, maybe not in the right direction but who would show her the way? She had to feel her way, and so did I. Now we were simply getting lightly bruised.

She didn't say much about those two instances. She only said that they both happened in that sandy village, a place where there was now no reason to return to. Then, after a few minutes of empty chatter she suddenly said:

"Do you think I regret anything? Strangely, although there is reason for regret, it never even occurred to me. Maybe it'll still happen, we'll see…"

Ira had recently finished her Teacher Training Course, obtained her certificate and made use of it: she taught English in a language school and sometimes gave private lessons. And she enjoyed that. I wouldn't have believed it had I not seen her eyes when she told me about it. I think that to be a teacher is an awful plight. But I take my hat off to those who find it's for them. It's an incredibly hard job, but she was coping.

We talked for a long time, almost all evening; or rather, she did the talking and I listened. I never thought that listening could be so pleasant. She would ask me about something, I don't remember what, and I'd give a quick answer, only so that she'd begin talking again. And she talked and talked... It was always interesting, always accompanied by a smile, inserting some unusual words, emphasizing some unusual moments, dragging me into her own memory which was full of all sorts. I doubt she even touched upon the tiniest fragment of what she could have. The evening ended and I left her. I left her to return.

She loves to drink water. I smiled like a fool as I sat in the empty office staring into space. Perhaps it was that love of liquid that made her eyes look slightly puffed – what did it matter anyway. Her eyes were beautiful and unlike anyone else's. I understand that now.

* * *

The sky was grey for half the day and around three it began to turn white. Snow covered rooftops and pavements and people were stepping through it, promptly leaving wet black footprints behind them. I sat on the windowsill, warming my feet by the radiator and my hands around a mug of burnt black coffee. I looked down. I felt that the gravitational force released from the tarmac was real. I knew that nothing would make me jump which made looking down extremely pleasant... As though I'd gained a victory.

But I'd lost or was close to it. It was nearly evening and I'd not written a single line. All I'd managed to accomplish in a day was to introduce myself to Katya, the nice girl whose desk was opposite mine, and drink five mugs of cheap complimentary sugarless coffee. Katya ran off somewhere after only twenty minutes in the office, having in that time smiled a couple of times, shown me where the coffee was kept and told me not to go and see Korpevsky that day because he wasn't there nor would be later. So that I spent that first day on my own and to no purpose, going over all that had happened the previous day, the day before and the day before that…and it was only an hour before the end of the work day that Katya returned. She stepped into the dark office with pink cheeks and a businesslike air and pressed the switch by the door. The light came on and I screwed up my eyes.

"Have you sat in the office all day?"

"Yes, in the dark though…" I smiled, trying not to yawn, but Katya gave me a somewhat unpleasantly stern look.

"That's no good. You've got to go out and mingle with people in order to write. What will you write about if you sit in the office all day? It's just as well that Korpevsky isn't here or he'd be lecturing you for at least an hour and a half…"

"I simply decided to get my bearings today, get used to the place, so to say…"

"You need to write an article or else Korpevsky will chuck you out without a second thought. He's hired hundreds before only to fire them… so don't hang around."

Katya lapsed into silence, threw off her jacket and without sitting down in her chair, turned on the computer. It began to hum and collect its thoughts; she made herself a strong cup of coffee and took a couple of sips, then sat down on the edge of her chair with her back to me. The screen lit up and she disappeared into her emails. While this or that letter was being downloaded, Katya examined the ceiling or the walls, hugging her warm mug with her palms. I was really tempted to stick my tongue out at her. It was just as well that she sat with her back to me so that when I did do so she remained unaware and didn't turn round. I too decided to withdraw – I began to open each document in turn on the screen, without understanding any of them and trying not to memorize anything. A sudden thought came to mind: should I delete all of them and to hell with it? I had no use at all for them. But no, I didn't nor ever would dare do that. Why? I know the reason so well that it's impossible to explain in simple terms.

"Has Minaev not been here?" I spoke clearly and Katya turned her head round sharply.

"Who's that?"

"The investigator."

"Oh, the one in charge of Skvortsov's case..." She muttered and went back to her screen. "I think he was here. I probably wasn't here when he came."

"Do you know if he had a look round here?"

"Of course he did. That is, I don't really know but am sure that he searched the computer," she said mockingly.

"What makes you so sure?"

"Andrei," she said somewhat condescendingly and looking me straight in the eye, "this is the crime department, this is where we write about murders. I myself have been doing this for nearly five years."

"That's quite a long time," I smiled. "I most probably won't hold out here that long."

"You won't hold out even a month if you're going to stay put."

"I would have gone out, but where to? I've no ideas in my head... what can I write about? I've written about Skvortsov – it's of no interest."

"Who told you that?"

"Korpevsky."

"Well, he says a lot of things and you should listen to him... I was told that your article would be published in the next issue."

"Really?" I somehow felt no pleasure at all.

"OK..." Katya sat down on the edge of the table so that she could see me without having to turn her head round. "I'll have to give you some help."

"You're going to teach me?" I said somewhat spitefully, though with no real malice.

"No, I'm not being paid to do that. I'll help you with information but you'll owe me."

"Fine, without questions asked."

"It actually doesn't amount to much... How I've come by this story I won't tell you. You understand that we're not being friends here. Well, the fact is that a director of a certain agency was killed. On the same day as our Skvortsov, only earlier that morning..."

"What agency?" I interrupted her.

"Some insurance agency, I wrote the name down but I can't remember it off-hand. Insurance Bureau or something. It's yours –you'll be following your first article with this one. A series in the making. The main thing is that he was also killed in rather a strange way; I think he too was found in a toilet, or near one..."

"Why don't you write the article?"

"I've a lot on my plate as it is, I don't think I can fit it in."

She said something else but all I could see was the button on her jacket: a large wooden button that had once been painted violet, but with the colour fading at the edge, its real skin poking through – maybe buttons also have a skin. For some reason I really wanted to grab that button, arm myself with paraffin and give it a good scrub. On its clear surface the swirls and rings of the wood pattern broke away, enticing my eyes beneath the thin sticky layer of a deadly shade, bright but inanimate. With every minute I moved further and further away from my surroundings, and closer to that tiny bit of dead material. Katya was speaking curtly, moving little, but I only saw the button, everything else was shoved into the background and I didn't want to hear another word. I was probably losing my mind.

"Why aren't you saying anything?" The words suddenly reached my ears.

"I don't want to write about it, sorry," I looked her in the eye and met astonishment. "I can't, simply can't…You must understand, I worked in that agency and knew the director. It's unethical. I mustn't write the article. You do it."

"If I can find the time…" she said reluctantly. "Although you'd do a better job of it as you worked there. You know more…"

I knew more than she could ever imagine. I was sick and tired of it all. I looked at her button one last time, then fixed my eyes back on the computer, settling down to more time-wasting. After opening one document I would instantly close it again, pressing on the mouse even harder. Katya pottered about quietly at her desk. Almost an hour went by, she got up, arranged her hair, pulled on her jacket and turned off her computer. The room became twice as silent. She said a brief goodbye and went out, quietly pulling the door shut. I waited a couple of minutes until her footsteps could no longer be heard in the hall. Then groping for the grey cable on the table, I frenziedly wrenched the mouse from its socket and flung it into the corner. It hit the wall with a faint thud and rolled onto the floor. But it didn't calm me down at all.

* * *

Winter had so brazenly settled on the city that I was slow to discover its beauty. Dreary colours, sombre masses of people muffled up against the cold, hideous slush on the roadside. Then I looked more closely: I smelled the morning frost and made out the intricate tree skeletons under a layer of powdered sugar or big balls of snow-white cotton wool. Then my soul found rest – winter is just a tiny bit more peaceful. In a cooler head your thoughts don't sting so.

I lay on the sofa covered by a thick blanket right up to my chin looking through the window with hardly any thoughts in my head, listening to the silence in the room and the howling wind outside. The light blue, almost transparent blinds masked the sight of the snowflakes hurled along in the blizzard as they were making a frenzied onslaught against the ice-patterned windows. I'd lost patience a few hours before, got up and pressed my face against the window – instead of a daytime sun, a yellow light hanging from a building crane shone brightly in the dark impenetrable night sky. It was so close that it felt as though the sky had fallen onto the rooftop. I looked up but couldn't make out anything. Even the stars had vanished in the gloom and the blizzard.

Across the empty road they were constructing a high-rise building. It completely blocked the sun from the lower floors of the house where I lived. But then, the large old light, suspended above it, was almost burning a hole through the window glass. It was really irritating and one day, or rather one night, I gave way to frayed nerves and in a fit of rage I moved my sofa further away towards the wall, knocking over some shelves in the process. The metal sofa legs scraped the floor with a grinding sound, every trinket rolled down from the shelves, books tumbled to the ground and, satisfied, I threw myself down with my head in my pillow and only put everything back in its place the next morning. Now that damned light only projected some pathetic shreds of its fiery rays into my face. Pushed into a corner the sofa was still dimly and unevenly lit up by that building site light despite the blinds. And there was apparently no getting away from it.

Across the whole façade of the fourth floor, where windows hadn't yet been installed, a projecting section of concrete slabs clearly stood out. It sliced the building with a single horizontal line almost at its base. But that base was on a level with my windows and some small lamps had been placed there, equidistant from each other. They were not always turned on, but if they were lit up at night they'd make me tremble, almost the same way as the annoying beam from that horrid light. At such moments I considered that it wouldn't be a bad thing to invest in some thicker blinds but in the end I only tossed some magazine at the wall and fell asleep in a bad mood. Now, however, with winter calming me down and listening in the silence and the warmth to the distant rustle of the cold wind, I suddenly looked at those lights in an entirely different way.

They were only visible to a certain extent. Just small bright fuzzy stains beyond the blinds. The wind, licking the window glass with its coarse tongue, made me believe that there, beyond them, was something vast, resonant, violent yet also free and empty … the ocean. And the lamps – they weren't burning on a grey building site but on a pier, with a huge white ship alongside, rocking slightly from the raging storm. Beyond that only water, grey or green, I'm not sure. But not icy. I didn't want it to be the Arctic Ocean; it could simply be the sea. The Mediterranean Sea. I'm in France, on the Côte d'Azur, I think in French about my past in a future context. With me is Natasha, Nathalie, Nat… I've no notion of what that country looks like. I've never even seen pictures nor do I want to. I cannot imagine how Natasha has ended up with me, but it's all part of my illusion.

Not long ago, when I said goodbye to childhood dreams, I began to dream as an adult – keenly aware that those dreams could never come true, nor wanting them to. God knows why I need those illusions, all kinds of them, but always mine. Frankly, I think that each person lives a separate life from others with his or her illusion, whether big or small, and no one knows which is more true, the reality or the illusion. Does reality actually exist? If I got up and went to the window I would see it. But lying by the dark window, I was happy with my ship and didn't care whether it was a phantom generated from something weird and hidden inside me.

I watched it for a long time and it was as though I found myself being someone else. They say that even if you run off to the other side of the planet it's impossible to get away from yourself. That may be so. But it's not always been that way with me. I would reach some big foreign city or a small village with just a dozen or so houses and I'd feel that the real me had actually stayed at home and my ownerless body would be knocking about streets and restaurants just wasting time. I couldn't understand whether I was afraid of missing out on something of utmost interest back home, or something of significance only to me. But it's happened that finding myself in transit in a small provincial station where I'd have to hang about for a whole day, I would open a book, shove some headphones in my ears and a meat pie in my mouth and I'd suddenly begin to hear myself. Strangely, I would not wish the hands on the clock to move faster but would, on the contrary, try to hypnotize them to a halt.

It was that way this time. As I fell asleep I began to hear myself. My ship had long vanished and I was left behind. Under the warm blanket I felt for her little palm, squeezed it lightly and glanced over at the neighbouring pillow – Ira was asleep, her mouth slightly open and her hair spread out. I was there. And I hadn't been there for a long time, ever since that day when life had taught me 'self-alienation'. It was better so, and tomorrow morning I wouldn't disappear again under my skin, nor shrink into nothing or be reduced to a little lump there where the neck becomes the head.

* * *

I can apparently put up with any human flaw. Every nasty trait, even if they're the only ones God has bestowed on a person. All this because I'm not at all convinced that I have the right to evaluate other people's characters, dishing out good and bad marks. All this because I feel awful when I think that someone else might size me up just as meanly. Perhaps it boils down to the fact that I don't want to touch someone who would then touch me back and I'm scared of making a mistake.

I'd always thought that I could figure people out better than most, but at the same time I didn't have the gall to establish their 'limits'. I just thought I did, but I now understand that I didn't see a damn thing. After all, every conclusion of mine was based on attire, cigarettes, figure, face, hairstyle and wallet... How could I really have thought then that you could be a murderer, whilst putting on a friendly smile and making a conspicuous sign of the cross when walking past a church.

Ever since I was a child I would hasten to ascribe good traits to people, commending myself for being humane and brave. It was so much simpler, you see, to bad-mouth everyone around you. I would then be like the brightest sunray among the other rays spread fanlike around the darkening sun. But was that the truth? To which I'd once sworn undying love?

Now I was aware of someone hidden in a tiny cage somewhere in my right foot's little toe or in the heel's dead skin. Somewhere where it had remained unnoticed, unfelt and unknown to me. And the feeling it gave me was both unpleasant and joyful. That someone was beginning to discover meanness and greed, stupidity and envy in people. It wasn't the fat belly that helped you recognize a scoundrel, but something that was beating inside him. I began to see inside people, without being afraid of the nausea caused by the sight of the blatant obviousness and deformity of the diseases they were stricken with. But now, as I looked at myself in the mirror or reflected in the window, I began to recognize bleeding sores inside myself too. And the more I looked the better I saw them.

Why had I changed all of a sudden? I'm not sure, but at a time when the only bad feeling within me had been some mild irritation I would credit everyone else around me with similar good feelings. But now that I felt the presence of a rat inside me I had no trouble thinking the same of others. I didn't have the slightest doubt that I was right. I saw this because I knew from experience what they felt and how their soul struggled against this. They might not even notice any of this themselves. And that scoundrel inside me was pleased as well as overcome by sadness. He'd only recently embedded himself in my body, but didn't show up straightaway.

He did show up for good on that morning when Katya, after checking an article on my computer, suddenly smiled spitefully and pointed out a couple of errors. Then she told me somewhat patronizingly that I should have done some more studying before seeking employment with the main city paper. I remained silent and a couple of hours later she offered me a cup of coffee as though nothing had happened. It would have been better if she'd not done that. I only drank coffee with her to avoid telling her to her face what I really thought of her. Stale burnt coffee makes you tongue-tied. It never occurred to me to replace the coffee because I wasn't the only one to have it and she didn't seem to care either way. Perhaps she did care, but she drank it to prove that she wasn't put off by the bitter taste, in other words, she was able to work without being daunted by anything. It was just nonsense but she wouldn't get that. Nor the fact that when she looked for flaws in me and barefacedly pointed them out, she was only convincing me even more of my unseemly thoughts and lack of skills.

I began to see but said nothing. Something might have changed but the main issue stayed the same: I still couldn't bear to analyze my own soul or my intellectual abilities. I feared still being touched by anyone and was therefore not in a hurry to touch others. I didn't say a thing to Ira when I clearly discovered something peculiar in her eyes. You see, she might then have looked into mine...

* * *

Half an hour before the end of the work day I ran away from Katya's recurrent taunting. No, I wouldn't show my cards. Let her judge me as spineless or a polite liar, but I wouldn't utter a single detrimental word against her. She just wouldn't get it and our relationship would be spoilt for good. But with each day there were more stinging comments. I could feel her breathing down my neck and to pressure me. I was afraid it might actually lead to my asking for another desk. But that would have cost me too much. I didn't want someone who didn't know anything about its previous occupant to sit in this chair. It would signal the end for all those folders and papers.

I came out of the metro, swept along by the wind and propelled forward with the other pedestrians. When I lived at home I only had about five minutes' walk. Now I had to walk for over half an hour until I ran into that grey apartment building, where, right under its windows, the building site had unscrupulously found its niche. I knew that Ira wasn't home.

She would turn up a couple of hours from now after finishing her evening classes. She'd go to the shop on the way home and call me from there to ask if we needed anything. I'd tell her to get sugar, so that I didn't have to suffer plain tea. I very rarely bought anything myself. All I had to do was hand over the money. No, I'm not lazy, it's simply that shops fill me with fear and I lose myself among their brands and smells. I've brought home totally unsuitable items more than once before. Women shop a lot more efficiently than men, or at least than me.

I'd moved across to Ira's at the beginning of winter. Our old building was poorly heated and I'd had enough cheek to ask her to put me up for at least a week. Since then neither she nor I had wanted for that very long week to end. I felt so much better there than in the murderer's den where the revolver held sway. It was still lying there in the corner, never touched once, its thick wrapping paper most likely covered with a thick layer of corrosive dust. At times, when falling asleep, I would remember it; there'd be a choking feeling in my throat and a hot, heavy weight in my chest. Nothing could chase away that heat except another kind of heat, the one Ira offered me.

Half an hour's walk in the cold is torture for me. But here was the long-awaited entrance door looming in the snowy wind a hundred paces away. I hurried my step, anxious to feel the warm air of the stuffy entrance hall. I reached for the key in my pocket. By the door I caught sight of a man, hopping from foot to foot wearing a hat covered in ice. As I opened the door he placed himself behind me and slipped in after me. Standing by the lift we both loudly stamped our snow-covered boots and shook the snow off our coats. Once inside the lift the man fixed his eyes on me, then turned away and said nothing. I was about to put him out of my head when he suddenly got out on the same floor as me. I let him go ahead and was extremely surprised when he suddenly, without any hesitation, rang my doorbell. Then again, two more times.

"Who are you looking for?" I asked, stopping beside him.

"Good evening," he looked at me rather suspiciously.

"Good evening. Who are you looking for?" I repeated coldly and he suddenly thawed.

"Zhenya."

"Zhenya who?" I smiled and inserted the key in the keyhole, nudging him aside with my shoulder. "Perhaps you've got the wrong floor?"

"No, that can't be. I remember precisely. This floor, apartment 112…There," he tapped the number by the door. "But it's possible Zhenya doesn't live here any more, and you're here."

"You're right. There's no Zhenya here. Goodbye!" I stepped into the corridor and the steel door began to shut slowly behind me.

"Goodbye! Only, Zhenya, he's my friend," he hesitated but when there was only a tiny crack left between him and me he suddenly rushed his words: "Tell Ira that Petrushin came by. I'm looking for Skvortsov, I've something to discuss with him." The door shut, the lock clicked, and the whirring in my head suddenly stopped. Everything came to a standstill.

* * *

I wouldn't allow myself to think. Two hours of no thoughts, two hours of waiting for a terrible verdict, two hours of happiness that I was still there. After a couple of hours I could vanish into thin air, as in a fairytale, as in a horribly bloody fairytale where there's nothing to be surprised at or to live for. For the first time I'd thought that there was still someone, unnamed and unassuming in my life who had a sensitive awareness of me. Or perhaps I was inclined to exaggerate my own role in my story. In the story that was being written not by me.

In the dark, an artificial yellow band of light fell through the door opening, onto the mirror opposite. That damned light – it wouldn't leave me alone, not even there in the hall, in the farthest corner of the hall, into which I'd shrunk without taking off my boots or jacket. It didn't touch me but its sickly yellowish sheen ate its way into my dim pathetic reflection. I looked at myself silently, but couldn't make out a single feature. Then I was horror-stricken – it was as though I didn't exist, as though the body I could feel myself in was a stranger's body and I'd entered it uninvited. No wonder that I felt clammy and cold and that my skin wasn't able to keep warm. It couldn't do so because it wasn't mine. And the eyes, which stared at their own reflection, couldn't recognize themselves. They weren't my eyes. They simply didn't exist. I just thought they were there. I'd made it all up.

I'd made up that house and that mirror which had gobbled me up without sound or craving. I'd made up that woman, who lived here like a phantom, and with whom I'd found peace. And that peace had been made up, pretending to conceal nerves quivering with fear, and when the inevitable scream rose in my throat, it would tenderly stroke the back of my head and my neck, digging its fingers into my Adam's apple. I wouldn't scream then but felt all the worse for not doing so. I'd buried myself in an imaginary grave, without having yet come to realize that it wasn't a soft bed with cosy pillows and a warm blanket. Of course, fool that I was, why was I so uncomfortable in the mornings? Because of the deadly cold, because it's always cold in a grave. And the cold was also an illusion of mine – it was an easier way to bear the pain. The cold shrinks any chinks inside drained blood vessels and the wind doesn't whistle too much down there. I didn't hear the whistle, I didn't understand how close the heart was to dehydration, mummification. Nor did I understand that by artificially slowing down its beat, I was weaning my whole body from life. As though I was, in good time, adapting the organs that were still pulsating to total stillness: constricting them day after day by lulling or cowing them. And they did gradually slow down. In the end they'd have to die or, having lost the habit of breathing, explode from life's last breath. But nothing was happening now; I'd made it all up, you see, and even fiction can only occasionally become a basis for reality. If fiction is easily altered it's almost impossible to do so with reality. The main thing was that my illusions and reality seemed to be all mixed up together like concrete. I just couldn't make head or tail of it all. Perhaps I'd just invented myself.

That man had certainly gone. Even if he'd been standing behind the door I wouldn't have got up or opened the door to him. I would have waited till dawn until he'd left and only then would I have begun to think about him, as a ghost who'd inadvertently stepped into our world. I'd have imagined him in white contours, almost transparent and light, swaying as he breathed in and out and then it would have been easier for me not to believe in him. Not to believe in that delirium in my head caused by one hastily spoken word.

Only then did I begin to grasp that I wasn't alone – did I begin to feel, as though in a daydream, my travelling companion's breath on my neck or straight in my face… my life's, my destiny's companion. He'd just climbed uninvited into my carriage and had never once shown his face. That was rude, extremely rude, if to top it all he also ventured to dig his filthy claws into me, taking it upon himself to thrust a revolver into my hands, press the trigger and type crazy strings of words… No, he'd knocked on my door much earlier, that time when I'd suddenly woken up, not alone, in my bed, with no recollection of the strange girl and the night spent beside her. He'd knocked and I'd opened up. He could clear off now. Whoever he was.

The clock on the wall ticked soundlessly. I wasn't expecting anything more. When my legs began to grow numb I stretched them and flopped onto the floor, just leaning my shoulders slightly against the door. Within a few minutes my neck began to ache. But I didn't care. I no longer felt any responsibility towards my body and only changed position automatically. I might have fallen asleep that way without any thoughts, gradually losing my mind, had I not heard the rattling of keys in the lock. I instantly came to – I jumped to my feet, threw off my jacket, pulled off my boots and opened the door.

Ira appeared before me together with the painfully bright strip of light behind her back. She was holding a shopping bag – I couldn't remember her calling me. She'd probably noticed that morning that we'd run out of sugar and she'd never been able to count on me. She passed it to me and wearily began to unbutton her coat and I, holding on to the bag, kept on staring at her. No, she was real. She emanated a smell of frost, her cheeks were just a little paler than usual. She always turned pale from the cold. I took her coat and hung it up in the closet. I didn't say a word.

"Has something happened?" she asked without any sense of foreboding, placing both her boots and mine in a row.

"Yes. Do you know Evgeny Skvortsov?"

I only had to utter that name for Ira to reel against the wall and clumsily sink to that same place where I'd lost myself only a moment before.

* * *

I'd only seen him once. For less than a minute. But it wasn't that fleeting moment that seemed improbable to me, nor the horrifying proof of its incredibility, but his half-dead body. As though his spirit had been squeezed out, but not quite. I'd never seen him before or after. But he still existed, he existed somewhere close by. It was still just as it was then.

Every time I sat on his chair and felt its ricketiness, caused by its previous occupant, I gave way to such thoughts. Although I wouldn't have lasted more than five minutes in any other chair that wasn't set to my height and with loosened screws, I left this one in peace. In that peace left of him. I nearly got used to stooping just a little and stretching my legs. I was no longer bothered by the rather narrow and almost redundant arm rests. It all suited me because I chose to accept it.

But those thoughts didn't go away. They unravelled even further in my mind when, holding the mouse, I moved the cursor across the clear screen with its lop-eared elephant background, a territory where for many days his hand had typed grey symbols. It was now my hand that simply nestled into that print.

Folders, folders, documents… images from other sites, excerpts from unnamed articles. Finally I decided to read through something. His writing was mundane. Worse than mine. And that discovery sparked off some kind of foolish pleasure, or rather a malicious pleasure in me. I don't know how I'd have reacted had his articles been much better than mine. Perhaps I'd have tried to ignore it.

There was nothing of interest in his articles. Simply sets of phrases relating a reality that could be spotted by just looking out of the window. Yet they were about murders, but kind of commonplace, as though there was nothing unusual about death, as though murderers were ordinary people, going about their business. After a while it suddenly occurred to me that he would have written in the same manner about his own murder. And he would have been right. After all, despite all its strangeness, it very simply had its place in the course of a lacklustre life.

"Katya." She slowly turned towards me as if tearing herself away from a good read. "That Skvortsov, was he a good worker?"

"So-so."

"Do you know if he liked his work?"

"Well, in any case, he made out as if he didn't." She smiled glumly. "And when his articles weren't printed he'd walk around with such a long face, as though he'd been told he had cancer."

"Really?"

"I'm exaggerating just a bit of course…"

Did I like my work? After taking over his place I couldn't stop making comparisons. I too take rejection very badly but I'm trying to get over that habit. The difference was that Korpevsky hadn't yet once returned any of my articles. I somehow believed in my own predestination. It didn't seem terrible now to make a mistake – I felt the taste of victories and hence could allow myself plenty. But was I happy with this? I don't know. I instinctively felt there was no getting away from it.

Besides articles, I also discovered a few games. He played when he didn't feel like working. Also some idiotic book with a modern title and masses of pages. I wasn't going to bother reading it. Among other documents I hit upon was one headed "Numbers". He'd probably been afraid that if he lost his phone he'd lose his connections. I too like to keep particularly important numbers in various places. I don't know why I opened this one. What could I find of interest in it?

I love it when names and numbers form two even narrow columns. As though random people surrender to my exact framework. Skvortsov also seemed to have that same attachment to order and unobtrusive manipulation. He put all his contacts down alphabetically without bothering whether they were long-term friends or casual acquaintances he'd perhaps call at some point in the future.

I was slowly scrolling down the pages without considering the meaning of what I saw, gradually working my way through the names, when I suddenly stopped. My brain instantly brought my thoughts to a standstill and I scrolled back abruptly. For a moment I sat motionless, then took my mobile from my pocket and, without looking, pressed 'contacts'. Familiar people arrayed in letters and symbols flashed before my eyes and I stared at that name. It was the same name as the one on the screen – and the same number. What of it? Those coincidences no longer surprised or overwhelmed me.

Without giving it another thought I rang the number. A recorded voice replied that that number didn't exist. It didn't exist now. He wasn't a fool, he'd changed it. Probably a while ago, on the day or the day after I'd called him to ask him to come and get his revolver. I wasn't upset, however. I really had nothing to say to him.

It was only on the way home that I recalled the day Pliukhin had first set foot in our loathsome office. He seemed so deliberately to have sought me out as a friend that I soon agreed to listen to him, to join him for lunch and for a smoke in the stairwell. And he often talked nonsense. The sort of nonsense that comes to many young people. Only once did I listen to him with interest. He told me about the fate of an old acquaintance who'd been suffering from having nothing to do and lack of funds, from constant moving from place to place and from misery in his private life, who'd then at the age of thirty plus had finally found a refuge. He was working for a newspaper, he'd found love with a beautiful girl and no longer strove for anything else. I thought then that it wouldn't have been a bad thing for me to find myself in that position. I thought then that there was still hope for me.

* * *

I lay on my back shielding my sore eyes and slowly sailed off in my rubber dinghy that smelled sharply of rubber. Small wet oars had been clumsily fixed to its sides. I chucked them aside in a fit of tiredness and sailed on unconsciously and peacefully for apparently a whole hour. The heat was quietly intense and the cool water licked the bottom of the boat. I could feel it and offered it all my thoughts. I wasn't as open with heaven as I was with water.

Every weekend I went on a binge. I drank the light, almost pristine air 80 kilometres out of town, in the old dacha settlement where loads of old people with their grandchildren, as well as a couple of idiots like me, spend their summers. Here everyone has long known each other but I don't remember any of their names. I was studying at university when I went there the first time. Later I thought that I'd lost the way there forever. Now I hung around in the place every day off, completely on my own, weeding, watering and digging. I was helping my parents out; they live off this land. They had little time that year. They had a lot of work and were much occupied with my pregnant sister. And I was glad. It was warm and quiet there. Our little house is in a remote area, almost next door to the rubbish dump. I liked spending days there because I'd recently bought myself an inflatable dinghy and now I sailed every evening along a small river where even at its deepest youngsters can walk on its bed. Along its banks there is impenetrable undergrowth, here and there a watering place for cows and sheep, tiny little beaches and paths and places for fishing. The stream isn't clean, but still it's cleaner than those within the city limits. And there's wildlife here.

Water rats, I don't know their precise name, swam past me more than once, large brown furry ones. I watched each one of them as it swam to the bank. I laughed out loud when I heard a child or woman's shriek and then a great roar when the poor rats had to swim past someone else.

I liked drifting in the middle of the stream that carried my boat along with no questions asked. As though I was of no significance there and so didn't have the slightest sense of responsibility. I moved with the current, watched the clouds, listened to the water... I talked to it and it only murmured in response. That's how I wanted it.

It took me a long time to recover from my last conversation with Ira. In the darkened room, having removed her mask and baring her soul she told me such things – things I didn't want to take in, and so I remained silent. And now, each time the boat carried me along on my solitary journey I recalled every word she'd said and tried to understand. I even answered her but only the water heard me.

There'd been a strange romance between her and Skvortsov. They tormented each other for nearly a year. She spoke of him softly, without anguish, with a chuckle. As was her way. Only now and then her voice would turn husky. I could have put this down to a recent cold. But I didn't. In the dark, I couldn't see her eyes but I felt her knees and fingers tremble. I sat at some distance, letting the odd word or even snippets of words drop. She didn't seem to notice them and continued her monologue. Yes, it was a monologue and she was speaking to herself. She simply needed a listener so as not to go mad. She couldn't understand my torment. It wouldn't even have occurred to a halfwit that her former lover had died at the hands of her present lover who was sitting opposite her right now and who'd not known anything about him or about their relationship. It's strange, but that's how it was.

"I was somehow infected by him, you know…dulling of the brain. I dreamt of him at night and got no rest from him morning, noon and night. I'd never been through anything like it. I'll be hanged if that's love. No, it's an awful disease as though the whole body were covered in sores… terrible words, but absurd and even funny at the same time…Well, I don't know, those blisters that when they dry up turn into scabs and you can't stop wanting to rip them off. They'll then stay with you forever, even if you rub them with antiseptic cream or iodine. Call me a masochist if you will. But you'll never understand me if you don't go through the same thing… And you won't, you don't have enough passion in you…"

It did seem that there was none in me. She'd hurt me deeply then – now I was rather grateful. What's wrong with always being calm? That's my temperament and I can't bear people who accuse me of not showing enough emotion. Today I would say to them that there should be harmony throughout the world. And if you're highly-strung or terribly cheerful then in the natural way of things there must be gloomy and quiet people too.

I looked at her through the darkness and saw that she was trying to stop herself from trembling. Everything was shaking inside her but she was covering this up with her strange chuckle – a dry cough-like chuckle. She was crossing her legs, twisting her hands, her fingers, almost doubling up and looking more and more towards the floor or to the side, only rarely at me. She could have done with a drink but she preferred a dry mouth as though it might have stopped her eyes from growing moist. It's just that when they don't scream with pain or even let out a groan, but laugh it away, it's so much more horrifying. I felt as though someone had wiped over her words with a rag so they were no longer mean or harsh…The truth is that I really just wanted her to burst into tears, to fall into my arms and shake and shake… Then I too would have burst into tears and shaken and she might not have noticed it. Because I was also holding back – and I found it harder and harder to breathe.

"Do you know why I'm sure that isn't love? At the bottom of my heart or subconsciously anyway, somewhere deep inside I had but one wish, an intolerable, unforgettable one, an obsession, a quiet one, as though someone was gnawing at my brain… a wish that he'd give me up. I could obviously foresee a bad ending. It was a stupid affair and its ending had to be a bad one. I'm not stupid, you know; I know people rarely change… But he wasn't a scoundrel, it was simply that love, an unusual love sometimes turns good people into those who wreak havoc with the other one's nerves. He didn't hit or insult me, he was even tender but that's what irritated me most. My head told me that it was all nonsense but my heart really wanted to be smashed, crushed, trampled on, abused… As soon as he felt my protest against the ordinariness of our relationship he'd leave and then during whole days and nights, like a madwoman, I'd do nothing but watch the phone and in the same prayer ask that he'd call and never call again, not once, that I'd forget his number, his address, his friends…But he tormented me. He'd only call me a week or two or even a month later and he'd tell me again that he couldn't live without me, and we'd be back to square one. From the first moment I met him I knew that I'd never forget that man in all my life, that I'd not even need a photo of him. I understood something else too: that we'd never be together. Then, when everything got screwed up, I wondered who'd be the first to scramble out of the hole. He began to disentangle himself first. He was the stronger one, he could split us up. It's sad he's no more. It was as though my leg or arm had been cut off and my heart about to be torn out too, and it would have been, had it not been for you."

At that moment I pinched myself, for some reason, below the knee, but without Ira noticing it. A small but bright bruise did subsequently appear. I wasn't out to hurt myself but my hand impulsively squeezed into a fist grabbing a piece of flesh with it. Clenching my teeth, I didn't let go for at least a minute. In due course I discovered with surprise that a month later I'd not relaxed my jaw yet. And every time I lay down to sleep I'd wonder why my chin was so painful. Ira was silent, gathering her thoughts. I knew for certain that she was about to talk about me and then having to cope with my shaking would be impossibly hard. And, damn it, I was prepared to jump up and make a run for the window when she began to talk with a voice that came from deep within her body.

"Had it not been for you, I'd have had a terrible time. I might even have thought of killing myself. You of course couldn't have known that. One thing is positive: I wouldn't have followed it up. I want to live too much. Whether on my own or with someone – sometimes I don't care which – as long as I can live. And you burst into my life so suddenly that I almost choked with amazement. Zhenya was still alive then but I'd done that sort of thing before. I'm not the slightest bit ashamed. I'd simply pulled through, that's all. He'd also sought relief, I know, but all that was useless, it was futile, like hitting your head against a brick wall…."

She was silent after that, looking up at the ceiling and the walls, along which the lights of passing cars down below occasionally flashed by. We'd not sealed up the windows for winter – cold air was coming in which was why Ira pulled down her soft cardigan sleeves over her fingers, sniffed and then noisily breathed out as though she had some blockage in the back of her throat. She seemed to be permanently ill. Only in winter and cold autumn days, she said. And in summer, on grey rainy days.

"He appeared to me in a dream… Just once, a few weeks after his death. It's strange – I thought I'd often dream of him. That's what happened when my grandmother died. She'd appear in my dreams every night with a few tiny breaks for almost a year. I thought then that the dead loved me. Really, that's what I thought. Zhenya only appeared once. He was very hot. We were sitting next to each other, in the yellow haze of a cinema auditorium, with a soft humming noise or even complete silence around us. He was sitting sideways – I could hardly see his face. But I saw his hand …I loved his hands, maybe that sounds funny…I like men's hands anyway, but only if they're beautiful. And his were beautiful, big, tanned, with rounded nails, and they were warm, sometimes hot and dry…I linked my arm through his, pressing against it all the way from his elbow down to his fingers, and talked some nonsense…"

She stopped. I couldn't hold back, though she was silent for all of a minute, and to my own surprise I asked her: "What nonsense?" She began to speak a few minutes later and I was taken aback at myself for having asked that idiotic question out loud.

"In that dream it was as though we'd long been apart, a year or more. As if he were alive but far away somewhere, inaccessible, living a life I knew nothing about… As though my cautious wishes had come true. But there I was, sitting by his side, seemingly by chance, with such heat emanating from him, there wasn't any smell, but you probably don't experience smell in dreams. He was very hot, his hand was hot…I can remember that heat now, as though skin has memory. Zhenya had warm blood. Everyone has, but he more so. Oh, yes, you were asking me. I don't exactly remember what I was saying, but this is what it amounted to. I gave him a choice: I told him that if he still wanted to be with me, then he should follow me as I walked out... So I walked out. I was to walk ahead without looking round or stopping, that's what we'd agreed. But I stopped at the spot where the cinema corridor turns off to the side... I looked at the door to the auditorium from where the odd person was coming out, but he wasn't among them. That's how the dream ended. I dreamt some nonsense after that."

I got up and went over to her. I towered above her crumpled silhouette. She was hunched up in the corner of her well-padded armchair, arms and legs twisted under her, contorted, trying to suppress her shaking. But she was in a bad way this time. I didn't know what to do. She didn't even stir when I was really close to her. She looked at my face but not into my eyes and then turned away again and gave a deep sigh. At that moment I felt like tugging at her, grabbing her by the shoulders and shaking them a couple of times so that they'd loosen up and then she'd stretch her legs as she used to, dangling them over the armrest, nestling like a grown-up child in a cradle. I looked at her and didn't dare destroy her tight cocoon. I stood upright before her, screening the feeble light trickling in through the window. Having stood there for more than a minute in that funny petrified pose, I suddenly couldn't endure it any longer and I pulled her roughly to me. She lurched like a rag doll and without a sound fell back heavily into the armchair. I grabbed her again, encircled her waist with an iron grip and felt her softly landing on my shoulder, where she buried her face and then drooped with her whole body over me so that I no longer needed to hold on to her. I carefully turned round and sat down in the armchair and she didn't pull away from my shoulder. She didn't want us to look into each other's eyes. Nor did I want to. Some time passed before she began to speak again but I no longer cared to listen. She spoke in whispers, softly resting her chin on my shoulder and I felt how hot her breath was. I could hear her heart beating in her chest and feel her hand tremble. She could see my profile, and this probably reminded her of her dream. I too began to sink into some kind of dark, warm, and cosy illusion, where there was no need to repent. Where I didn't have to answer for myself.

"It wasn't like that before... it's strange to live and feel as though someone's missing, as though you'd lost someone and not found that person again. Yes, lost him, in a previous life perhaps... So that when you came crashing down next to me in bed, reeking of alcohol, when you drew me towards you with your hand under my arm and suddenly began to snore, I felt I was going mad. Because to me it was as if I'd found you. I wanted to snuggle up to you, touch your skin – I stroked your cheek, your neck, your shoulder, a few times very gingerly so as not to wake you. I felt like a tiny, crazy woman, wet with tears, useless tears from past sufferings, desperate only for you and there you were beside me, not going anywhere... Yes, you stank, your snoring was repugnant and you even kicked me a couple of times in your sleep. I find it odd to think that I forgot about Zhenya then. I always had him in my mind but that time I forgot him, or rather, I forgot to remember him. And when I realized that, I was glad and that's why I didn't tell you about him. The fact that you work for the same newspaper as him might have finished me off, but he's dead now. I don't know whether one can love the dead more than the living but I do know that you saved me. That's why I didn't say anything. I thought that he'd left me. I still believe that..."

She talked for a long time, and her voice gradually lost its dryness, became moist, then tearful. I knew how it would all end. My arms hugged her more tenderly, I wanted to protect her even more, but from what? From herself. It's true that she'd said she was calm when she was with me. I felt the same. Although, at the beginning of the conversation, words had been struggling to break free like spirited little birds, words about my own worthlessness, about being that murderer who'd deprived her of her man, shamefully and deceitfully pinning his mask onto my own crazy face, I thought that my confession would scarcely help her now. I knew that she loved me. I knew that she was the one I loved. I knew that after the tenderness we were gradually moving towards, I would disappear in the dark. And she'd never see my remorse and my anguish.

* * *

I killed a man. But I didn't know there was a man there. I only understood it later. Not having seen a gesture or heard a word of his, I concluded that he was a man when in that motionless mute torso I detected the breath of life ebbing away. I decided that I was the one who'd caused its loss. I was a murderer. And a murderer has no right to love. Love is life-giving. If with willpower and imagination you draw the pluses and the minuses together, you mix good with bad, black with white, you could go mad from the resulting staleness and stench. But what if that's already happened?

It was only through other people's words that I knew he'd existed. It seemed to me that he was a product of another age. His life had run its course along some other river, on the other side of the planet, somewhere underground or above the heavens, somewhere else, not here. Then why, when I'd killed him, did he suddenly grab me by the chest, shake me with terrible force, dump me into his own river, move me over to his side, bury me underground or hurl me up to heaven? Why had I all of a sudden begun to be aware of him, a dead man, as though he were alive, when I hadn't known of his existence before his death? Why had he slipped so plausibly and masterfully into my life? To take revenge for my intrusion into his death? That had been unpremeditated and revenge is seldom so. Are the dead capable of doing something like that? They probably know more than we do. I therefore just have to wait for my eyes to be opened, when it's my turn to close them.

I was now filled with doubts about everything, about love, death, life. Another one's life and my own. About each word, glance, even about the existence of anything. I wouldn't have been surprised had I been told that we were all phantoms, living in a vacuum in the middle of a black hole where nothing exists except fantasies. And those are not our fantasies, or mine or theirs. They are no one's. They don't exist either. Such thoughts both terrified and calmed me. If there's nothing there, then there's no suffering. It means that there's just emptiness and you can do as you please. The main thing is for me to want something, but what? I've long stopped thinking on that score, as if to punish myself for that one accidental pull of the trigger. As if depriving yourself of life, because you once allowed yourself to grant someone death. I threw away everything as if I'd live better for having made this strange sacrifice. I placed everything on an altar – I gave him my whole life…But no, I couldn't deceive myself. He was dead after all, and I was in charge.

I threw away the revolver of course. On some rubbish dump not far from town. I stood looking at it for a long time with my head and arms hanging down, my eyelids drooping more than usual, with not a thought in my head. I only felt my chest swelling up with heat. Then I gave up my apartment. For nearly a year I moved from one friend to another, making up stories every time, about my apartment being flooded or having repairs done or that my parents had come over. Then I got fed up with the newspaper as well as with Korpevsky, Katya and other learned rats and irksome creatures. As much as I tried to hold on to Skvortsov's place, I seemed to be getting nowhere. I once arrived at the office and found a system administrator in his chair. A virus had gobbled up all his folders, and later a cleaner cleared all his notes from the cupboard and even his chewed-up pencils flew into the bin. As I left I turned off the light and thought that I'd been unable to hold on to anything. Not a trace, not a line. Up there in heaven he was probably very upset. But he must have seen that at least I tried.

Time flew past me like a bullet, and I'd dug myself in knee-deep, never ceasing to stare blankly at everything around me. It all passed me by without touching me but I had to move, because a motionless wheel can't keep its balance for long. I wasn't looking for anything ahead, and behind me lay a bunch of unfulfilled hopes. One evening when there was little money left in my pocket, I bought myself a train ticket to a small town where I'd once been held up for twenty-four hours. I remember how, having bought myself a big greasy meat pie and having opened a paperback by an unknown author, in French, understanding only half of what I read and giving in to the tasteless meat pie, I suddenly heard my own voice whispering to me. I liked hearing it. This time I sat in the stuffy waiting room of the train station waiting for the train that would rush me off from the present to the future. From an artificial fantasy land to what was right and true. I had that absurd hope.

The waiting room was crowded with people. I used to enjoy watching them – now I didn't notice either their faces or their bodies, as though they'd been produced by the wind. The huge windows across the entire wall let in too little light. The voices, shrieks, mutterings and whisperings all blended into one well-coordinated chorus and I absorbed it as a whole. The steel white chairs were arranged in strange rows across the centre, the sides, at the front and the back in such a way that the people who sat on them looked like refugees salvaging their pitiful existences on a buffeted old ship. I too was sitting there among bags and trunks, rustling parcels and children crawling everywhere. All those people had somewhere to go to while I felt that I could have sat there the rest of my life. They all seemed to be fenced off from me by a transparent but solid wall, which I didn't knock on or bang my feet or head against. I simply looked at them thinking how close yet far away they were. How I didn't understand them and didn't give a damn. I wasn't in the same river current. The stormy current of their river was unfamiliar to me. The gentle waves of the greenish water I was on were warmer and quieter so that death could appear almost unnoticed and therefore painless. But it's been said that pain is a sign of life. Does that mean that you could, at the same time, be alive and dead? I don't know; I only know that I still carried a pain inside me, a tiny, silent, inoffensive pain. The pain of incomprehension. The pain of ignorance. The pain of emptiness. As though I was moving my legs in vain, getting nowhere even if I'd taken a step or two.

My train was delayed. I still had the blurry grey wall before my eyes when suddenly, among the phantoms and illusions I caught sight of a face. It was a baby boy's face. He was looking at me with watchful earnest eyes. Big eyes – children's eyes are often out of proportion with their faces. He was holding on to his mother's shoulder with his little arms and she was gently rocking him with her back to me. He had a rattle in his hand, an attempt to calm the poor little thing down with all that racket going on. But he had no intention of closing his eyes, he was staring at me as though peering at an alien among a lot of boring glum faces. He followed me with his eyes as he would an animal, now knitting his tiny fair eyebrows, now opening his eyes wide. I found it incredibly funny. I smiled – he smiled back and shrieked gleefully with a high-pitched little voice. He was so tiny and fragile, he knew and understood so little but I didn't see him as something presupposing a long life, maturity and full height. I basically didn't see the man in him. He and I were in the same time bubble and that put us on a level. We were identical. In that moment in time and space we had the same destiny, perhaps only for an instant, but we made contact.

The little boy began to pull faces. I desperately wanted to do the same back, but as happened every time children paid me close attention, I began to feel awkward and afraid of being taken for a fool. Not by adults but by them. As though they were matchless when it came to acting like fools and where did I fit in with my jokes and funny faces that sooner or later took on an offensive or vulgar tone. My brain has long been poisoned by life. So I simply looked at him, smiled and winked when he stretched out his little arms towards me and laughed out loud without the slightest sense of urgency. I would have gone on sitting there, quietly placid, had he not dropped his rattle on the ground after more squealing and throwing up his little arms. The woman who'd till then stood with her back to me, turned round sharply and we saw each other. I instantly recognized her but I didn't shrink back or overwhelm her with kisses; I didn't say a word but stood there like an idiot with the rattle in my hand and feeling the touch of a tiny palm on my forearm.

My God, how much time had gone by. She'd changed, but only slightly. I couldn't actually see where those changes had occurred. In her face, her bearing... After that night of revelation I'd only seen her a couple of times and then only through the office window. She'd been looking for me and I'd hidden away. Like a scared cat who'd fouled the sofa. How she must hate me now! Why didn't she slap me across the face? Why didn't she turn away? I scrutinized her eyes – no, she held no bad feelings. But I couldn't make out any other ones. There was no evidence of love, tenderness, fear or joy. She looked at me as though I'd gone out five minutes before to get some cigarettes. We stood for a few minutes without saying a word and barely moving. I wanted her to cling to my shoulder, at least for a moment. But she simply looked at me, perhaps trying to read my feelings. Then I couldn't hold out any longer and turned my eyes away. I don't know in which direction she was looking when she said:

"This is not your child."

I looked at the little boy. He had moist grey eyes. He was still staring at me.

"I know," I said, smiling at the child who let out a happy cry. "This is Skvortsov."

That moment I still felt nothing. I just understood that I no longer needed to go anywhere.

Irina Bogatyreva was born in 1982 in Kazan (Tatarstan) and grew up on the Volga. In 2005 she graduated from the Literary Institute in Moscow. Today she is widely published in the leading literary magazines, and in 2008 her first novel, *AutoSTOP* (published in English as "Off the Beaten Track"), was shortlisted for the Debut Prize and also won the Eureka, Ilya-prize, and the *Oktyabr* magazine's prize. She has several published books to her credit, all on most topical Russian problems. Her recent novel *Comrade Anna* was short-listed for the Belkin Prize.

Yaroslava Pulinovich (b. 1987) comes from Omsk (Siberia) and currently lives in Yekaterinburg (the Urals). A graduate of the Yekaterinburg Drama College, she writes plays which have been widely staged in Russia and other countries as well as winning her many prestigious prizes, including the Debut in 2008. *Natasha's Dream* was produced in London and Baltimore. Her other plays include *Beyond the Track, I Won't Come Back*, and *Washers* (Grand Prize at the Kolyada Play Festival in Yekaterinburg.) "Yaroslava Pulinovich may be the next big thing in the world of young Russian playwrights. That was the word, at least, at the Towson Studio Theatre, where two of her monologue plays were given a workshop performance." (John Barry)

Victoria Chikarneeva was born in 1987 in a little town near Rostov in the South of Russia. She has a degree in Sociology and Political Science from the South Federal University in Rostov. In 2012 she graduated from the Literary Institute in Moscow. Chikarneeva divides her time between

Rostov and Moscow and, after a succession of various part-time jobs, she now works as a script writer. She was a Debut finalist in 2008 with the story "I Simply Wanted to Live", and again in 2009 with her short novel *Everyday Life*.

Anna Lavrinenko, born in 1984, lives in Yaroslavl (Central Russia) where most of her stories are set. A Law graduate she works as a company lawyer in Yaroslavl as well as taking an active part in the city's cultural life: she leads the largest reading group there and reviews books and films for the local press. Her short stories and essays have been published in the top literary and art magazines. She won the Debut Prize in 2006 for her short stories.

Kseniya Zhukova, born in 1981 in Moscow, has a degree in Journalism from the Institute of Journalism and Literature. Worked as an editor, reporter, proofreader, composer of crossword puzzles, etc. She has twice won the Debut Prize: in 2003 for her play *Accidents,* and in 2011 for her long story "Twenty Letters from the Twentieth".

Anna Babiashkina, born in 1979 in a small town in Central Russia, has a degree in Journalism from Moscow University. Currently she works as chief editor of a women's magazine with a circulation of 180,000. She has several published novels to her name. In 2011 she won the Debut Prize for the semi-fantasy novel *Before I Croak* which also won the Bestseller Prize as the best "urban novel".

Olga Rimsha, born in 1988, lives in Novosibirsk (Siberia). A graduate of the Siberian Institute of International Affairs she currently works as a literary editor and assistant stage-manager. She has a number of long stories and plays to her name. Her short novel *Still Waters* won the Debut Prize in 2010. It was also published in Chinese. She describes her prose as "pessimistic optimism".

GLAS BACKLIST

Arslan Khasavov, *Sense*, a novel
Political struggles and youth movements in today's Russia

Off the Beaten Track
Two Stories about Russian Hitchhiking

Mikhail Levitin, *A Jewish God in Paris*, three novellas

Roman Senchin, *Minus*, a novel
an old Siberian town surviving the perestroika dislocation

Maria Galina, *Iramifications*, a novel
adventures of today's Russian traders in the medieval East

Sea Stories. Army Stories
by **Alexander Pokrovsky** and **Alexander Terekhov**
realities of life inside the army

Andrei Sinyavsky, *Ivan the Fool: Russian Folk Belief*,
a cultural history

Sigizmund Krzhizhanovsky, *Seven Stories*
a rediscovered writer of genius from the 1920s

Leonid Latynin, *The Lair*,
a novel-parable, stories and poems

The Scared Generation,
two novels by **Vasil Bykov** and **Boris Yampolsky**
about political persecutions in Russia of the 1930s and '40s

Alan Cherchesov, *Requiem for the Living*, a novel,
the extraordinary adventures of an Ossetian boy set against
the traditional culture of the Caucasus

Nikolai Klimontovich, *The Road to Rome*,
naughty reminiscences about the late Soviet years

Nina Gabrielyan, *Master of the Grass*,
long and short stories by a leading feminist

Alexander Selin, *The New Romantic*, modern parables

Valery Ronshin, *Living a Life*, *Totally Absurd Tales*

Andrei Sergeev, *Stamp Album*, *A Collection of People,
Things, Relationships and Words*

Lev Rubinstein, *Here I Am*
humorous-philosophical performance poems and essays

Andrei Volos, *Hurramabad,*
national strife in Tajikstan following the collapse of the USSR

Larissa Miller, *Dim and Distant Days*
a Jewish childhood in postwar Moscow

Anatoly Mariengof, *A Novel Without Lies*
the turbulent life of a poet in flamboyant
Bohemian Moscow in the 1920s

Irina Muravyova, *The Nomadic Soul,*
a family saga featuring a modern-day Anna Karenina

The Portable Platonov, a reader
for the centenary of Russia's greatest 20th century writer

Boris Slutsky, *Things That Happened,*
a biography of a major mid-20th century poet
interspersed with his poetry

Asar Eppel, *The Grassy Street*
vivid stories set in a Moscow suburb in the 1940s

Peter Aleshkovsky, *Skunk: A Life,* a bildungsroman
set in the Northern Russian countryside

ANTHOLOGIES

Squaring the Circle, anthology
The generation which never lived under the Soviet system.

Mendeleev Rock, two short novels from Debut

War & Peace, army stories versus women's stories:
a compelling portrait of post-post-perestroika Russia

Strange Soviet Practices
short stories and documents illustrating
some inimitably Soviet phenomena

Captives
victors turn out to be captives on conquered territory

NINE of Russia's Foremost Women Writers
a collective portrait of women's writing today

Beyond the Looking-Glas, Russian grotesque revisited

A Will & a Way, women's writing of the 1990s

Childhood, the child is father to the man

Booker Winners & Others-II. The mid-1990s

Booker Winners & Others, mostly provincial writers

Love Russian Style, Russia tries decadence

Jews & Strangers, what it means to be a Jew in Russia

Bulgakov & Mandelstam, earlier autobiographical stories

Love and Fear, the two strongest emotions
dominating Russian life

Women's View, Russian women bloodied but unbowed

Soviet Grotesque,
young people's rebellion against the establishment

Revolution, the 1920s versus the 1980s

NON-FICTION

Michele A. Berdy, *The Russian Word's Worth*
A humorous and informative guide to
the Russian language, culture and translation

Contemporary Russian Fiction: A Short List
11 Russian authors interviewed by Kristina Rotkirch

**Nina Lugovskaya, *The Diary of a Soviet Schoolgirl:
1932-1937*, the diary of a Russian Anne Frank**

Alexander Genis, *Red Bread*, essays
Russian and American civilizations compared
by one of Russia's foremost essayists

A.J. Perry, *Twelve Stories of Russia: A Novel, I guess*